"Who are you?

"You already know the

She put her fingers against his lips to still his words. "Don't play me for a fool. I did the best I could with your injuries, but now that you're part of reality again, you owe me answers."

His voice was low, soft and very serious. "Lauren, please don't ask. I can't—"

"I don't want to hear I *can't*." She fixed him with a hard stare. "I want answers, Kyle."

He tugged on her hand until he had closed the last small gap between them. His lips brushed against hers, then he captured her mouth fully in a hot and sensual kiss.

She closed her eyes for a moment, savoring the warmth that flowed through her, until it almost obscured her thoughts. When she spoke, her words were barely above a whisper. "Who are you, Kyle Delaney? Why are you here? And what am I involved in?" She had to ask...but she wasn't so sure she wanted to hear the answers

He took her hand again, bringing it to his lips. "You have to let this go, Lauren. You can't become involved. You have to trust me—and I have to trust that you'll maintain your silence."

Her voice a barely discernible whisper, Lauren said, "I don't think I can do that...."

Dear Reader,

They're rugged, they're strong and they're *wanted!* Whether sheriff, undercover cop or officer of the court, these men are trained to keep the peace, to uphold the law. But what happens when they meet the one woman who gets to know the man *behind* the badge?

Twelve of these men are on the loose...and only Harlequin Intrigue brings them to you—one per month in the LAWMAN series. This month meet Kyle Delaney, a tall, dark stranger in the waterfront town, who's got secrets he's not about to share....

Be sure you don't miss a single LAWMAN coming to you in the months ahead...because there's nothing sexier than the strong arms of the law!

Regards,

Debra Matteucci
Senior Editor & Editorial Coordinator
Harlequin Books
300 East 42nd Street
New York, NY 10017

Lover Unknown
Shawna Delacorte

Harlequin Books

TORONTO • NEW YORK • LONDON
AMSTERDAM • PARIS • SYDNEY • HAMBURG
STOCKHOLM • ATHENS • TOKYO • MILAN
MADRID • WARSAW • BUDAPEST • AUCKLAND

ISBN 0-373-22413-3

LOVER UNKNOWN

Lauren's
Business and
Living Quarters

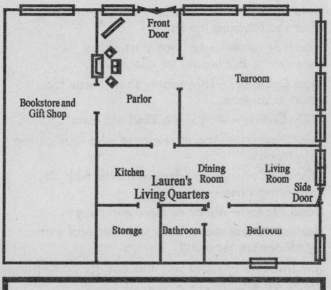

Front Door

Tearoom

Bookstore and Gift Shop

Parlor

Kitchen

Dining Room

Living Room

Side Door

Lauren's Living Quarters

Storage

Bathroom

Bedroom

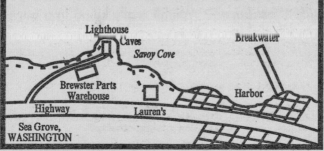

Lighthouse

Caves

Savoy Cove

Breakwater

Brewster Parts Warehouse

Harbor

Highway

Lauren's

Sea Grove, WASHINGTON

CAST OF CHARACTERS

Lauren Jamison—She desired a dangerous man.

Kyle Delaney—Would Lauren still want him after she learned the truth?

Frank Brewster—He was part of the conspiracy, but would be eliminated.

Max Culhane—This county sheriff was too good to be true.

Milly Evans—Was she a kind old lady?

Tony Mallory—Local newsman who was giving Kyle trouble.

Mitch O'Connor—A deputy sheriff with an interesting past.

Irene Peyton—Pillar of the community?

Harvey Sherwood—Why was this real estate developer so nervous?

Joe Thurlow—What was this easygoing deputy sheriff up to?

Billy Washburn—Was he really killed in a car wreck?

Prologue

"We've been over his psychological profile before, Chief. Kyle Delaney is not a team player. He's a loner. No one ever knows what he's doing, or for that matter what he's already done. His paperwork is sketchy at best, assuming that he actually takes the time to even do a report. In fact, I suspect the reason his reports are noticeably lacking in details is because of the way he bends the rules to suit his needs. His expense vouchers, although eventually explainable and deemed legitimate, read more like a fiction novel than anything else. He thrives on the adrenaline surge that comes with danger."

The psychologist placed the file folder on the chief's desk. "I think you should bring him in and put him behind a desk—let him chill out for a while. You can't live on the edge the way he does without eventually losing it."

"I can't do it, Fred. That's exactly why Delaney's so perfect for this particular assignment. His instincts are excellent. He has an uncanny ability to take seemingly unrelated little bits of information and form them into a cohesive picture. He improvises. He makes do with what's at hand. His qualifications are the best. He's a former Navy Seal. He has a near photographic memory and is a whiz with disguises and accents. He possesses a chameleonlike ability to blend in with his surroundings to the point of becoming almost invisible, or he can go just the opposite and stick out so obviously that everyone completely accepts his chosen cover without question.''

''That's all well and good, but—''

''The mere fact that he's able to distance himself emotionally works in his favor. It allows him to be objective about everyone he encounters without having his judgment clouded by personal sentiment.'' The chief picked up the file and glanced at the top page. ''He's one agent who would never allow himself to be tied down to a desk or to a daily routine. That same adrenaline surge that seems to bother you is exactly what keeps him on his toes.''

''Well, I don't have any concrete facts that would allow me to overrule your decision.'' The psychologist furrowed his brow in concentration for a moment. ''But I think he's on a collision course with a severe case of burnout.''

''I DON'T LIKE IT. He's just a kid, only nineteen years old. He works as a parts clerk at the warehouse. Maybe he's done a little snooping, has some suspicions, but he doesn't know enough to really hurt us.'' The lean man in his midforties with the thinning brown hair furtively glanced around the unlit parking lot for the fourth time, noting that it was still vacant. ''I'll keep an eye on him. It'll be okay.''

The larger, older man eyed him skeptically. ''He's a smart-ass kid with a big mouth. It won't be long before he tries to put the squeeze on us. It ain't like it's the first time, you know.''

''Is it really necessary? I mean, you're talking murder—''

''You're not goin' soft on us, are you?''

''No!'' The smaller man swallowed nervously. ''No...I don't have any problem with it. Nothing like that. It's just—''

''Don't get yourself in no uproar.'' The larger man snorted his disdain. ''It ain't your hands what's gonna get

irty. I'll see it's taken care of, neat and clean. Two…three
ays tops. It'll look just like an accident. Won't be no one
iving it any serious investigation.''

"Sure, that sounds good." He ran his fingers through
what was left of his thin brown hair, then shoved his hands
nto his jacket pockets to hide the trembling. He cleared
is throat a couple of times while awkwardly shifting his
weight from one foot to the other. "What do you want me
o do?''

"Go back to your office and do nothin'. Just follow your
normal business routine." He glared at the younger man,
barking out the words like a drill sergeant. "And wipe that
scared look off your face before someone sees it and won-
ders what's wrong with you." He gave one last snort of
disgust then walked off.

The younger man watched as the older man climbed into
he cab of the mud-spattered pickup truck and drove away.
He pulled a handkerchief from his pocket and mopped the
beads of sweat from his brow, then took three deep breaths
before turning toward his car. He shook his head and mut-
tered under his breath. "I don't like it. We're asking for
trouble…big trouble.''

Chapter One

The vision had been very real, jerking Lauren Jamison out of a sound sleep. It had lasted only a few seconds but left a vivid impression. A man, she could not see his face, lurching off the cliff into the blackness of night—falling toward the crashing waves below. Who was he? Why had he fallen from the cliff? Was it a mystery from the past or a portent of things to come? She did not know. The ability was there, but she had never learned to command it or properly use it. The visions seemed to come from nowhere of their own volition. She closed her eyes for a second and tried to force the vision from her mind.

She glanced at the clock. It was almost time to get up anyway. She forced herself to think of other things as she took her shower, slipped into a warm robe and padded barefoot to the small kitchen.

She carried the mug from her living quarters in the back of the building to the front area, which housed her business, a combination bookstore and gift shop on one side of the entrance parlor and a tearoom on the other side. She built a fire in the fireplace of the parlor, then sat in her favorite chair sipping her herbal tea and staring at the flames. She occasionally looked out the window. The early-morning drizzle obscured most of the dawn light.

Try as she might, she had not been able to shake the

disturbing vision from her mind. She sensed something very powerful in the works—dramatic changes hovered on the horizon. She tried to collect her thoughts and focus her energy and concentration.

The Siamese cat jumped from his favorite perch atop the large antique Hoosier cabinet. The small gold bell around his neck jingled softly as he darted across the parlor then jumped into her lap. A tremor of expectancy caused her to shiver. She closed her eyes as she stroked the cat's fur. "I think, Ty-Ty, that we're about to become involved in an exciting adventure."

She held the cat a moment before shooing him from her lap. She carried her empty mug into the kitchen and refilled it. A loud buzzing at the front of the building startled her. As soon as she stepped through the connecting door into the business section of the building she saw the dark silhouette of a large man, his hands cupped around his face as he pressed against the front window. Again, the tremor of expectancy darted through her. Whatever was going to happen somehow involved this stranger who had mysteriously appeared out of the early-morning mist.

She crossed the parlor and opened the front door, tilting her head to one side as she looked at him. "Yes? May I help you?"

The smooth, masculine voice had an almost seductive quality about it. "I'm sorry to disturb you so early in the morning, but I saw your lights and—"

"Please, come in out of the cold." She stepped aside. He hurried past her and went directly to the fireplace, holding his hands out toward the flames. He was tall. His dark good looks projected an aura of mystery that she found very exciting.

His glossy brown hair was a little long, resting thick and shaggy across the back of his neck and the tops of his ears. The tousled front hung in disarray across his forehead. A stubble of whiskers covered his cheeks and chin but could not hide the two-inch scar that cut across his jawline. His face was drawn and haggard. His sky blue eyes looked tired and slightly bloodshot, as if he had been up all night.

She watched as he continued to rub his hands together, allowing the warmth of the flames to take away his chill. His gaze traveled slowly around the room, then came to rest on her.

"I was hoping this might be a restaurant. The sign says tearoom. Is there any chance you also serve coffee?"

"I think I might be able to find you some." Lauren disappeared into her living quarters in the back of the building, leaving him alone in the front parlor.

His gaze lingered on her retreating form until she had vanished completely from sight. She seemed to move with a fluid motion, her floor-length robe making it seem more like a glide than a walk. The lighting caused her copper-colored hair to glow as brightly as the flames in the fireplace. A wave of heat surged through his body, filling him with a sensual warmth that had nothing to do with the fireplace. He reluctantly shoved aside the moment of hedonistic self-indulgence, which had produced the starting of a delicious fantasy, and turned his attention to more practical matters.

The entry was a warm and inviting area. To one side was a room of high-back chairs and tables covered with crisp white linen cloths. To the other side lay an area that first appeared to be a confused combination of books, greeting cards, handmade crafts, houseplants and various gift items. On closer inspection he realized it was a series of small rooms extending into other rooms with areas clearly defined yet conveying an informal flow. He seemed to be in a kind of middle zone that separated the tearoom from the rest of the business.

It suddenly occurred to him that in addition to not questioning who he was or what he wanted, she had left him alone in the room. That had been very foolish of her.

"You're wrong, you know."

Her voice startled him but her words confused him even more as he whirled around to see her standing in the doorway holding a coffee cup. Her sound was low and throaty and seemed to float magically on the air. He forced a casual manner as he continued to warm his hands in front of the fireplace. "Oh? And just what am I wrong about?"

"We're not alone. Ty-Ty is standing watch." He followed her gaze to the top of the antique Hoosier cabinet. The Siamese cat sat very still, almost like a statue—its blue eyes staring at him, watching his every move. "I have no reason to fear you."

Her eyes immediately captured and mesmerized him. They were green, a brilliant emerald color, and seemed to glow with some inner light. A captivating smile lit her face, touched with an unmistakable hint of amusement. Her finely sculpted features created a truly beautiful face that momentarily robbed him of the ability to speak. It was almost as if he had not really noticed her when she had first opened the door to him, although he could not imagine how that would have been possible.

If there was only one truth about Kyle Delaney's life, it was that he maintained control of all that went on around him. But this... He detected the slight increase in his heartbeat and a tightening across his chest. He was not sure whether it was the result of his immediate physical attraction to an extremely desirable woman or her very disconcerting manner. Either way, he needed to know just who this woman was who seemed to have read his mind.

As if in answer to his unasked question, her words again startled him. "I'm Lauren Jamison. This is my place of business and my home." She handed him the cup of coffee. "Black, no cream and no sugar." It was not a question, it was a statement of fact. Her captivating smile pulled at his senses, filling him with a variety of thoughts—all of a truly erotic nature.

He took the cup from her, returning her smile with a dazzling one of his own. "Kyle Delaney...and yes, that's the way I take my coffee." For some inexplicable reason he felt the need to add the words, "Good guess."

"It wasn't a guess." She crossed the parlor to her favorite chair.

"Oh?" A slight grin tugged at the corners of his mouth. "Does that mean you read minds?"

"No, I don't read minds. But I sometimes get feelings."

"You mean like those commercials on television that you call and they give you a reading?"

"Not at all. I don't tell fortunes." She was not sure if he was making fun of her or not. "It's just that I sometimes get feelings about things... Well, it's not important."

She indicated a chair across from hers, then abruptly changed the subject. "Tell me, Kyle—" she took a sip of her tea "—what brings you to my door so early in the morning and in such disagreeable weather?"

He declined her offer of a chair, preferring to stay in front of the fireplace. He flashed a teasing grin, refusing to let the subject drop. "You mean you don't already know what brings me here?"

She took his teasing in stride, returning a mischievous grin of her own. "Why don't you tell me and I'll see if I was right?"

"It's the lighthouse." He noticed her immediate reaction to his words, a response she quickly covered by lowering her head to take another sip of her tea.

"The lighthouse? What would your interest be in it? It was shut down decades ago. In fact—" she suppressed a grin "—it's haunted. The last lighthouse keeper died mysteriously, and his spirit still lives there. Sometimes at night you can see lights moving inside the attic of the living quarters or around the upper level of the tower—the keeper trying to light the lamp to provide safe passage to all the ships at sea." She paused, then went on. "The land and structures were purchased from the government many years ago. The keeper's living quarters, adjacent to the tower, were restored about ten years ago to their turn-of-the-century appearance by the local historical society as part of our city's heritage project. It's now open to the public.''

He eyed her curiously, a hint of skepticism written across his features. "Have you seen this…spirit?"

She gave a little shrug. "We've encountered each other on occasion over the years."

A sudden silence enveloped the space between them as their eyes locked together in an intimate moment. A little tremor of excitement tingled in her stomach as she read the unmistakable earthiness in his eyes, a look that divulged a very lusty nature and imparted one very clear thought. It was Lauren who broke the increasing pull working its way into her consciousness. She looked away from him and took another sip of her tea.

She forced her attention to the topic of the lighthouse, as much to calm the decidedly erotic effect his presence seemed to have on her as to satisfy her curiosity. "What's your interest in the lighthouse?"

"I'm a…paranormal researcher. I'm here to verify or disprove the rumors of some sort of entity occupying the lighthouse." He suddenly became very aware of the 9 mm semiautomatic pistol nestled securely in his shoulder holster—certainly an unusual piece of equipment for a researcher to have. "Actually, our reports indicate several different types of…activity taking place there."

He reached in his pocket and handed her one of the business cards that had been printed to add credence to his cover story. He continued as Lauren glanced at the card. "I believe the head of the Sea Grove Historical Society, Mrs. Irene Peyton, received a letter about my arrival and intentions."

She tilted her head again and leveled an appraising look

at him. Her emerald eyes seemed to be reaching into his very soul to dig out the truth. An uncomfortable feeling shivered up his spine. This Lauren Jamison was a very unsettling woman who was becoming more intriguing by the minute. If he believed in all this psychic stuff he would be tempted to say she really did have some kind of gift, some level of knowledge beyond what was normal. But, of course, that was ridiculous. It was all a bunch of nonsense.

"A paranormal investigator." She could not stop the slight smile that curled the corners of her mouth—an inward, almost enigmatic smile. Irene had mentioned the letter to her. Lauren had been confused about what there was in the small community of Sea Grove, Washington, with a population of less than two thousand people, that would attract the attention of a paranormal researcher. And to think that this man was that person—this was not what she had expected.

"How interesting. As I mentioned, I have a certain amount of expertise in that and other related areas. Perhaps I could be of some help." She rose from the chair. "I'm going to pour some more tea. Could I warm up your coffee for you?"

LAUREN WATCHED from the window as Kyle climbed into his van and pulled out of her parking lot. Her personal observation was that of a handsome man with sex appeal that nearly knocked her socks off—a magnetism that could not be hidden even though he had driven all night and was exhausted. He was a dynamic man with many hidden contradictions and shadowy secrets.

She did not believe the paranormal investigator bit for even a moment. He had done his homework well, knew the proper jargon and buzzwords and would probably be able to fool most people—but not her. There was an energy about him, a flow she immediately tapped in to that told her he was definitely a skeptic. It was not anything specific he had done or said, just his manner and the slightly mocking edge in his voice when he referred to fortune telling and mind reading.

A frown wrinkled her forehead. Why would someone pretend to be a paranormal investigator? There was nothing at the lighthouse, regardless of all the weird stories that periodically circulated, that should have attracted the attention of any outsiders.

She glanced at the top of the Hoosier cabinet. ''Well, Ty-Ty, if Kyle Delaney is the skeptic I believe him to be it will be interesting to see what he does if he encounters Jeremy.'' The cat jumped from his perch, landing on her shoulder. She lovingly stroked the cat's fur. ''Don't worry, Ty-Ty. We'll find out what he's all about.''

KYLE STRETCHED his tall frame out on the bed in his motel room, his hands resting behind his head as he took in his new surroundings. It was an okay room, large enough to keep that caged-in feeling from enveloping him after a few weeks had passed. Luxury it was not, but it would do. He emitted a sigh of resignation. It was the luck of the draw. He had been on this case too long, and it had too many intricate little pieces. It made no sense for someone else to take it over now.

His jaw tightened and he furrowed his brow in anger as he recalled the heated argument he and the chief had gotten into because of the report the psychologist had done. *Job burnout...losing my edge. That'll be the day! The jerk compiled his stupid report without even talking to me. Even the chief admitted the guy may have been a little out of line. Damn fool psychologist!*

His thoughts turned to the two hours he had spent early that morning with Lauren Jamison. She was the most mysterious and mystifying woman he had ever come across in his life. She was very easy to talk with, but there was something very disturbing about her—something he did not understand. His natural skepticism made him wary of her, but a much stronger force attracted him to her.

He closed his eyes and conjured up a mental image. First, she wore no wedding ring. He always made it a point to notice whether or not a woman was married. That kind of trouble he did not need or want. He sized her up as being about five foot eight, a perfect fit for his height. But mostly it was her eyes—they were the most extraordinary emerald color and filled with a bewitching mixture of honesty, intelligence, curiosity and a hauntingly disturbing hint of mystery.

He cleared his mind of the disturbing thoughts. The idle musings were getting him nowhere—except into an unwanted state of extreme distraction. He had been up for over thirty hours straight and was in desperate need of some sleep. In a matter of only a few moments he was oblivious to everything.

Kyle did not know how long he had been sleeping when the strange sound finally penetrated his consciousness. He slowly moved toward wakefulness as he tried to decipher exactly what he was hearing. It sounded like some sort of a raspy rumble with a jingling sound occasionally joining in. The sound seemed to emanate from just next to his head. He turned his face toward the sound and slowly opened his eyes.

"What the hell—" His body stiffened, his heart jumped into his throat, and he felt his eyes widen in startled surprise as he stared into another pair of blue eyes.

The purring Siamese cat stared back at him as it licked its front paws, each movement of its head causing the small gold bell around its neck to jingle. Kyle reached for the cat, but it quickly darted out of the way and scurried under the bed.

Kyle sat upright, shaking the sleep from his head. How had the cat gotten into his room? It was an inexcusable lapse on his part for something like that to have happened without his being aware of it. His very life depended on his being aware of everything that went on around him.

He picked up his watch from the nightstand and was surprised to find he had been sleeping for nearly six hours. He looked around the room with a critical eye. The window was open a little bit—just enough for an agile cat to squeeze through. Odd. He certainly did not remember the window being open. He quickly closed and locked it.

"All right, cat. Where are you hiding?" He looked under the bed, in the closet, in the cabinets, behind the door, in the bathroom. Nothing—the cat was nowhere to be found. Then the sound came again. The same raspy rumble filled the air, as if the cat were mocking him—daring him to find it.

"WE HAD A PRETTY good day today, Milly. Especially considering the miserable weather." Lauren glanced at the clock. It was ten minutes to six. "Why don't we go ahead and close up. I doubt there'll be any more customers during the next ten minutes." She picked up the stack of mail the postman had left a couple of hours earlier. "Anything here other than bills?"

The gray-haired woman in her mid-fifties looked up from her work. "You have another letter from Shane Nolan. That makes two this month instead of his usual one. Even Mr. Erskine mentioned it when he delivered the mail this afternoon."

Lauren stared at the familiar handwriting on the envelope postmarked Dublin, Ireland. "You're right, this is unusual." She slipped the envelope into her pocket so she could read the letter later.

Milly began efficiently checking the log of books and cards sold that day so that the reorder list could be updated. She paused and watched Lauren for a moment before she spoke. "Tell me…what happened between the time I left here yesterday evening and the time I came to work this morning?''

Lauren felt the flush cover her cheeks as she looked at her mentor. ''I...uh...I don't know what you mean.'' It had been almost seventeen years since Milly had taken the frightened and lost eighteen-year-old under her wing and acted as a surrogate mother following the death of Lauren's parents in the car wreck. It was Milly who had helped her recognize and define her newly emerging psychic abilities and had taught her about folk medicine and healing herbs. Milly had also been there for Lauren seven years ago following the traumatic circumstances that surrounded the death of her fiancé.

The older woman placed her hands on Lauren's shoulders. ''I'm talking about the marvelous glow that surrounds you, something new and exciting that's entered your life.''

She looked away from Milly's searching gaze, glancing out the front windows just in time to see the van with the dark tinted windows pull up in front of the door. She knew she would be seeing Kyle again some time soon. She felt the tingle of excitement as she called to him when he walked in the door. ''Hello, Kyle. Did you get some sleep? You look rested.''

Milly smiled knowingly and quickly gathered up her purse and jacket. Her words were whispered. ''I'm sure you can handle the closing chores by yourself. I'll make myself scarce and see you in the morning. Besides, I have a dinner engagement tonight and need to be on my way.''

Lauren smiled knowingly. ''Another date with your mysterious admirer? When are you going to tell me who he is?''

Milly stammered nervously. ''Maybe some day soon.''

Lauren glanced at Kyle, then at Milly. ''Oh... uh...Milly, this is Kyle Delaney. Kyle, this is Milly

Evans. She's my right hand here at work and my dear friend."

"I'm pleased to meet you, Milly." Kyle extended his hand and offered a charming smile.

"Thank you." Milly accepted his handshake. "It's nice to meet you, too." She shot Lauren another sly look then edged toward the door. "Well, if you'll excuse me I was just about to call it a day."

Kyle glanced out the front window, then focused his attention on the squad car that pulled into the parking lot. Milly seemed slightly flustered as she stole a furtive glance around the parking lot. The driver opened the passenger door from inside the car and Milly slid in. Kyle continued to watch as the car pulled away, then returned his attention to Lauren.

Small white flowers adorned her head and were woven in with her French braid. The heady fragrance caused his senses to tingle with an intriguing sense of seduction. He felt the heat rise low in his body and a tightness spread across his chest.

He crossed the parlor, unzipping his jacket as he made his way toward the fireplace. "I have something here that I think you want." He reached inside his jacket and brought out the Siamese cat.

"Ty-Ty!" The smile lit up her face. "You naughty boy, where have you been?" She looked at Kyle. "Where did you find him?"

"Odd as it might sound, I found him inside my motel room. It's a mystery to me why he was there."

She reached to take the cat from his hands. "Shame on you, Ty-Ty. You shouldn't have been bothering Kyle." The cat squirmed free, jumped to the floor and headed for the Hoosier cabinet.

Their hands touched, their eyes met. An undeniable arc of energy sizzled between them.

Lauren felt it the second they made physical contact,

then she immediately saw it in her mind's eye. Life-threatening danger surrounded him. It was more than just his mysterious aura, more than his pretending to be something she knew he was not, more than the many secrets he kept. It momentarily frightened her. She knew danger would bind them together, that his danger would somehow be hers. She covered her concern by shuffling through some receipts at the cash register even though she had checked them earlier.

Kyle was not sure exactly what had happened or what to do about it. This was a completely different sensation than any he had experienced. This was not the familiar feeling of excitement associated with a new sexual attraction, it was more—much more. It was as unsettling to him as was Lauren herself. He peered around the corner into the tearoom. "Do you—" he tried to regain his composure and project a casual manner "—serve dinner here?"

"No, just lunch. In fact—" she glanced at the clock above the fireplace "—we're closing the bookstore and gift shop in just a few minutes."

He could not stop the disappointment that quickly presented itself. "I haven't eaten since dinner yesterday, and I'm starved. Could you recommend a good restaurant?" He offered her his best smile, then the words came out of his mouth without his consciously meaning to say them. "Perhaps you could join me for dinner. I'd appreciate the company."

She knew this man was destined to be the one great love of her life, a love far more intense than anything she had previously experienced. She also knew it would be a love fraught with setbacks and complexity.

"I have a better idea. Why don't you let me fix us some dinner right here? I'd really like to hear more about your investigation of the lighthouse, and this atmosphere is much more conducive for quiet conversation." She saw the quick look of uncertainty cross his face. Beyond his initial statements, which she did not believe, he had managed to avoid all her questions about his job. She wanted to know why he was being so evasive.

He was thoughtful for a moment before responding to her offer. He flashed a confident smile. "I accept. Maybe you can fill me in on the local scene. I know how it is in small towns when strangers come in and start poking around in local business. Perhaps you could steer me toward the right people. I want to interview several of the longtime residents and also search through the newspaper archives."

He pretended an offhand, casual manner, as if a thought had just struck him. "Tell me, that large warehouse located on the lighthouse road close to the end...what is it and why is it so isolated from everything else?"

"That's Frank Brewster's warehouse. He owns the hardware store and the auto parts supply store. He does a lot of regional business encompassing the four surrounding counties, especially in auto parts, so he keeps a lot of inventory stored there. The property has been in his family for generations. Since he already owned the land I suppose he felt it was the logical place to build the warehouse."

"Well, that certainly makes sense."

"THAT WAS DELICIOUS." Kyle placed his fork on the empty plate. "You're a very good cook."

"Thank you." Lauren picked up the dirty dishes. "I enjoy cooking but it's just too much of a bother for only one person." She carried the dishes into the kitchen, leaving him alone in the small dining room.

He had assumed they would eat in the tearoom. Instead, she had invited him into her living quarters behind the business part of the building. The surroundings were comfortable—a living room with separate dining area, a kitchen and, he assumed, a bedroom and bathroom beyond the closed sliding doors. The air was filled with a scent, the same scent that permeated the bookstore and gift shop. He had smelled it that morning but did not recognize it.

"It's bayberry."

"What?" He whirled around to face her. Again her words and sudden appearance startled him, just as they had early that morning. "You were wondering about the fragrance...it's bayberry. It's good luck. I always burn it in the shop, either incense or a candle."

"That's very unsettling the way you seem to read my mind." He allowed the hint of an impish grin. "It could also end up being very embarrassing. That is—" his expression turned serious as he traced her jawline with his index finger and plumbed the depths of her eyes "—if you can tell what I'm thinking right now."

Her breathing quickened as the heat of his touch warmed her senses. She recognized the look in his eyes, the intensity of a man of many passions—not the least of which was a sexual magnetism he could not have hidden even if he wanted to. She stepped back from his all-too-tempting touch and rubbed her hand across her nape in an attempt to force the tremor away. She needed to steer the conversation toward safer ground. "Tell me more about your job. How did you become interested in paranormal activities?"

He launched into his carefully prepared cover story, relating the educational credentials and experience he would be expected to possess in order to accomplish the task as he had presented it.

She listened politely and quietly until he had finished. "That's an impressive list of qualifications. You've even been with the Institute for Psychic Research. That's located in Connecticut, isn't it?" She looked at him, her face all innocence.

"No, it's in Boston." He immediately recognized her effort to trip up his story, to test him.

"It's funny, though..." She eyed him carefully.

"What's funny?" He was not pleased with the suspicion he detected in her voice and the wariness in her eyes.

"You don't seem old enough to have accomplished all that." She paused, as if turning something over in her mind, then continued. "Just how old are you, if you don't mind my asking?"

Perhaps he had laid it on too thick. He needed to reserve the full line of psychobabble for the totally uninitiated. Lauren was obviously too knowledgeable about this type of thing. He decided the best defense was a good offense. "I don't mind at all. I'm thirty-two. And how old are you—" a mischievous grin turned the corners of his mouth "—if you don't mind my asking?"

Chapter Two

Lauren stared him straight in the eye. "I just turned thirty-six last month."

Kyle could not stop the look of surprise that darted across his face. She had done it to him again, caught him off guard with her straightforward manner. "Really? Thirty-six, huh?"

She cocked her head, a hint of a teasing grin pulling at the corners of her mouth. "What was that look all about...did you think I was older than thirty-six?"

He quickly recovered his balance then began to laugh. "Not at all. I was just surprised that you told me. Actually, I prefer older women." His smile faded and his manner turned serious again. He skimmed his fingertips across her cheek. A touch of huskiness surrounded his words. "And I don't use the word *older* in any type of a negative context."

Younger women seemed to play coy little games. He preferred the maturity and confidence of older women. Actually, he did not seem to have time in his life for much of anything other than his job.

Now it was Lauren's turn to experience a moment of disquietude caused by Kyle's directness. His sky blue eyes captured her in the web of his magnetic aura. She felt a shortness of breath and a tightness in her chest. She took in a calming lungful of air and changed the subject. "Have you been to the lighthouse yet?"

"Well...no, not yet." He found no reason to mention the aerial survey he had done a week ago and the blueprints of the original construction he had studied after procuring them from the government archives.

"Since you're here to investigate the lighthouse, you really should take a tour with someone who knows it." She looked at him questioningly. "Why don't I show it to you right now?"

"You? Now?" Surprise covered his face.

"Sure...if you're interested in the presence that inhabits the lighthouse, night is the best time."

"The...uh...presence." His eyes narrowed slightly, and his look turned skeptical. "How can we get into the lighthouse? This certainly isn't the regular time for it to be open. I had planned to contact Mrs. Peyton in the morning to see if I could get a key of my own for the duration of my investigation. Obviously I need to do my work when the building isn't open to the public."

"I'm the head of the lighthouse committee." She allowed a soft chuckle. "It's more a matter of convenience due to proximity than any type of special honor. Even though Irene is head of the historical society, her pet project is the restoration of the Victorian homes and the old railroad station the society was able to purchase and thus save from the unrelenting march of progress. She's done a monumental job of raising funds for their restoration and the purchase of land surrounding the railroad station for the creation of a heritage park. The Victorian houses will eventually be moved to that location."

She cocked her head and gave him a questioning look. "Are you ready to go? I'll get my wrap."

Kyle shrugged into his jacket. He was not happy about this. He did not want any onlookers in the way. All the little bits and pieces of information he had put together over the past six months had pointed to one thing, as far as he was concerned. The old lighthouse had to be the focal point.

"Are you ready?" Lauren called to him as she came out of her bedroom. She wrapped the warm, floor-length cape around her shoulders and fastened it at the neck. She indicated the side door. "Let's go out this way." She pulled the hood over her head, then opened the door.

The night was even darker than normal. Whatever moonlight might have been available was completely hidden behind low-hanging dark clouds. The cold mist swirled around Lauren and Kyle as they walked toward the bluff, the path through the tall, wet grass so narrow they had to walk single file. He berated himself for having given in to her suggestion.

He reached inside his jacket and touched the pistol through the fabric of his shirt, reassuring himself that the weapon was in place and ready. He pulled his jacket collar up around his ears then stuck his hands in his pockets to keep them warm. There was just enough of a breeze coming in off the ocean to make it seem colder than it really was. They walked along in silence for several minutes. Up ahead, the dark shape of the old lighthouse loomed through the swirling mist.

Lauren's voice broke the silence. "We're almost there."

Kyle stopped short. He squinted as he tried to stare through the mist. His intense gaze locked on the upper deck of the tower. He saw it again. He blinked several times, but it was still there—a light moving past the window. "What's that?" He pointed toward the tower, but when he looked again the light had vanished. There was only darkness and silence.

Bewilderment clouded her voice. "What's what?"

"I...there was a—" His irritation caused him to snap out the words. "It's nothing!" Confusion swirled in his head. His logical mind knew there had to be some rational explanation. He looked at the dark angry sky then toward the road. Whatever it was it could not have been the reflection of moonlight or car headlights.

A frown wrinkled across his brow as he clenched his jaw. He had formulated a theory in his mind. He hoped it was right and he was not wasting his time. The chief suspected that the center of activity was fifty miles down the coast, in a much more heavily populated area of the next county.

Since the moon was currently in its first-quarter phase, Kyle suspected it would probably be three weeks before anything of consequence happened—a time when the darkness of the new moon would bring more reports of ghostly sightings and the town would be abuzz with yet another rash of mysterious happenings at the lighthouse. Meanwhile, he would see how much he could dig up without causing any suspicion.

They finally arrived at the entrance to the lighthouse, the cottage in front with the tower rising up behind. Lauren unlocked the front door and reached inside for the switch, flooding the interior entry hall with light.

"As you can see, the restoration has been done with precise attention to every detail, re-creating the living quarters as they were in 1895 when they were originally constructed."

Her edge softened and the warmth came through as she conveyed her fondness for the subject. "Many of the antiques and period touches were donated by local merchants and longtime residents. The cottage consists of a large parlor, dining room, kitchen and pantry on the ground level with five bedrooms upstairs. The first lighthouse keeper had a wife and seven children—thus the necessity of so many bedrooms."

"My, my...seven children." Kyle shot her a lascivious look followed by a decidedly wicked grin. "I always wondered what a lighthouse keeper did with his spare time, his job being so isolated from everything else.''

She felt the flush cover her cheeks as she tried to ignore his comment. ''The last lighthouse keeper was a bachelor.'' She paused as she thought about his untimely death and the ensuing accusations. ''The tower originally had two doors, one from the outside and the other connecting from the kitchen. The outside door was removed and the wall repaired at the time the structural reinforcement was done. The tower contains only the winding stairs that lead to the top level where the lamp was installed. Both the cottage cellar and the tower are closed off and not part of the restoration for public viewing.''

Kyle followed her into the room designated as the parlor. ''Do you have a key for the tower? Isn't that where most of the sightings have occurred? There and the attic of the cottage?''

''Well…'' She was hesitant, not sure how to answer his question. It amused her each time she heard a new story of the strange and frightening happenings. She did not know how or why the stories had gotten started. As the person with the closest proximity to the lighthouse, she had never seen or heard the things others had claimed to have experienced.

She paused for a moment, her brow furrowed in concentration. ''I don't have a key for the connecting door. In fact, I'm not sure who does have a key. To the best of my knowledge no one has actually been inside the tower since the construction crew completed the structural work ten years ago.''

She gave him a quick tour of the downstairs rooms, then they ascended the staircase to the second floor where he inspected the bedrooms. Everything was just like the photographs he had studied, nothing out of place or suspicious in any way.

He paused inside the door of the largest bedroom, then

went over and sat on the edge of the bed, his expression telling her how uncomfortable he found it. He shot her a sly grin. "Well, now I understand why he had so many children. This bed certainly isn't any good for sleeping, so there must have been something else they did with it...."
He allowed his words to trail off while he waited for her response. Everything about her excited him, making it very difficult for him to maintain his distance. He was anxious to see how she would respond to his clearly sexual teasing.

She returned his grin with a wry one of her own. "Well, seven children and two adults did give them their own baseball team."

His laugh was open and easy. He was satisfied with her retort. He rose from the bed and followed her to the attic. It contained four gabled windows, two looking out to sea and the other two facing the road and parking lot.

He poked around in some storage boxes. They contained pamphlets and other material used as handouts for visitors to the lighthouse. There was nothing stored in the attic that was of any interest to him or pertinent to his investigation. He stared out each of the four windows in turn, noting the scope of the view across the parking lot toward the bluff and out to sea.

After several minutes he abruptly whirled around and faced Lauren. "This damp night air really chills right through to the bone." He zipped up his jacket. "What do you say to abandoning this tour and doing something to warm up?"

Even in the dim light of the attic there was no mistaking the glint in his eyes as he crossed the room toward her. There was also no mistaking his definition of doing something to warm up. A little tingle of excitement shivered through her body.

"Sure. How about a couple of logs in the fireplace and an after-dinner drink?"

He slipped his arm around her waist and guided her

toward the stairs. His voice and words teased her. "If that's the best you have to offer, then I'll accept."

They left the cottage and returned to Lauren's place. She opened the unlocked side door into her living quarters. They went inside then she closed the door behind them.

A disapproving edge clung to his words. "Don't you ever lock your doors?"

She studied his handsome features for a moment, noting the open concern crossing his face. "The business is locked up, and as far as my side door is concerned, we were only gone for a little while. You're obviously from a large city. This is a small community. There's very little crime here. Our sheriff probably has the easiest job of anyone in the entire county. Max Culhane used to have his own construction company but decided to change careers and run for sheriff."

She furrowed her brow in thought. "It was ten years ago. His company did the structural work on the lighthouse. It was right afterward that Max was elected sheriff. He's probably retirement age, although you wouldn't know it. He's very strong and active."

"That may be all well and good for the people of your community, but this place is located on the main highway and in a sparsely populated area on the outskirts of town. Anyone wandering through could target you for whatever bad intentions they might have in mind. Look at me, for instance, a total stranger knocking at your door at the break of dawn and you just—"

"Are you trying to tell me that you have bad intentions?" A slight grin tugged at the corners of her mouth as she took off her cape. "That I'm not safe with you?"

"Bad intentions?" A sly glint sparkled in his blue eyes. "Of course not. I'm a model of perfect behavior, above reproach, a man who wouldn't dream of stealing anything from you. But—" he reached out and brushed his fingertips lightly across her cheek then cupped her chin in his hand "—are you safe with me?" His gaze turned serious as it wandered across her features. He quickly withdrew his hand. "Hmm…that's a difficult question."

"Perhaps…" His nearness was intoxicating. A sense of reckless abandon charged through her body. "Perhaps a better question might be, are you safe with me? What would you say—" she rested her hand lightly against the taut hardness of his chest "—if I told you I have magic powers and could easily cast a spell over you?"

Their gaze locked for a long, intense moment. The innocent flirtation had turned decidedly serious. She experienced the full impact of his masculinity, the unsettling way he caused her heart to beat a little faster and her pulse to race.

"Well…" A rush of embarrassment filled her as she took half a step back. "You must think I'm awfully forward."

"Not at all." A smoldering intensity burned in the depth of his blue eyes. He reached out toward her. A noticeable huskiness surrounded his words. "I think you've already cast that spell."

He again touched her cheek then stepped toward her, wrapping her in his embrace. He captured her mouth, softly nibbling at the edge of her lips before totally claiming her as his.

She had been thrown into emotional turmoil once before by an ill-fated love. She had put her life back together and had pretty much resigned herself to the fact that she would never find love again—then Kyle Delaney walked through her front door. He made her feel like no one else ever had before, not even Jim Franklin, her fiancé from seven years ago.

She felt the heat of his passion, his intensity almost taking her breath away. His hot kiss promised things yet to be and spoke volumes about the sensuality of the man. She ran her fingers through his thick hair, then reached her arms around his neck. It was a delicious kiss that got better with each passing second.

He took complete control. His mouth demanded everything without really being demanding. The very air surrounding them crackled with sexual energy. The length of his body was pressed against hers. It was the type of seduction that could not be ignored—smooth, experienced, filled with a scorching heat that seemed to be rapidly heading in only one direction.

Then a totally unexpected surge of anxiety took control of her. It had started as just a slight tickle but quickly escalated into full-blown panic. There was no reason for her to be experiencing this sudden embarrassment and uncertainty. She was a mature woman, yet at that moment she felt just like a schoolgirl involved in her first crush. She broke off the kiss and took a step back.

An almost imperceptible frown wrinkled his brow, followed by a quizzical look. He spoke with strength and confidence, yet there was a soft quality that surrounded his words. "Did I misinterpret—"

"It's...it's getting late. Perhaps we had better say goodnight." She felt the anxiety well inside her. She lowered her gaze for a moment, then regained eye contact with him. "I want you to know that I'm not the type of person who plays teasing games then walks away."

His voice was soft, his words sincere. "I never for a moment thought that you were."

Once again he caused her to experience tremors of delight. In spite of the mystery that surrounded him and the danger she associated with him, she was sure he would reveal the truth when he felt the time was right. She could afford to be patient—after all, they would have the rest of their lives together.

A totally unexpected jolt of icy cold shivered up her spine. The rest of their lives...that might not be as long as it sounded. She tried to shake away the disturbing feeling that had forced its way in.

"Good night, Lauren." His gaze lingered for a moment on the kiss-swollen lushness of her mouth, then he turned and walked out the door.

He was not as easily appeased as his controlled manner would indicate. He had often experienced an immediate attraction to a woman on a purely physical level, but nothing like this. No one had ever captured his senses and desires as quickly as Lauren had. The kiss they had shared had become a sensual experience he could still feel. He shook his head. He needed to clear thoughts of her from his mind and keep his attention focused on the job. He could not afford to let any diversions distract him from what he needed to do, no matter how enticing.

He drove toward the lighthouse rather than to his motel. He wanted another crack at checking the lighthouse before his presence and accompanying cover story became common knowledge. He turned off the headlights and continued on for the last quarter mile. He parked a hundred feet from the lighthouse, then sat and stared at the dark, foreboding structure for a couple of minutes before opening the door and sliding out from behind the wheel. The swirling mist had turned to a light rain. He pulled the hood of his jacket over his head, grabbed a flashlight and shoved it in his jacket pocket. He closed the van door and stole silently up the road on foot.

He rounded the corner of the cottage, stealthily moving in the darkness to the back of the structure. He pulled a set of lock picks from his inside pocket. A moment later the lock clicked. He pulled open the heavy wooden double doors that led directly to the cellar and descended the steps, closing the doors behind him.

The darkness surrounded him. He remained still, listening for anything that did not belong. He heard only the whistling of the wind and the gentle patter of the light rain. He snapped on the flashlight and slowly shined it around.

The cellar was a jumble of miscellaneous storage— pieces of furniture and accessories, boxes of various sizes, gardening tools and maintenance supplies. It was divided into two rooms—the large main part with pillars and ceiling beams to support the floor of the cottage above, and a smaller room off to one side, which also had a couple of ceiling beams. It was an odd little room not much bigger than an oversize walk-in closet. The back wall appeared to have been damaged at one time resulting in a patched area.

He cautiously ascended the stairs to the ground level inside the cottage, pausing for a moment when he hit a squeaky step. He picked the door lock to gain entrance to the main part of the cottage. He quickly made his way to the kitchen and went to work on the connecting door leading to the tower. After repeated tries the rusted lock finally clicked open. He turned the handle and pushed the heavy wooden door. It creaked on its hinges as it swung wide, ripping loose the cobwebs that tried to hold it shut.

He shined the flashlight beam ahead of him as he stepped through the door, its brightness penetrating the inky black interior of the tower. Particles of dust floated down, crossing the bright beam of his flashlight then settling on the floor. Every step he took echoed off the walls. He slowly shined the light around the cylindrical room. The winding stairs went up inside the tower, disappearing into the dark.

The oppressive gloom closed in around him. The loose dust particles tickled his nose, threatening to make him sneeze. It was an eerie feeling, one he could not clearly define. He had been in lots of dangerous situations over the course of his career, life-threatening scenarios that caused the adrenaline to pump and his heart to pound. But they were always situations where he had a feeling of control. This was different.

He listened again but all he heard was the rain and wind. He started up the long spiral staircase. About two-thirds of the way up he paused and snapped off the flashlight. He squinted as he peered into the black cylinder of the lighthouse tower.

A cold shudder of anxiety darted through him, then his heart began to beat faster. Up the winding staircase, high above him in the tower, a dim light suddenly appeared then grew brighter. It continued to glow for several seconds before disappearing, leaving only blackness.

Kyle gulped in a lungful of cold air while trying to bring the pounding in his chest under control. Surely it must have been a flash of lightning. He listened for the accompanying sound of thunder he hoped would follow, but the only booming he heard was the pounding of his heart.

He took a calming breath as he unzipped his jacket and reached under his shirt. He pulled the pistol from his shoulder holster and snapped off the safety. He peered through the darkness toward the top level, the place where the glowing light had come from. He took another calming breath, then quietly climbed the rest of the way. As he approached the opening onto the top level, the blackness gave way to shades of gray and he felt the movement of air. The increased cold and dampness chilled him to the bone.

He peered through the opening at the top of the stairs, then stepped onto the deck of the lamp housing level. The cold wind blew across his face, numbing his cheeks and nose. He began walking the circular decking, his pistol at the ready and all his senses on alert for anything out of the ordinary. He was immediately struck by the commanding view, a far better lookout point than what he had observed from the cottage attic. A person stationed on the top level with night-vision binoculars could easily keep anyone below apprised of the movements of unwanted visitors from either land or sea.

An old kerosene lantern across from the stairwell opening caught his attention. He started to reach for it, then yanked his hand back. Heat radiated from the old lantern. Even in the cold damp air it was still hot. Someone... A quick shiver darted up his spine. He glanced around, then took a steadying breath. He looked at the lantern again.

There had to be some rational explanation for the lantern being hot to the touch. Then his gaze lit on something else. He pulled the small penknife from his pocket, knelt next to the lantern and carefully dug out the object that had dropped between the top planks of the decking. A cigarette butt...a nice, fresh one that was not even wet from the light rain. He withdrew a small plastic evidence bag from his inside jacket pocket and put the cigarette in it.

He could not stop the gratified smile that tugged at the corners of his mouth. He had never heard of a ghost who smoked real cigarettes. The discovery did leave him with one puzzling question, though. He was positive no one had been through the connecting door between the tower and the cottage kitchen. So how had someone gotten to the top deck? He glanced around once more, his gaze lingering for an uncomfortable moment on the lantern, then he returned to the circular stairs that led to the ground.

LAUREN LAY IN BED snuggled under the blankets. A vision flashed across her mind, lasting only a fraction of a second. It was the same as before. A man—she could not see his face—hurtling off the cliff into the blackness of night, falling toward the angry ocean far below. She closed her eyes and shoved the vision away, just as she had done earlier.

Ty-Ty jumped onto the large bed and curled up next to her. She stroked the cat's fur, the gesture intended to soothe her own nerves as much as to show her affection for the Siamese. Her thoughts moved from the disturbing vision to Kyle Delaney—his darkly handsome features, intense blue eyes and dazzling smile. She placed her fingertips against her lips. The reality of his kiss still burned hot against her mouth as well as in her memory.

Chapter Three

"Mrs. Peyton, it's a pleasure to meet you." Kyle offered his best smile as he shook the elderly woman's hand. "Thank you for making time for me today."

"That's quite all right, young man. I'm happy to be able to help you in any way I can." She indicated a chair for Kyle then seated herself in her favorite rocker. "May I offer you some tea and cookies?"

"That would be very nice." He carefully lowered himself onto the chair and tried to get comfortable. He inwardly winced as he heard the chair creak. His large frame just did not work well with her delicate furnishings. He quickly scanned her living room with a practiced eye. It seemed to suit her.

Several framed photographs rested on an antique oak sideboard next to his chair. He picked up one of the pictures and studied it for a moment. He glanced at Irene, then looked at the photo again. It showed a very pretty girl with two boys. The physical resemblance between the boys indicated that they were probably brothers, even though one appeared to be quite a bit older than the other. "This is you, isn't it?"

Irene took the photograph from his hand. "Oh, my." She seemed slightly flustered as she placed the picture on the sideboard. "That was taken such a long time ago. I was fifteen years old.'' She poured tea into a delicate china cup and handed it to him along with a small china plate containing two oatmeal cookies.

''Thank you, Mrs. Peyton.''

''Actually, it's *Miss* Peyton...I've never married. But you may call me Irene.'' She reached into one of several dishes containing hard candy. She unwrapped one of the candy balls and put it into her tea instead of adding sugar. He watched as she methodically folded the candy wrapper in an intricate pattern and added it to the stack of similarly folded candy wrappers on the table next to her chair. It was a little ritual she seemed to perform without really thinking about it.

She returned her attention to Kyle. ''Now, how may I help you?''

He took a bite from one of the cookies. ''These are delicious, Irene. Did you make them yourself?'' Again, he extended his best smile—pure charm as he smoothly worked his way into her good graces and confidence.

''Listen to me, young man. My seventy-eight years of age might dictate that I move around at a slower pace than I used to, but I'm still strong and healthy and my mind is sharp as a tack.'' She leveled a steady gaze at him. ''I suggest you save all that practiced charm for someone else. I've lived too long to be easily taken in by the smooth manner of an attractive young man.''

She leaned back in her chair and offered him an engaging smile. ''Now, your letter wasn't very specific. Exactly how may I help you?''

He was taken aback, but quickly recovered. Irene Peyton may have seemed at first glance like a doddering little old lady who lived in a world of Victorian houses, gardening and afternoon tea rituals, but there was a lot more to her than that. There was something about her manner that said things would be on her terms or not at all.

Lauren had already filled him in on Irene's pet projects

with the historical society, but he had also picked up on her hesitation. It was as if she was trying to be gracious in spite of mixed feelings. She had mentioned Irene's self-appointed position as community social leader and head of various and sundry civic projects.

Kyle spent close to two hours with Irene, outlining his work and what he planned to be doing at the lighthouse—at least as far as his cover story went. He told her he needed to do his work at night when the lighthouse was closed to tourists. He asked if he could have a key so that he did not need to bother anyone with his inconvenient schedule. He also mentioned that he would be making several trips in and out of town over the next few weeks so for her not to worry if she did not see him for a few days at a time. Before he departed she provided him with a key to the lighthouse cottage. He was left with the impression that Irene considered appearance and status to be all-important, that she needed the adulation and respect her work garnered and that was what kept her going.

His next stop was the county office building and the sheriff's office. He found it wise to have the local law enforcement agency know of his presence and purpose, at least as far as 'his cover story went, especially in small towns where everybody seemed to know everybody's business. That usually eliminated all suspicion when he went around asking questions, poring through the local newspaper archives and checking into city and county records.

Kyle was informed that Max Culhane was at the sheriff's station on the main highway. He left one of his business cards with the secretary then drove to the station. He was ushered into an office and introduced to the sheriff.

"It's a pleasure to meet you." Kyle extended his hand and was surprised by the strength of Max's grip. Lauren had not exaggerated about his physical condition.

"Well, you managed to track me down, so what do you want?"

Kyle handed the sheriff one of his business cards. Max looked at the card then tossed it on the desk. "Irene mentioned someone wanted to snoop around in the old lighthouse." He leaned back in his chair and lit a cigar. "Just what is it you expect to find that everyone don't already know? You plan to find out about all them ghosts and goblins everyone thinks lives there?" He allowed a sneer of disdain, pointedly directed at Kyle.

Kyle's senses shot on alert. Max Culhane was challenging him, but why? "There have been so many reports about paranormal activity at the lighthouse that it's hard to ignore." He shifted his weight in the chair and continued with his original purpose for meeting with the sheriff. "I'll be going through old courthouse records, the local newspaper archives and talking to longtime residents. I'll try to stay out of everyone's way."

"Bunch of nonsense, if you ask me. Things is just fine as is. This here's a small town. Folks don't take to strangers pokin' into their business."

Kyle adopted a casual, friendly manner. "I certainly don't intend to pry into anyone's personal life. I'm interested in any historical events that might relate to a presence remaining at that location. I also want to collect local stories and firsthand accounts of specific sightings and encounters."

Max clamped his cigar between his teeth and growled more than spoke. "Well, it's a damn fool waste of time if you ask me—"

"Sheriff, we've got a bad wreck down by—" The intruder halted in midsentence, carefully scrutinizing the stranger in the sheriff's office. He turned his attention to Max. "I'm not interrupting anything, am I?"

Max jerked his head toward the young man who had burst into the office. "This here's one of my deputies, name's Joe Thurlow." The sheriff indicated Kyle. "This here's Kyle Delaney, the fellow Irene says is gonna be hunting for ghosts at the lighthouse." He relit his cigar and leaned back in his chair again. "Now, what's the problem, Joe? Some sort of traffic accident?"

"Fatality…Billy Washburn dead at the scene. His car went off the road and into a ditch a couple of miles south of the lighthouse. Mitch O'Connor spotted it while on patrol. Must have happened some time last night. The body has been removed to the county morgue and the car is being towed to the impound. About a dozen empty beer cans in the back seat."

Max sat up straight, a scowl covering his face. "Damn fool kid. I thought he had straightened out after that run-in we had with him a couple of years ago at the beer bust down on the beach. Drunk as a skunk, he was." He looked at his deputy. "Sam Washburn been notified yet?"

"Yep. We told him about his boy. He's real steamed, Sheriff. Says there was no way Billy had been drinking. He's screaming—"

An angry man in his mid-fifties crashed through the front door, the loud bang reverberating through the office. He quickly descended on the sheriff. "Max Culhane, you lousy son of a bitch! You ain't whitewashin' this death like they did that other one. Ain't no way my boy was drinking. Just ain't no way!"

Kyle saw the rage contorting the man's face and the intense pain in his eyes. His hands were balled into tight fists making him look as if he were about to take a swing at someone. Kyle quickly rose to his feet and gingerly stepped to one side, not wanting to get caught in the middle of what appeared to be an imminent cross fire of flying punches over a clearly local matter.

The sheriff also jumped to his feet and rushed out from behind his desk. He grabbed the man's raised arm and twisted it behind his back. "Now, calm down, Sam. I know you're upset about Billy. Damn shame about the boy, but all the evidence is there. Car littered with empty beer cans, no skid marks on the road, no other car involved. And it ain't like it's the first time, either. We had your boy right here in the drunk tank followin' the high school graduation party.''

Max steered Sam Washburn toward the door, his voice softening a little. "You calm down and go on home. I'm sure the coroner will release the body real soon. Now, you go on home."

Kyle watched Max Culhane escort Sam Washburn out to the street, followed by Joe Thurlow. It was just as well. It had been obvious that his conversation with the sheriff was at an end.

Kyle left the sheriff's station and walked down the sidewalk, his mind going over everything that had just taken place. Of particular interest was the sheriff's stated surprise about the accident, yet he knew the details even though his deputy had not filled him in. He glanced across the street at the offices of the *Sea Grove Gazette,* paused a moment, then crossed and headed toward the building.

Kyle introduced himself to Tony Mallory, the publisher, editor and chief reporter for the local weekly newspaper. He handed Tony one of his business cards while giving him a brief overview of his cover story.

"Sure, Kyle." Tony's attitude was enthusiastic. "I'd be happy to provide you with whatever archive material you need. I think the paper's morgue is complete—issues back for seventy-five years, when the newspaper was founded. If you could tell me exactly what it is you're looking for, I might be able to give you more help."

"I'm not sure *exactly* what I'm looking for. I'm just gathering background information about the lighthouse— anything that might have been newsworthy enough to have made the paper."

"Well, if you want to go back to the beginning—the land under the lighthouse had been in the Brewster family for generations. They sold a small parcel out on the bluff to the government for the lighthouse. It was closed down in 1952. The closure coincided with the completion of the new, modern signal beacon, and the unfortunate accident that resulted in the untimely death of the lighthouse keeper, a man named Jeremy MacDonald. He fell from the top landing of the lighthouse tower.'' Tony paused for a moment then added, almost as an afterthought, ''The coroner's inquest ruled it an accidental death and the case was summarily closed but not without some controversy and hard feelings.''

''You seem to have a pretty clear knowledge of the events, considering it all happened before you were born.'' It was an innocent enough statement, but Kyle noted the way Tony momentarily clenched his jaw into a hard line.

''That's easily explained—1952 is the year I just finished transferring to a computer retrieval system. I started at the beginning and have been working my way forward as time and money permit. Since I did most of the actual computer input myself, the information is fresh in my mind.''

''That sounds like a pretty ambitious project.'' Kyle shook hands with Tony. ''I appreciate your help. I'll be in and out of town over the next few weeks, but I'm sure we'll be seeing a lot of each other. If you don't mind, I'll just find a quiet corner and try not to interfere with your daily routine.'' He turned to leave then paused as if a thought had occurred to him. ''I was just at the sheriff's office when the deputy told him about a car wreck fatality. I understand the victim was a local resident…had graduated from high school right here in Sea Grove. Terrible tragedy.''

''Yeah…we just got in something about that.'' Tony rummaged through several pieces of paper on his desk then picked up one of them. ''Billy Washburn, nineteen years old. Worked at Frank Brewster's auto parts warehouse out on Lighthouse Road. Apparently he had been drinking and fell asleep at the wheel.'' He shook his head in dismay. ''These kids think they're invincible. When will they ever learn? Drinking and driving just don't mix.''

Kyle left the newspaper office with mixed feelings about Tony Mallory. The newspaperman was outwardly friendly and certainly went out of his way to be cooperative, but there was something a little troubling about him. Maybe it was the way he avoided making eye contact as they talked. Kyle was not sure, but it kept nagging at him as he walked down the street.

''Hey, there…Mr. Delaney, isn't it? Wait up a minute.''

Kyle turned toward the source of the intrusion. He eyed the paunchy man in his late fifties who seemed to waddle more than walk as he hurried down the sidewalk. By the time he caught up to Kyle, the stranger was totally out of breath.

The man stuck out his pudgy hand. ''I'm Harvey Sherwood of Sherwood Development.''

Kyle accepted his handshake. ''It's nice to meet you.'' The man's palm was sweaty and there was a nervousness in the way his gaze darted from place to place. ''Just what is it you develop, Mr. Sherwood?''

''Real estate ventures are my main area of operation, land development. Take that land where the lighthouse sits. I was putting together a really sweet little deal for the construction of some condominiums—a country club type of setting that would have eventually included a golf course.'' Harvey pulled a handkerchief from his pocket and mopped his perspiration-laden brow. ''Yep, it was a real sweetheart of a deal.''

The weather was cool. There was no reason for Harvey to be sweating. ''That's interesting, Mr. Sherwood—''

''Please, call me Harvey…everyone does.''

''All right, Harvey. That's all very interesting, but what does it have to do with me?''

''Well, I thought you might be in a position to influence

the historical society people…convince them that it's all those tourists making the ghosts unhappy, that they should close up the lighthouse or maybe move it to another location. That way the ghosts would be happy and would go back into hiding.'' Harvey lowered his voice as he furtively glanced around. ''I'm sure my investors could come up with some tangible way of showing their appreciation for your efforts. Know what I mean?''

Kyle took a steadying breath. He did not like Harvey Sherwood, did not like him at all. ''I appreciate your offer, Harvey, but I doubt the historical society would be interested. The lighthouse is an integral part of the history of Sea Grove and its people. In fact, of this entire stretch of coastline.''

''Yes, well…'' Harvey reached into his pocket, withdrew a business card and handed it to Kyle. ''You think about what I said. If you change your mind, give me a call.''

He watched as Harvey waddled down the sidewalk and around the corner. Even for a small town, word of Kyle's arrival had gotten around in record time.

KYLE SNAPPED OFF his flashlight and stood in the darkened attic of the lighthouse cottage. He stared out the gabled window toward the ocean, the view obscured by the mist of another stormy night. His thoughts were lost in the events of the day. It had been an enlightening series of meetings.

Irene Peyton was the driving backbone of the historical society and was very dedicated to her cause. She was one very sharp, matter-of-fact woman.

Max Culhane was questionable. He was the county sheriff, and therefore someone to be trusted. Only Kyle did not trust him.

Tony Mallory was intelligent, quick, organized and seemed like he would be very resourceful. But still, there was something nagging at the back of Kyle's conscious-ness, a wariness that told him to keep his distance and not trust Tony's overly helpful manner.

Frank Brewster was on his list of specific people to con-tact. The Brewster family owned several parcels of land in town. The story of them having built the warehouse in an isolated location next to the lighthouse because they al-ready owned the land did not sit well with Kyle.

And Harvey Sherwood...the real estate developer had openly offered him a bribe seemingly without concern for any adverse consequences. The land with the lighthouse was not enough for his condominium project. He would need a great deal of the surrounding land, as well. Most of it was owned by Frank Brewster...and a small parcel belonged to Lauren Jamison.

A sound from downstairs jerked his thoughts to the pres-ent. He heard the front door open and close, followed by the almost imperceptible creak of footsteps on the stair-case. He had not expected trouble this soon. He pulled the pistol from his shoulder holster and silently moved behind the door.

A shadowy figure entered the attic room. Kyle threw his arm across the trespasser's neck in a choke hold and placed his gun against the intruder's temple. His voice was a men-acing whisper. "Don't even think about moving. Don't even breathe."

"Kyle?" The fear coursed through Lauren's body and came out in her voice. Her insides churned and her heart pounded as she tried to swallow her panic.

"Oh, my God..." He released her and stepped back. "Lauren...what are you doing here?"

She turned to face him as she reached for the light switch on the wall, then pulled the hood of her cape away from her head. She could not stop her eyes from widening in shock as her gaze fixed on the gun in his hand, the weapon he had pointed at her. For a dizzying minute, she was taken back to that horrible night just forty-eight hours before her wedding when she had discovered her fiancé's body. Jim Franklin had been shot, the blood staining his living room carpet a sickening color of red.

Things were beginning to make sense to her, the awareness that danger surrounded him and would subsequently engulf her. "I..." Her jangled nerves still were not quite under control. "I was taking my regular nightly walk and saw a light shining around the attic and—"

"And what?" His voice held an edge of anger, an anger tinged with a hint of anxiety. "You thought you'd just casually saunter over and check it out? Isn't that a little foolish?"

"Not at all." Her clipped words and indignant tone told him she resented his comments. "I assumed it was you. Irene told me she had—" she pointedly stared at the gun he still held in his hand "—given you a key."

The moment was truly an awkward one. Kyle did not know quite what to do or say. He quickly slipped the pistol into the holster, covering it with his shirt. "Lauren..."

"A gun, Kyle? Why do you carry one?" The trepidation in her voice was tinged with anger. There was no question in his mind about the anxiety this bit of knowledge caused her. He could see it in her eyes.

"Why does a paranormal investigator need to carry a concealed weapon? What could there possibly be about your work that would require a gun?"

"It's, uh, well, you're right. A gun certainly wouldn't be of any use against some sort of spectral entity." He tried to sound light and casual as he emitted a nervous laugh while his mind raced to find an acceptable explanation. "In the course of my work I've occasionally found myself in strange, out-of-the-way places dealing with some very weird people. I've even had my life threatened a couple of times. It's just for my own protection."

For his own protection...that was what her fiancé had

said about the gun he kept in his house—the very weapon that had been used to kill him. She leveled a clearly skeptical look at Kyle and took a calming breath. Her heartbeat had almost returned to normal, but she was unable to totally conceal her animosity toward the unexpected turn of events. "And you thought you might encounter some hostile spirit here?" She looked around the attic. "Some sort of otherworldly danger that could be handled with a gun?"

His voice softened, his words coming from some unexpected place deep inside him. "The only danger that exists in this attic at this moment is an emotional one." He reached his hand out toward her face, allowing his fingertips to lightly brush against her cheek. He cupped her chin in his hand and searched her face for a moment before bending his head toward hers.

He captured her mouth with a soft kiss that quickly escalated. He wrapped his arms around her, drawing her into his embrace. He needed to repair the damage he had done, calm the awkward situation he had created. But that would have to wait. Right now, all he wanted was the taste and feel of her mouth. He slipped his tongue between her lips and sensually brushed it against the texture of her tongue.

He was being drawn in by her just as surely as he had captured her. She was totally different from any other woman he had ever known. He felt a heated desire that came from an entirely new place for him. It was a place of caring that was quickly turning into emotional involvement—a connection he knew he did not dare allow but did not know how to stop.

Lauren did not know what to think. A gun—one minute he had the vile thing pointed at her head and the next minute he was methodically driving her crazy with desire. Even with his clothes and her heavy cape as a barrier, she could still feel his growing hardness pressed against her body.

"Kyle..." Lauren forced a calm to her highly charged

passions as she pulled back from his kiss. "This is too much, too fast. One minute you're pointing a gun at me and the next minute you're…" She took another calming breath as she dropped her hand to his taut chest, the feel of his strong heartbeat resonating to her fingertips. "I can't deny that I'm very attracted to you—"

He drew her into his embrace. "Then there isn't any problem. Why don't we try out one of the bedrooms here in the cottage?" His words tickled across her ear in a teasing whisper. "Let's pretend you're the lighthouse keeper's daughter and I'm the shipwrecked sailor—"

"Wait." She exerted a minimum of pressure against his chest in an attempt to stop him. "There is a problem."

An uneasy feeling stirred inside him. He saw the uncertainty in her eyes and felt it pull at his senses. He was not accustomed to being turned down. But then, in his line of work he was not in one place long enough to be able to afford the luxury of a leisurely game of subtle persuasion and gentle seduction. That was probably why he chose the type of partners he did—women who were not looking for any more of a commitment than he was.

His voice held a hint of apprehension. "What's wrong?"

The intensity in his eyes carved a path right through her common sense directly to her heart. She had to look away for a moment in order to break the magnetic hold he had on her. "Who are you, Kyle? Who are you really? Why have you come to Sea Grove?"

"I told you who I am and why I'm here." He brushed his fingertips across her cheek. "What more is there to tell?"

"I know what you said, but I don't believe it." Her words were emphatic. She saw the caution dart through his eyes. "There's a very real danger surrounding you, Kyle—life-threatening danger. And it doesn't come from any paranormal activities at an old lighthouse."

He was not sure exactly how to respond to her words. "What kind of danger are you talking about?" He slowly pulled her into his embrace, allowing his lips to nibble at the corners of her mouth. He tried to make light of her concerns. "Why do you think so?"

She turned her head from his attempt to renew his seduction, but she did not step back from him. "Don't make fun of me, Kyle. I saw it, I felt it. The first time we met, the moment our hands touched—even before I knew you carried a gun."

"So, what are you saying?" He unfastened the clasp at the neck of her cape and dropped the garment to the floor. "That you had some sort of premonition about me?" He caressed her shoulders then let one hand slide down her spine, coming to rest at the small of her back.

She was barely able to speak, unable to concentrate. "As an educated and intelligent man you shouldn't treat that concept with such obvious disdain...and someone in your stated line of work shouldn't have any reason to be carrying a gun."

"I already explained that."

"No, you didn't. Not to my satisfac—"

He captured her mouth before she could finish her sentence. After a long, heated moment, he finally released her from the kiss. His voice was husky, attesting to his aroused state. "You know as surely as I do that we're going to make love. Apparently not tonight, but it will happen." He was not making any demands of her, he was simply stating what they both knew to be true.

"Oh?" She tried to make light of the words that had sent a tremor of delight through her body. "Is it *your* psychic ability that tells you so?"

His voice was soft and so very sincere. "No, it's your kiss that tells me so. It's destined to be."

He stooped to pick up her cape from the floor. He placed

it around her shoulders then grasped her hand in his. "Come on, I'll take you home."

FRANK BREWSTER perched on the edge of his chair and leaned forward with his elbows on his desk. He held the phone receiver in one hand while his other hand gently massaged his throbbing temple.

The voice on the other end of the phone connection was impatient and angry. "Stop worrying, Frank. As long as you keep your head when this Kyle Delaney talks to you everything will be all right."

Frank's voice trembled with apprehension. "I don't understand why he would need to talk to me. I don't have anything to do with the lighthouse. Besides, what if he stumbles onto something? What then, huh? What then?"

"Everything's under control."

Frank's left eye twitched a couple of times. He took a clean handkerchief from his pocket and mopped his brow, then ran his fingers through his thinning hair. "I sure hope you're right. I don't like this, I don't like any of it."

KYLE STOOD at the edge of the bluff. The high tide crashed below as the waves beat against the base of the cliff. He closed his eyes and inhaled the cold night air. He had to clear his head. All he had thought about for the past hour had been Lauren Jamison and where his desires might have taken them had she not put a stop to things. It was no good. He needed to put any personal thoughts about her out of his mind and concentrate solely on the assignment.

He heard a twig snap and whirled around into a crouch as he reached for his shoulder holster. He had let down his guard. It was only for a moment, but it was long enough. A shot rang out. A searing pain tore through his body and sent him reeling backward. He struggled to regain his balance, but could not prevent himself from hurdling out of control over the edge of the bluff. He fell for what seemed like forever, then the salt spray stung his eyes and the icy reality of the ocean closed around him.

Chapter Four

Lauren jerked upright into a sitting position. Again, it had been a vision so real and so vivid that it woke her from a sound sleep with her heart pounding. She saw a faceless man falling from the cliff to the dark swirling waters below, only this time a shadowy figure stood at the edge of the cliff watching him fall.

She wrapped her arms across the front of her body, hugging her shoulders as she tried to stop the trembling. She hated this particular vision. It frightened her right down to the depths of her very soul. She had to put it out of her mind. She forced herself to relax. She finally drifted off into an uneasy sleep, plagued by strange dreams and confusing visions.

LAUREN had no idea how long she had been sleeping. She swatted at the intrusion, not sure exactly what it was that had invaded her troubled sleep. There it was again. It tickled her nose and prodded her cheek. Then she felt a weight press against her chest. She shook her head to clear the fuzziness as she forced her eyes open. The Siamese cat batted at her face again, demanding her immediate attention.

Her words were thick with sleep, her voice filled with irritation when she finally realized what woke her. "Ty-

Ty, what's the matter with you?'' The cat flicked his tail back and forth in an agitated manner, then paced in a circle. His fur was damp and his paws muddy. He paused every few seconds to let out a plaintive cry.

Lauren's eyes popped wide open as a sudden jolt of fear rippled through her consciousness. She sat up, her thoughts suddenly coming with crystal clarity. "What is it, Ty-Ty? Is something wrong?''

The cat jumped off the bed and darted toward the door, pausing long enough to see if she was following. Lauren threw back the covers and leaped out of bed. She grabbed her robe and jammed her feet into her slippers. She tried not to concentrate on the cold fear that jittered in the pit of her stomach. "Okay, Ty-Ty. I'm up. Now, what's going on? What's the matter with you?''

She followed as the cat led her to the side door. As soon as she opened it the Siamese darted out into the cold night air, Lauren close behind. She came to an abrupt halt about twenty feet from the building. Her heart thudded in her chest. A sick feeling tried to push up from her stomach, but she forced it down. Her feet were leaden, refusing to move. Just ahead of her, facedown and motionless on the ground, lay the body of a man.

She felt it in her bones and in her soul. She did not need to see his face to know it was Kyle. With great difficulty she forced herself into action, moving through the wet grass until she reached him. She swallowed hard then tried to take in a calming breath as she knelt next to the body. She heaved a sigh of relief when a soft moan reached her ears. He was alive.

Taking care not to jar him, she slowly rolled him onto his back. His clothes were sopping wet and covered with mud. She noted his ripped jeans and the scrapes and cuts on his hands. He had obviously dragged himself for quite a distance but lacked the strength to go the final twenty feet.

"Kyle? Can you hear me?" She tried her best to keep her voice calm and not show the fear churning inside her. She smoothed his wet hair from his face, removing pieces of kelp in the process. Other bits of kelp clung to his clothes. The smell, the feel, the look—he had been in the ocean fully clothed and then had dragged himself across the bluff.

"Kyle?" A quaver crept into her voice and would not go away. He lay there like a wrung-out washcloth, the only signs of life the violent shivers that suddenly convulsed his body. She needed to get him inside where it was warm. She tried to prop him into a sitting position, but as soon as she grabbed his shoulders he groaned and recoiled in pain. It was too dark and his clothes were too wet and dirty for her to determine where and how he was injured.

"Kyle...please, speak to me. Say something." The tears filled her eyes as another stab of fear shot through her body. She cradled his head against her body, the sand and grit rubbing off on her robe. "You can't die on me, Kyle. I won't allow it!" He was two hundred pounds of dead-weight, and somehow she had to get him to his feet. "You've got to help me. I can't lift you by myself."

"Lauren?" He did not know how, but she had managed to find him. The relief he felt far surpassed the pain. "Yeah...I..." He was not sure which part of him hurt the worst, the shoulder that had taken the bullet or the muscles that had done battle with the cold ocean then been strained to the limit as he tried to make his way to her house—to what he hoped would be a temporary safe haven. Kyle tried to raise himself up, but the second he put the slightest strain on his right shoulder he winced in pain and fell back.

"Give...just...rest a minute..." His voice was weak, barely above a whisper, but it was the sweetest sound she had ever heard. He was conscious and lucid.

The tears of joy ran down her cheeks, almost choking

her words. "Try to stay calm. I'll call the paramedics and—"

"No! You can't call anyone. Just…get me inside."

"Can you stand up?"

He made another attempt, but it was no good. On top of the fatigue that engulfed him, he had also lost a lot of blood. He tried to focus on Lauren's face. He saw her deep concern, made all the more noticeable by her apprehension. He reached toward her, his trembling fingers making brief contact with her cheek just before everything went black.

Lauren's joy was short-lived. The panic boiled inside her to the point she could almost taste it. Even in the dark she could tell how ashen and drawn his face was. She frantically searched her mind for some way to safely transport him. Then it hit her…it was just what she needed.

She did not know whether he could hear her. "I have to get something. I'll be right back." She kissed his forehead. "You're going to be all right. I won't let anything happen to you." She took off her robe and covered him as best as she could.

Lauren ran to her house, desperation spurring her to a faster pace. She rummaged around in an old storage room until she found what she was seeking. It was two years ago when Milly had broken her leg. Lauren still had the wheelchair. She raced to Kyle. She found him struggling to get to his feet.

She positioned the wheelchair and helped him sit in it. "Hang on. I'm afraid the ride will be a little bumpy." His body continued to convulse with hard shivers. Beads of perspiration stood out on his face, and his breathing had become labored. She was afraid, truly scared. She silently prayed that she would be able to get him to her house before he passed out again.

She knew she had to keep him talking, keep him focused. She could not keep the urgency out of her voice.

"Kyle, can you hear me? Say something. Don't quit on me now. I'll get you a doctor—"

"No!" He was not able to give it much volume, but his meaning was unmistakable. "No doctor."

"But—"

"No. Promise me." It was obviously an effort for him to talk. It was equally obvious that he was highly agitated and seemed to be on the verge of panic. "No doctor. No one must know...promise me."

"Okay. Calm down, don't try to talk. No doctor." Confusion swirled inside Lauren. He was injured, perhaps seriously, yet he had been so emphatic. The anxiety jittered through her stomach. Somehow she had to make sure no one knew where he was while making sure his injuries were tended to.

She managed to get him into her bedroom, then struggled to help him out of the wheelchair. He collapsed across her bed. She flipped on the light, and the sight that greeted her frightened her even more. His jacket was torn, as if a hole had been ripped through it by some outside force. His shirt was bloody, fresh blood rather than remnants that had not been washed away by the ocean water. The only thing comforting about his appearance was the way his chest rose and fell with his breathing. He was alive...but would she be able to keep him that way without any outside help? Lauren tensed her jaw for a hard moment while steeling her nerves for the difficult task ahead.

The first thing she needed to do was get him out of his wet, dirty clothes and try to figure out where he was injured and exactly how serious it was. She untied his shoes and pulled them off. But when she reached for his jacket he stopped her. "No. My van...you've got to get my things from it...bring them here...now...can't wait..."

"Just as soon as I get you out of these clothes and—"

"No! Now." He struggled to raise himself, but only

succeeded for a couple of seconds before falling back. "Immediately...before anyone can get to it."

"But why? What's so important—"

"Now, Lauren. No time..." He lifted his head from the pillow and fixed her with as much of a level gaze as he could. "Don't let—" he winced in pain "—anyone see you." He forced the words, straining to make himself heard and understood. For some reason, something in his van was more important than his own well-being. "Hidden space under back floorboards...two suitcases...get them..."

"Where is the van?"

"Behind—" His body shuddered as a hacking cough ripped through him. He gasped for air, sucking in a deep lungful in spite of the obvious pain it caused him. "Behind lighthouse cottage. Off the road, hidden from sight. Key." He tried to reach for his zippered jacket pocket.

"You lay still. I'll get it." She unzipped the pocket and withdrew a set of keys. She suppressed a sob as she watched his face contort in pain. "I can't leave you here like this."

"Go." He reached for her, then fell back. "Those suitcases...can't let anyone else get them."

"Just the suitcases? What about your van?"

"Leave it. Can't have whoever shot me wondering what happened to it...why it's missing...be careful...don't let anyone see you."

Kyle. He needed help. What he really needed was a doctor. "I can't leave you here like this."

"Go." He left her with no room for disagreement.

Lauren pulled on a pair of boots and wrapped her cape over her pajamas. She leaned over and kissed him on the cheek. "I'll be right back." She gave one last worried look in his direction, then hurried out the side door.

Ty-Ty twitched his tail then nudged his face against Kyle's cheek. He tried to shove the annoyance away. "Not now, cat." He had a vague memory of the animal being there when he finally collapsed in the wet grass. He had almost made it to Lauren's house, but not quite. That had been the last thing he remembered until she had rolled him over. He tried to clear his head. He took a deep breath and held it in an attempt to ward off the pain as he forced himself into an upright position.

He sat on the edge of the bed for a moment, trying to clear his head. His shoulder throbbed and continued to ooze blood. The cold ocean water had helped by temporarily slowing the flow. The bullet wound, however, was the least of it. He had been wounded more seriously than this during the course of his career. The fall from the bluff followed by the fight against the strong waves and cold ocean current had been a far more deadly battle. Any normal man would have succumbed to those elements, even without a bullet wound. It was his Navy Seal training that had saved him.

He tried to remove his jacket, but his right shoulder refused to cooperate. He took a deep breath and clenched his jaw. He had to get the wound washed before infection set in, if it was not already too late. He made one last effort and managed to get his jacket and shirt off, then dropped his shoulder holster and gun to the floor next to the bed. He struggled out of his wet jeans, then stumbled into the bathroom dressed only in his briefs and socks.

Kyle slumped against the shower wall, allowing the warm water to soak through his matted hair and rinse the sand and grit from his body. He slowly sank to the floor, the last of his strength swirling down the drain with the dirty water. He did not know how long Lauren had been gone, but he knew she needed to get back quickly while he could still function. He also knew if the waves of nausea he had been fighting and the recurring bouts of dizziness were any indication, he could not remain clear and in control much longer. He desperately needed the medical kit from one of his suitcases. He thought he heard something in the other room, but was not sure. He could not force himself to move.

LAUREN ENTERED through the side door, pausing only to lock it behind her. She struggled with the two heavy suitcases until she got them to the bedroom. She came to an abrupt halt. Kyle was not on the bed. In fact, he was nowhere in sight. A trail of clothes led toward the bathroom. She set down the suitcases, then cautiously made her way toward the sound of the shower.

He sat in the corner of the shower with his back resting against the wall as the water splashed against his body. Only the fact that his eyes were open and he seemed to be looking around in a dazed manner told her that he was conscious. She turned off the water and bent next to him. Her gaze became riveted to his shoulder. She immediately recognized the injury for what it was.

It was not the first time she had come in close contact with a bullet wound. A sick feeling churned in the pit of her stomach as the memory flashed through her mind. She had found Jim sprawled out on his living room floor in a pool of his own blood with a gaping wound in his chest and the pistol about ten feet away—the gun he owned for his own protection, the gun that had been used to take his life. She sucked in a deep breath to fight off the uninvited images. That was seven years ago, and this was now. Kyle needed her help, not painful memories from her past.

She tried to make her voice sound as authoritative as possible. "Come on, Kyle. Can you get up?" She tried to help him, being careful of his shoulder. "We have to get that wound cleaned out and put a dressing on it. Fortunately the bullet seems to have passed clean through your shoulder."

He winced in pain, but finally managed to get to his feet. "Do you...my suitcases—"

"They're in the other room."

He staggered toward the bathroom door. "Medical kit."

"I'll get it." Lauren quickly retrieved the medical supplies. "This is quite a collection of emergency provisions." She leveled a curious look at him. "Certainly an odd assortment of things for a paranormal investigator to be carrying around with him, especially hidden away under the false floor in your van." There was no mistaking her implication, but she quickly moved on. This was not the time for such a conversation. She worked efficiently, putting everything else aside until later—not the least of which was the inappropriate tingle of excitement caused by his near-naked body.

"I'm sure this is going to sting." She took the antiseptic and cleaned out the wound after carefully washing it. She felt him flinch, but he gave no other indication of the pain. Next she applied a penicillin ointment, then covered it with a gauze dressing.

She helped him to her bed. "I've done everything I know to do." She smoothed the hair from his forehead. "You really need a doctor. You've lost a lot of blood. The wound is clean now, but between the ocean water and the field on the bluff and wherever else you might have been, I'm worried about infection."

"No, no doctor. No one. It'll be okay. I just need a little rest, that's all." He drifted off almost before he finished the words. She was not sure if he had fallen asleep or lapsed into unconsciousness. She felt his forehead again. A fever had already taken hold.

LAUREN WATCHED as Kyle slept. It had been thirty-six hours since she had returned from retrieving his suitcases. A day, a night and another day had come and gone in which she had to juggle her time between her business and tending to Kyle while not arousing suspicion among her employees and customers. She had come so close to calling a doctor or driving him to the emergency room, but he had been emphatic about total secrecy.

She had changed the dressing every two hours, finally resorting to a home remedy, a poultice of healing herbs to draw out the infection and fight the fever. He had continued to drift in and out of consciousness. She had tried to clean his jacket and had washed his clothes, but she had refused to touch the shoulder holster and gun. They lay on the floor where he had dropped them. She had placed a towel over them so she did not have to look at them.

She sat next to the bed sipping herbal tea and watching him as he slept. Who was this man who seemed to live with constant danger? Was he a criminal? That would certainly explain his insistence that she not contact anyone. She furrowed her brow as she shook her head, almost an involuntary action. All she had were questions, and he was unable to give her any answers.

His face contorted. She jumped to her feet and mopped the perspiration from his brow with a cool cloth. He thrashed restlessly for several minutes, his face laden with beads of sweat and a thin sheen of perspiration covering his chest. He tried to kick off the covers. The blanket slipped down to his waist. Then suddenly he became very still. His fever had finally broken.

She could not help but notice his physique...again. His upper torso was well-toned, with just a smattering of hair across his muscled chest. He was obviously in excellent physical condition, a fact that had undoubtedly gone a long way toward saving his life. She vividly recalled her adverse reaction when she first saw the ugly scar that ran across his right side. Had he been shot before? Was it some kind of occupational hazard? She pulled the blanket around his shoulders, careful of his injury.

Ty-Ty jumped on the bed and curled himself next to Kyle's body. He sat with his front paws tucked under and stared at Kyle as if he sensed some sort of change in the condition of this man who had been staying in Lauren's bed.

A few minutes later Kyle moaned softly, then opened his eyes. An instant surge of panic grabbed him. His gaze darted around the semidark room. He frantically sought out anything familiar. The relief settled inside him when he spied Lauren sitting on the edge of the bed, her face covered with deep concern.

"How are you feeling?" Her voice was soft and caring, but her eyes told him a different story. They were filled with a multitude of very serious questions about things other than the state of his health.

"I feel like hell...like someone beat me up then ran over me with a truck." He saw her eyes narrow. He did not like the silent signals they sent his way.

"Really?" She cocked her head and raised an eyebrow. Her words were cloaked in sarcasm. "I thought you might have felt as if someone shot you then dumped your body in the ocean."

Her eyes seemed to be delving into his consciousness, forcing him to look away to avoid the feeling of having his soul stripped bare. His gaze lit on the Siamese resting comfortably on the bed watching him. "Well, cat...I seem to recall your being around a lot lately, in fact every time I've opened my eyes."

"It was Ty-Ty who found you. He came to get me, otherwise I never would have known." A sob caught in her throat. "I knew something terrible had happened, but I didn't know you were out there. You could have—" She refused to finish the sentence.

He tried to reach from beneath the covers, but the sharp pain that grabbed him put a halt to his actions. Lauren touched his arm. It was a light touch, but it served the purpose. Kyle sank back onto the bed.

"You can't go moving around like that. The bleeding has stopped, and I think the infection is under control, but you really should have some stitches." Her voice took on a disapproving edge. "We won't even discuss the fact that this is insane, that you should be in the hospital where you could get proper care."

He tried to project a light attitude even though he felt anything but upbeat. He forced a smile. "You're right, we won't even discuss it." He turned his head to look at the cat, who had not moved from his resting place. "Well...it seems that I owe you a vote of thanks, Ty-Ty."

It was almost as if recognition was what the cat had been waiting for. Ty-Ty jumped off the bed and disappeared through the door, the gold bell around his neck jingling softly as he ran.

Kyle tried to sit up. Lauren saw him wince in pain, but it did not deter his efforts. She was immediately at his side, assisting him. "You can't exert yourself like this. You're far from okay." She arranged a couple of pillows as a backrest. "Are you comfortable?"

"Relatively speaking."

"Is that relatively speaking in general—" she leveled a serious look at him "—or relatively speaking for someone who was on the receiving end of a murder attempt?"

He squirmed uncomfortably. He knew he was going to have to answer some questions, but he was not sure exactly how to do it. He needed to play it very carefully. He also needed to stall for time, he had to think—now that his head was clear enough for lucid thoughts. "What time is it? Or maybe I'd be better off asking what day it is. How long have I been incapacitated?" He ran his hand over the whisker stubble on his chin and cheeks.

"It's not been that long." She smoothed his hair from his forehead. She checked the dressing on his shoulder, her senses tingling with excitement when she came in contact with his bare skin. This was different than when she had earlier dressed his wound, when she was not even sure he would live. This time he was conscious and alert. His eyes were a clear sky blue, and he seemed to be taking in everything that surrounded him.

She saw it in his eyes—the secrets, the wariness, the mystery that shrouded the truth. She felt it and she sensed it, but she could not clearly define it. "Now that you seem to be doing better you can tell me what happened."

He ignored her comment, preferring to pick up the thread of the previous conversation. "Just how long is not that long?"

"Don't play games with me, Kyle." She swallowed hard and took a deep breath. "Who are you...what are you?"

"You already know that. I'm here to—"

She put her fingers against his lips to still his words. "Don't play me for a fool. Against my better judgment I've complied with all your wishes. I retrieved your suitcases from your van. I did the best I could with your injuries and didn't call the doctor. I've tried to maintain a normal work schedule in an attempt to ward off any questions while you were in here vacillating in and out of consciousness and fighting off fever and infection. Now that you seem to be part of reality once again, I think you owe me some straight answers." She brushed his hair back, allowing her hand to linger against his face for a moment longer than necessary.

He attempted to reach for her hand but stopped midway, carefully lowering his right arm to lessen the throbbing in his shoulder. He switched to his left arm instead, capturing her hand in his and pulling her toward him. His voice was low, soft and very serious. "Lauren...please don't ask. I can't—"

She angrily blurted the first words that came to mind. "I don't want to hear *I can't*." She fixed him with a hard stare, a task made all the more difficult because he still clasped her hand and had pulled her face very close to his. "I have to have some answers, Kyle."

Her manner softened as she continued. "You've been shot. You don't want anyone notified, which I assume also applies to reporting this incident to the authorities. You won't allow me to get you professional medical attention. That didn't make any sense to me at first, but now I understand. A doctor, by law, must report a bullet wound."

She closed her eyes for a moment and collected herself. "You don't leave me with too many choices about what's going on here. The most obvious—" She felt the pressure as he gave her hand a squeeze. The warmth flowed through her, almost obscuring her thoughts. "The most obvious answer is that you're involved in some sort of criminal activity."

He tugged on her hand until he had closed the last small gap between them. His lips brushed against hers, then he captured her mouth fully. He felt her initial hesitation. It was not reluctance on her part, more like uncertainty. The thought crossed his mind that perhaps she was concerned about his injuries, about his shoulder wound reopening.

He felt her hesitation gradually melt away as his mouth settled comfortably on hers. It was no ordinary physical attraction that grabbed his desires. There was nothing ordinary about her. She may have proven herself cool in a crisis, but everything else about her made his blood race hot and fast.

The kiss increased in intensity, becoming heated and sensual while at the same time conveying a softness that said he was making no demands. He ran the tip of his tongue along her lower lip, then brushed against the texture of her tongue while sampling more of her taste. Thoughts began doing battle with feelings. The more he tasted, the more he wanted—but he knew those desires would have to wait. His entire investigative plan had blown up in his face, and he had lost valuable time. He desperately needed to assess his situation and formulate a new plan immediately.

Kyle reluctantly broke off the kiss as he shifted his weight. Much more than just his desires had been aroused. He had become acutely aware of his lack of clothes. He needed to hide the fact that despite the unsettled circumstances and confrontational nature of their conversation, the heated kiss had a decidedly physical effect on him. He drew his knee up, pulling the blanket so it no longer lay against his body.

"I think I need to find some clothes."

She leaned back to put some space between them. "I washed what you were wearing. I'm afraid your jeans are ripped and there's the—" a shudder moved quickly through her body "—bullet hole through your shirt and jacket, but everything's clean."

He tugged the blanket a little higher around his waist. "I have clean clothes in one of those suitcases. I'll go—"

"You'll do no such thing. I'll get what you need from your suitcase, just as soon as you quit trying to change the subject." And a good job he had done of it, too. If the kiss had lasted any longer she just might have forgotten what they had been talking about. "I want you to give me some straight answers." She continued to sit on the edge of the bed, refusing to give him enough room to get up without wrenching his shoulder.

Her words turned soft, barely above a whisper. "Who are you, Kyle Delaney? Why are you here? What am I involved in?" She had to know, but she was not sure she really wanted to hear the answers.

He took her hand again, bringing it to his lips for a moment. There seemed to be no recourse other than to address her concerns head-on. He looked up and was immediately captured by the intensity and deep concern in her eyes. "You have to let this go, Lauren. You can't become involved. All I can do is ask you to trust me, and in turn I have to trust that you'll maintain your silence."

"I'm already involved. In fact, I could probably be in

trouble just for hiding a person with a bullet wound. So, as you can see, it's too late for you to shut me out.''

"You have no idea what you'd be getting yourself into.''

"We can solve that problem by you telling me about it.''

He shook his head, almost an involuntary gesture. "It's far too dangerous." He lightly trailed his finger across the back of her hand. ''I can't take a chance on you being hurt. Look what happened to me, and I know what I'm doing. The less you know, the safer you'll be. I'll get out of your—'' His quick intake of breath told of the pain when he tried to put his weight on his right arm. He fell back against the pillow and closed his eyes. ''I'll get out of here in a little bit.''

She inhaled deeply, held it for a moment, then exhaled slowly in a sigh of resignation. ''No, you won't. You'll need someone to change the dressing on your wound. Besides, you'll be safe here, at least until you can get your strength back.'' She hesitated, trying to get the proper words together. ''One thing, though...I have to know, are you...are you wanted by the law? At least tell me whether or not you're involved in something illegal.''

His words were soft. ''Would it make a difference?''

She studied him for a moment before answering, her voice a barely discernible whisper. ''No.''

"Lauren, I... No, I'm not wanted by the law. I'm not a criminal.'' He wanted to tell her more. He wanted to get out of there before his presence caused her harm. He did not know what he wanted. He had never been so uncertain about anything in his life.

"Then what are you? Why would someone shoot you and why would you not report it?''

"You're asking questions I'm not at liberty to answer. You already know too much.''

"You haven't told me anything. How can I know too much?"

He fixed her with a deadly serious look, and his voice told her just how perilous the situation was. "You know that I'm still alive."

He did not want to deceive her, but telling her the truth was against everything logical and prudent. He could not put her in danger any more than she already was. The very nature of his job made sharing something that did not come to him naturally, even under normal circumstances.

He smoothly slipped into one of his many personas—the charming rake without a care in the world. He flashed her a smile and a wink. "I don't suppose I could talk you into handing me my pants. As much as I'm enjoying lounging around in your bed, I really do feel it's time to get dressed and take care of a little business."

She rose without saying a word and produced some of his clothes. She dropped them on the side of the bed, then moved his two suitcases next to the nightstand. She presented him with an expressionless mask. "Will you be staying for dinner or are you in too much of a hurry to bother?" She knew the sarcasm was there, but at that moment she did not care. She turned to leave the room so he could get dressed.

Before she could go anywhere he grabbed her arm and brought her to a halt. Her display of anger and hurt tugged at him. He did not know what to do. Kyle Delaney—a man of action who lived on the edge and liked it—did not know what to do.

"Lauren, please believe me. This is for your own good."

She gently removed her arm from his grasp and ignored his words. "Are you sure I can't fix you something to eat before you leave? What do you feel you can handle? Would you like some soup or something more solid?

You'll have to give me a hint. I've never prepared a meal for someone recovering from a bullet wound."

He could not keep the frustration and exasperation out of his voice. "Dammit! What I'd like is for you to tell me you understand, that you're not angry with me."

She whirled around, her green eyes flashing fire. "Well, I can't do it! I *don't* understand and I *am* angry. You don't need to worry, I'll keep your secret if that's all that's important to you. No one will know you've been here or even that you survived the shooting and the ocean." Her eyes narrowed as she leveled a hard stare at him. "But perhaps you need to be reminded that this is a small town. Whatever you try to do, wherever you try to go and whoever you pretend to be, everyone will notice you."

She was right. He needed a new cover and a disguise to go with it, and it would have to be something that would not arouse suspicion. He was not able to curb his irritation as he asked, "Do I take that to mean you have some sort of an idea or suggestion?"

"First I need some honesty from you. Then I think I have the perfect solution. So, what do you say? Are you willing to trade? I get answers to my questions, and you get an acceptable identity."

"You're a tough negotiator, Lauren Jamison." He had made his decision. Against his better judgment he would take her into his confidence...in a limited capacity. He forced out the words. "My name really is Kyle Delaney. I work for the government." He saw her eyes widen in shock immediately followed by a quick look of relief. "I'm an investigator with the Customs Service on an undercover assignment." He could not stop the involuntary chuckle as he glanced at the blanket covering his near naked body. "Apparently literally as well as figuratively."

Lauren shook her head in shocked silence, then finally managed to blurt, "I don't believe it!"

Chapter Five

"Why don't you believe me?" Confusion covered Kyle's face. "It's the truth."

"I *do* believe it, but I'm flabbergasted—that's what I meant." She tried to get her thoughts together. For someone with her ability she had sure missed calling this one, but now things were beginning to make sense.

"So, I've shown you mine and now it's your turn to show me yours—" he allowed a hint of a devilish grin "—so to speak." He was making an extra effort to keep the conversation light, even though the subject matter was anything but carefree. "What's this marvelous new identity you can give me? Something that will allow me to go about my business without garnering suspicion?"

Lauren's mind was still in a whirl. "I'm afraid it's going to take me a few minutes to assimilate all of this." Not only was he surrounded by danger, his very life was dedicated to it. A man who carried a gun for a living. And someone had tried to kill him. Someone in her quiet little town of Sea Grove was a dangerous criminal and had tried to murder this man who had stepped out of the early-morning mist and into her life.

She was almost afraid to ask the next question. "Do you know who shot you?"

He tried to keep it light. "I was hoping you could tell

me, maybe come up with some sort of vision..." He immediately deferred to the stern expression on her face, the one that said she was not amused by his attempt at a joke about her abilities.

"No, I didn't see who it was. I was caught—" His attention momentarily drifted to that moment when he had been so filled with thoughts of Lauren that he had let down his guard. "It was dark, and I only caught a glimpse of a shadow, then the flash of the shot." It was a bit more than just a shadow he had glimpsed, but not much more. He had his suspicions, but they were only a gut feeling and certainly not anything he would ever share with anyone.

He turned the intensity of his blue eyes on her. She felt herself being drawn inside him as surely as if he had a physical hold on her. "You still haven't answered my question. Who is it I can become without arousing the curiosity of the locals?"

"This identity..." She tried to carefully choose her words. "It doesn't allow you—"

He sat bolt upright, suddenly all business as his face took on a hard edge. "I thought we had a deal."

"We did...we do. But what I have in mind won't allow you to wander around by yourself. It only works if you're with me."

"That wasn't our deal, Lauren." He snapped out the words, making no effort to hide his irritation.

"It has to be. It's the only way it will work. First, I'll have to find a disguise for you. Maybe bleach your hair and..." She furrowed her brow in concentration as she studied him.

He displayed the control and authority that were part of his nature and his training. "Just tell me what this great plan is and let me worry about the disguise."

She tried not to show her amusement, but could not stop the slight grin that tugged at the corners of her mouth.

"Just what's so damn funny?" He had passed irritation and was headed directly toward anger.

The amused chuckle escaped her throat despite her efforts to the contrary. "Well...here you are flat on your back, unable to show your face in public—as you so eloquently pointed out, at my mercy—and yet you're barking orders like some drill sergeant."

She brushed his hair from his forehead. He reached up and tried to swat her hand away. He welcomed her touch, but not now—not when he was trying to regain control of the situation. "You're having quite the grand old time at my expense, aren't you?"

"We're certainly going to have to figure out some sort of a compromise to our working relationship if we're going to be able to pull this off."

His anger exploded. "Dammit! I keep telling you this is not a case of *we*. You don't seem to understand that this isn't a game. This is real—this is life and death." He clasped her hand and brought it to his lips. He calmed down, even allowing a little tenderness to creep into his voice. "I can't do my job if I'm preoccupied with worrying about the safety of an innocent civilian." He pulled her closer until his mouth reached hers. The kiss was soft and gentle and very real. "And I can assure you, Lauren, that you would certainly be a major distraction."

Her heart beat a little faster, and her pulse quickened. A *major* distraction? Had she heard him correctly? She quickly shoved the inappropriate musings aside and forced her thoughts to what needed to be done. "You might want to hold off on your negative assessment of my idea until you've at least heard it."

He leaned against the pillow and let out a loud sigh of resignation as he closed his eyes. "Okay, tell me all about it." There was a noticeable lack of enthusiasm to his words.

"I have a pen pal. His name is Shane Nolan, and he

lives in Dublin, Ireland. For the past seven years he's been writing me once a month. I just received another letter from him, three weeks early. He said he was going to be involved in an archaeological dig for the next few months and wouldn't be able to write. Everyone in town knows about Shane, and with our letter carrier's penchant for spreading the news faster than he delivers the mail, I'm sure everyone knows I just received a letter way ahead of schedule."

Kyle opened his eyes and sat up straight, his mind rapidly clicking off the possibilities presented by this intriguing set of circumstances. "And?"

"And...I can say the letter announced that Shane was coming for a visit and would be here in a few days. That would give you some time to regain your strength and for your shoulder to start healing. It's only natural that Shane would be staying with me. There would be nothing suspicious about my showing him all around town. It's only logical that he would show particular interest in the lighthouse, since that's something I'm involved with."

She watched as his eyes narrowed and his stare took on a new intensity. He seemed to be mulling her words over. There was a new energy about him, an excitement that had not been there a minute earlier.

His words came out slowly and carefully. "Your idea has some merit." *Some* merit—it was damn near perfect, and for all the reasons she said. He did not like the aspect that dictated her personal involvement, but he also had to admit she was right about being seen with him. It was the only way it would work.

He settled back into the comfort of the bed as he warmed to her idea. "Tell me about Shane Nolan, starting with what everyone already knows then giving me his background and anything else that might help me get inside this character."

"I have all the letters he's written me. Would those help?"

"They sure would." He started to reach for his clothes, then paused. "Did you say something about food? I'm starved."

"I have some nice thick homemade beef stew with lots of vegetables. How about that along with a green salad and some French bread?" An amazing transformation had taken place before her very eyes. He almost seemed like a different person. There was a strong energy about him, a positive reinforcement, something akin to a reaffirmation. He was a truly complex man who seemed to march to his own drummer and respond to his own internal beat.

"Yeah, that sounds great." He cocked his head and extended a questioning look, his words tentative. "And maybe a piece of pie with a scoop of ice cream on top?"

She smiled, trying to hide her sense of relief that he had apparently decided to stop challenging her and accept her help. "Well, you certainly do seem to be feeling better."

"And some coffee?"

"Some herbal tea would be better for you."

He ignored her comment as he reached for his neatly folded clothes. "As soon as I get dressed I'll get some supplies from my suitcase and we'll get started."

He had used the word *we*. Just as her revelation had prophesied, his danger had now become hers. She glanced to where she had placed his suitcases. "I'll get what you need. You shouldn't be up and around yet."

He shot her a lascivious grin. "I'm going to get out of bed now and put on my clothes. You can either leave so I can have some privacy or you can stay here and help me get dressed—since you seem to be intimately familiar with my various articles of clothing." He edged his way toward the side of the bed. He reached down, grabbed a towel from the floor and tossed it on the chair.

He saw the flush of embarrassment cover her cheeks as

she averted her eyes. She was so genuine, so real...so unlike any of the women he had known over the years. Then he saw something else. He saw a combination of anxiety and fear mixed with repulsion that suddenly froze on her face. He followed her line of sight. She was staring at the shoulder holster containing the pistol, lying where he had just uncovered them.

Her eyes snapped to him. He could not read what was in them, but he knew it made him uncomfortable. Why was she willing to risk her life to help him, yet at the same time be so averse to the tools of his trade? What was there about her that he did not know? His words were tentative. "Lauren? What is it? What's wrong?"

She turned away from the clear blue fathoms of his eyes. Once again she felt herself being pulled into the depths of his soul. "I...uh...I'll go and fix you something to eat, then I'll find Shane's letters." She hurried out of the bedroom.

Kyle pulled back the covers and swung his long legs over the side of the bed. The pain in his shoulder throbbed, but he had suffered through a lot worse.

He checked the bandaging Lauren had applied to his shoulder. He did not know what concoction she had put on his wound, but he did know it was not the penicillin ointment he carried in his medical kit. Whatever it was it sure seemed to be doing the trick. He had only intermittent memories of the time following his attempt to get to her shower—of the fever and the pain. All of it appeared to be under control now.

He dressed as quickly as his injuries allowed, then turned his attention to the gun. Almost an hour in salt water followed by a couple of days lying on the floor while the salt tried to eat into the metal had certainly not done the weapon any good. He would have to take it completely apart and clean it very carefully, and even at that, he would put it aside until he could get it to headquarters and let the experts check it out. He would have to use one of the two spare pistols from the suitcase.

His next order of business was to contact the chief, using his cellular phone and a scrambling device. Kyle allowed a self-satisfied smirk at what he knew would be the chief's surprise at hearing from him during an undercover assignment. It might even produce a *positive* entry in the file that fool psychologist seemed to be fond of flashing around.

Kyle gave the chief a rundown on what had happened.

"Are you crazy, Kyle? Involving a civilian like that?" The chief's voice was understandably angry. "The one time you make an effort to follow procedure by actually checking in when something goes wrong and the only thing you have to tell me is that you've gone even farther afield than normal?"

There was an obvious hint of amusement in Kyle's voice. "Gee...and I thought you'd be pleased to hear from me."

The chief's voice crackled with exasperation. "Of course I'm pleased to hear from you, and I'm relieved that you're safe. I received a phone call about your van. The sheriff's department in Sea Grove assumed they were talking to a leasing agency that owned the van. They were reporting that they had found it abandoned. They claimed to be making a routine inquiry about who it had been leased to and where that person could be located. The call only came in an hour ago. I was about to send someone to Sea Grove when you called."

Kyle's sarcasm was mixed with contempt. "My, my, my...how efficient of the local constabulary. Are you going to pick up the van?"

"No. The sheriff's office said it would remain impounded until the lessee could be located and they had an opportunity to determine whether foul play was involved—an unusual procedure but not unheard-of. There wasn't a lot we could do in the guise of a leasing agency without arousing suspicion." There was a slight pause before the chief asked his next question. "What about your supplies?"

"Lauren got my things out of the van that same night. The belongings I had in my motel room were only normal clothing and toiletry items and a few books and notes relating to my cover story. There's nothing to worry about."

"Nothing to worry about. You were nearly killed, you're improvising on the fly again and this time you've taken a civilian in tow. Nope. Nothing to worry about, that's for sure." The sarcasm in the chief's voice left no doubt about his mood. "You will keep me apprised of what's happening, won't you? I mean in light of this Lauren Jamison's involvement and your having put the agency in the position of needing to protect her—"

Kyle's tone was upbeat, displaying a barely hidden teasing quality. "Good. Since we're obviously in agreement on the matter, I'll get back to work." He immediately disconnected the phone call without waiting for what he knew would be the chief's response.

He opened the bedroom door and stepped into the living room just as Lauren came from the other direction.

"Come on in the kitchen. Your food is nice and hot." He was neatly dressed, the scrapes and scratches on his face and hands providing the only clue to the life-threatening ordeal he had been through. His manner and movements showed nothing wrong.

The hunger pangs rumbled through his stomach as the aroma of home cooking filled the air. He was acutely aware of his weakened condition and the fact that he would have to feel a whole lot better than he did to even work his way up to calling it lousy. Food was what he needed, and a good night's sleep. He allowed his gaze to drift along Lauren's enticing curves. Food and sleep were not the only things he needed.

He seated himself at the table as he inhaled. "Smells

good." He glanced at her, once again raking his gaze across the lines of her body. "Looks good enough to eat. Care to join me?"

"I've already had dinner."

He shot her an undeniably lascivious grin, then a quick wink as he took a sip of his coffee. "Who said I was talking about dinner?"

KYLE FROWNED as he stared at himself in the mirror. The reddish-blond wig did not look quite right. He adjusted it so it sat farther back on his head. It was the smallest fraction of an inch, but the change met with his approval. He smoothed in the nose putty so it blended perfectly with the rest of his face, giving his nose a different shape.

He applied the neatly trimmed beard and mustache, a shade or two darker than the wig. Years of practice allowed him to work very quickly and efficiently without any wasted motion. It not only altered the appearance of his face, but it also covered the scar across his jawline. His complexion was now a more ruddy shading, with the beginnings of some wrinkles across his forehead. Next came the brown contact lenses to disguise his sky blue eyes. A little padding in his clothes and the final touch, a pair of glasses, completed the transformation.

He double-checked his appearance in the full-length mirror then turned toward Lauren. "Faith and begorra, 'tis the luck of the Irish that dictates. And tell me, my pretty one, does this meet with your approval?" The soft Irish accent was perfect, the voice unrecognizable as that of Kyle Delaney.

She looked him over with a critical eye. The effect of his efforts was a man of totally different appearance who looked at least ten years older and twenty pounds heavier.

"That's some disguise kit you carry with you. I think I can safely say I wouldn't recognize you if I passed you on the street. It's an amazing change." She noted that he still favored his right shoulder when he tried to do something requiring any pressure.

He saw the silent concern on her face and read the question in her eyes. In answer he grabbed a jar from his disguise kit using his left hand, tossed it in the air and caught it. "I'm pretty adept with my left hand. I can even write with it. I'm not ambidextrous in the true sense of the word, but I can get along well enough to be convincing. I even qualified expert at the pistol range with my left—"

He saw the look of disapproval cover her face. The gun had not been mentioned during the past four days of his convalescence, but he could see it was always at the forefront of her concerns. She had refused to enter the room while he was cleaning and oiling the weapon that had been in the ocean.

That was not the only thing he had tried to ignore over the past four days. At the very top of that list had been their sleeping arrangements. He had done the honorable thing by offering to sleep on the couch in her living room rather than assuming she would allow him to share her bed. She had insisted that he take the bed, but to his dismay she had been adamant that she would sleep on the living room couch. She had steadfastly argued that he needed to get good solid sleep if he was going to recover as quickly as he wanted.

It was not at all what he wanted. His mind had been filled with thoughts of her body snuggled next to his, of the feel of her silky, smooth skin pressed along the length of his torso. He knew the taste of her kiss and he wanted to intimately know the rest of her.

He mentally kicked himself. He had to get his mind on business. He had committed to memory all the pertinent facts in Shane's letters. Not only had they given him a good picture of the man, they also provided him with an insight into Lauren. She had not mentioned that Shane Nolan had been a close friend of her former fiancé, a man named Jim Franklin. In fact, she had not mentioned being engaged. Kyle did not know what happened, only that some tragedy had taken her fiancé's life a couple of days before the wedding. Immediately afterward Shane began writing to her.

Shane Nolan seemed to be a decent and caring man. Kyle felt a strangely unexpected sense of gratitude that he had been there for Lauren in her time of need, even though Shane and Lauren had never met in person. He wished he could have read her letters to Shane.

She had brought him a couple of books on Ireland from her bookstore and he had boned up on the history, geography and current political climate. The only other thing that needed to be handled was the report of Kyle Delaney's *death*. As previously arranged, the chief generated a news release stating that the Coast Guard had fished the body of an unidentified man in his early thirties out of the ocean off the coast of Sea Grove.

Lauren and Kyle were ready for a trial run. They decided to test out the disguise on Milly. Lauren told her friend she would be leaving early that morning to drive into Seattle to pick up Shane at the airport. They would be back that afternoon. The stage was set. They put Kyle's suitcases in the trunk of Lauren's car and left just before sunrise so no one would see them.

"I DIDN'T KNOW what to do so I called you. It's obvious the fellow didn't just skip out on his bill. I mean, all of his things are still here." The motel manager unlocked the door to Kyle's room then stepped aside so the sheriff could enter. "It's just that his weekly rent is due and no one's seen him for several days. The housekeeper says his bed hasn't been slept in."

Max Culhane walked around the room, stopping occasionally to open a dresser drawer or pick up a book and leaf through it. He looked inside the closet and into the small bathroom. Everything looked as if the occupant of the room expected to return.

He turned to the motel manager. "I guess you'd better pack up all this stuff and send it over to my office. If he shows up, or if anyone calls for him or comes to see him, get their name and notify me. Meanwhile I'll check around and see what I can find out."

"You know, Max, it occurs to me that perhaps that guy on the news might be Mr. Delaney...you know, the body the Coast Guard found off Lighthouse Point? The man was about the right age. Maybe you could check on that?"

"Sure thing. Don't you worry. You just send his things over and I'll take care of it."

"Is it okay if I rent out the room?"

"Yeah, it's okay. We don't know that anything happened to him and if it did, it sure don't look like it occurred here. Besides, the room's already been cleaned so there wouldn't be much to find. You go ahead and rent it out."

A smile crossed the motel manager's weary face. "Thanks. I'll get this stuff over to your office right away."

LAUREN AND KYLE were only half a mile from the tearoom. He studied her profile as she drove. The nervousness twitched across her features. She had a tighter grip on the steering wheel than necessary. He reached over and brushed his fingertips across her knuckles. "If you don't relax your grip you're liable to break that steering wheel in two." A slight sigh of exasperation escaped his throat. "It's not too late for you to change your mind."

She gave a quick sidelong glance in his direction then returned her eyes to the road. "I won't change my mind. This is the only way it will work, and you know it, even if you don't like it."

He focused his gaze out the front window. "You've got that one right—I don't like it." He turned in the seat until he half faced her. "I want you to promise me that you'll do exactly as I say without trying to second-guess me. Both our lives might depend on that fraction-of-a-second edge. And when I tell you it's time for you to get out, I want you as far away from here as quickly as you can go. Do you understand that?"

She tried to lighten his mood and ease the tension that filled the air. "You're such a nag. For the millionth time, I understand that."

"Stop it, Lauren!" He snapped out the words, making no effort to hide his annoyance. "Also for the millionth time, this isn't a game. You've already shown me how clever and resourceful you are. Against everything that's logical and rational I'm reluctantly allowing you a limited amount of involvement in this, but I don't want to end up with someone praising your sterling qualities to the towns-folk at your funeral." He knew the words were harsh and he made no effort to soften them.

She pulled the car to the side of the road and braked to a halt almost within sight of their destination. She turned to face him. "And I don't want to be telling people how you swept into my life one misty morning only to be taken away far too soon by a bullet with your name on it. I know that sounds like a corny cliché, but it's the way I feel." She quickly turned toward the road when she felt the tears begin to well in her eyes. She put the car in gear, making sure he could not see how much the thought truly upset her. She had already lost one man to a bullet and had no intention of it happening again.

His exasperation came across loud and clear. "Can we at least go over today's plan one more time?"

Lauren flipped on the turn signal then pulled into the parking lot. She recited the plan as if it was an oft-repeated litany. "We arrive with a flourish. I introduce you to Milly. We see what her response is. If she buys it we go to Billy Washburn's funeral so you can listen, snoop, and with luck get a chance for an innocent little conversation with Billy's father."

She pulled the car around back and turned off the engine. He took her hand in his, stopping her from opening the car door. "Lauren..." The words were difficult for him. "I'm not sure what I'm trying to say here...I want you to know—"

"Whatever it is, I suggest you say it with an Irish accent because it's show time!" She had to cut him off. She did not want to hear anything that might indicate he was going to change his mind. They would do this together or die trying. A little tremor of anxiety rippled across her skin. She hoped those words were not as prophetic as they sounded. She swallowed her trepidation and reached for the door handle.

Chapter Six

Kyle and Lauren entered through the side door and placed the suitcases on the floor of her living room. They had driven to the Seattle airport, where Kyle checked with the customs inspection office to procure the proper airline tags and stamps for his luggage. After that they had an early lunch then drove to Sea Grove.

Lauren shot him a tentative glance, which he answered with a subtle squeeze of her hand. Then they stepped into the early-afternoon activity of the tearoom. Milly was busy at the cash register. As soon as she had a quiet moment, Lauren called to her.

"I'm back. Is everything okay?"

Milly turned toward the sound of Lauren's voice. The wide, friendly smile spread across her face as her gaze settled on Kyle. "So, this is Shane Nolan." She rushed toward them, her hand outstretched. "I am so delighted to finally meet you in person, although I do feel as if I've known you for years."

The physical transformation had been handled with Kyle's disguise expertise, but the metamorphosis that took place before Lauren's eyes was startling. He had absorbed every nuance from Shane's letters and had become an entirely different person.

The Irish accent flowed naturally from his mouth, surrounding his words like a soft caress. "Ah, this can only be the charming Milly Evans." He accepted her hand and brought it to his lips in a gallant gesture. "Every bit as lovely as Lauren described you."

"Oh, my." Milly giggled like a schoolgirl. "I think you must have kissed the Blarney stone once too often."

Kyle flashed her a dazzling smile. "My dear lady, one does not need to kiss the Blarney stone to recognize true loveliness."

Lauren interrupted before things got too far afield. "Has this morning's business been hectic, Milly? If everything's under control I want to give Shane a quick tour around town before he totally collapses from jet lag."

"Things are running smoothly. The two of you go along and enjoy yourselves. Don't give this place another thought."

Lauren turned toward Kyle. "Well, Shane. Why don't you take a few minutes to unpack, then we'll do a quick turn through town. If you don't have any objections, I would like to stop by the services and pay my respects to Sam Washburn. I know how tired you must be, but it will only take a few minutes."

"Oh, yes. You mentioned him. The man who lost his son in the automobile accident. Of course, 'tis only fitting and proper."

"I'M SO SORRY about Billy." Lauren's words were sincere as she extended her condolences to Sam Washburn following the funeral.

Sam could not hide his grief as he spoke. "Thanks, Lauren. You were always real good to Billy, recommending those books for him to read and helping him to expand his interests. I know it was real hard for him his final year of high school, and then a year ago when he developed the medical—" Whatever Sam was going to say never made it out of his mouth. He cut off his words, but not before they had captured Kyle's interest.

Sam turned his attention to Kyle, extending his hand. "It was nice to meet you, Shane. Thank you for coming to the services." He turned to Lauren as if a sudden thought had occurred to him. "Why don't the two of you stop by the house? There won't be too many people there." Sam glanced toward a small group of men, a scowl quickly covering his face.

Kyle followed Sam's line of sight. The man the sheriff was talking with exuded pure anxiety, right down to the beads of sweat standing out on his forehead and upper lip. He ran his fingers nervously through his thinning brown hair. The two men had been joined by two others. One of them Kyle recognized as the deputy, Joe Thurlow. Sam's words jerked Kyle back to the conversation. "Just a few close friends and some relatives."

Kyle jumped at the invitation. "That's most gracious of you, Mr. Washburn. We'd be honored." He watched as Sam left the graveside, then quickly scanned the area. He saw Irene Peyton making the rounds, speaking to almost everyone before turning in their direction.

"Lauren, dear. I've been meaning to call on you but I've just been so busy. Between the railroad station restoration project and the annual charity ball I haven't had a moment's rest." She scrutinized Kyle for a moment. "And this must be your friend, Shane Nolan."

"Yes, indeed. Shane, this is Irene Peyton, president of the Sea Grove Historical Society and as you just heard the head of the annual charity ball committee. In fact, Irene is involved in just about every social, charity and civic function that happens in Sea Grove."

"And 'tis a pleasure to make your acquaintance, dear lady. Lauren has written so many nice things about you and your ceaseless efforts to preserve the history of your beautiful area. I feel as if I already know you."

They exchanged a few moments of conversation, then Irene continued on her rounds, stopping to talk with the sheriff for a few minutes. Kyle spotted Tony Mallory taking a few photos and making notations in his reporter's notebook. He tried to discreetly turn away from the camera every time he saw Tony ready to snap another picture. Lauren introduced Kyle to several other people.

Kyle spotted Harvey Sherwood in a huddled conversation with another man. Harvey furtively glanced toward the sheriff and the man he was talking to and occasionally in Lauren's direction.

During the course of the service, and afterward at the grave, Kyle had caught little snippets of conversation about the Washburn family history and the people of Sea Grove. From what he could piece together, Billy's grandfather, Henry Washburn, had been linked to the death of Jeremy MacDonald, the last lighthouse keeper.

Lauren and Kyle returned to her car. Kyle whispered, "Did you hear what Sam said? About a year ago Billy developed some sort of medical problem. Do you know anything about it?"

"I'm not aware of Billy having any medical problems."

"I'm not surprised. The way Sam cut off his own words tells me no one was aware of it. It's possible there might still be some of Billy's medication in the house, something that would tell me what Sam was trying to hide."

Lauren eyed him curiously, her confusion putting a slight furrow across her brow. "I'm not sure I understand what the significance of that is."

"Oh, it's probably nothing. I'm just trying to fit some loose pieces together that may not even belong together, and even if they do, they probably don't have anything to do with my case." He needed to be cautious in what he said, not indiscriminately divulge his speculations. He wanted to get a look at the autopsy report, to see the official cause of death and whether alcohol was involved. He knew it was not likely he could, though, unless he broke into the coroner's office. He reserved that idea as a possibility.

He also toyed with the possibility that there was a life insurance policy on Billy Washburn. If so, the insurance company would be entitled to information about the circumstances of Billy's death before paying the beneficiary. Perhaps there was some sort of group insurance policy connected with Billy's employment.

Kyle paused, scanning the area with a practiced eye. Max Culhane's expression might have been benign, but his eyes were nervous. Kyle leaned toward Lauren and whispered in her ear without taking his eyes off what was going on around him. "The man the sheriff and Irene are talking to, who is he? Also who is the man with Joe Thurlow? And lastly who is Harvey Sherwood talking to?"

"That's Frank Brewster with Max and Irene. The deputy with Joe Thurlow is Mitch O'Connor, and Harvey is talking to Dennis Kendrick, the mayor."

Lauren cocked her head and pointedly stared at him. He ignored her obvious question. He was more concerned with finding something at Sam's house that would tell him why someone would be interested in killing a nineteen-year-old boy and then going to a great deal of trouble to make it look like an accident.

They arrived at the Washburn home, a modest house in a middle-class neighborhood. There were about half a dozen cars parked in front. Sam greeted them at the door and introduced them to a couple of cousins and an uncle from out of state. Lauren engaged Sam in conversation while Kyle discreetly headed for the bathroom.

As soon as he closed the door he opened the medicine cabinet and studied the contents. There were a couple of prescription bottles.

He picked up the first and read the label. It belonged to Sam Washburn and was blood pressure medication. The other bottle also belonged to Sam and contained a very mild painkiller. There was nothing that belonged to Billy.

Perhaps the teenager's bedroom would yield some useful information. He opened the bathroom door just enough to observe what was happening in the living room. No one seemed to be paying any attention to his activities. He slipped out of the bathroom and down the hall.

On the surface the bedroom seemed to be typical of a nineteen-year-old. It was also obvious that Sam had not touched the room since his son's death. Kyle spotted an ashtray on the nightstand next to the bed. He retrieved a couple of cigarette butts, studied them for a moment, then placed them in an evidence envelope he took from his pocket.

He tried to open the nightstand drawer, but was surprised to find it locked. A quick turn of a lock pick granted him access.

There it was, the answer to the riddle of Billy's medical condition—an insulin kit. He read the pharmacy label. He noted the doctor's name and address. It was from Springfield, a city of about one hundred fifty thousand in population located in the next county. There was something else in the drawer. Next to the insulin kit was a small black notebook.

Kyle glanced over his shoulder toward the door, then picked up the notebook and looked at the first page. It appeared to be a series of dates and times coupled with a few key words. A familiar tingle of excitement darted through his body, a feeling that told him he was on to something.

There was no question in his mind that the notebook contained surveillance notes of some sort. He started to tuck it into his inside jacket pocket. His breath caught when a spasm of pain shot through his shoulder. He cautiously transferred the notebook to his left hand, slipped it in his pocket, then left the room.

LAUREN SPOTTED KYLE out of the corner of her eye and caught his silent signal as he crossed the living room toward her. She extended her hand toward Sam Washburn. "I think we'd better be going. As I mentioned, Shane arrived from Ireland just this morning, and I think the jet lag has caught up with him."

"Of course. I understand."

"You know, Sam..." Her words were hesitant. "I was surprised you waited so long to have the funeral. Was it due to out-of-town relatives needing time to get here?"

"No." An angry scowl crossed his face. "The county wouldn't release Billy's body. Said they had to do some kind of tests or something, I don't know exactly what. All I wanted to do was put my boy to rest next to his mother...." Sam's voice faltered.

"Well—" the moment was an awkward one for Lauren "—if there's anything you need don't hesitate to give me a call."

"Thanks, Lauren. There's lots of folks in this town that I got no use for, but you've always been real decent to Billy and me. I especially appreciated all your kindness seven years ago when my wife died. Even though you had your own grief to deal with you still found the time to check in on Billy and me." He turned toward Kyle. "I hope you enjoy your stay in our country."

"Thank you, Mr. Washburn."

As soon as they returned to Lauren's place, Kyle removed the disguise and took a shower. He disliked the false beard and mustache. While he was doing that, she tended to the end-of-day business functions and bid Milly good-night. When the front had been locked for the night, she returned to her living quarters.

Kyle was stretched out on her couch, his rapt attention focused on Billy's notebook. He had pulled on a pair of jeans and some socks. His shirt was unbuttoned, his hair still damp from the shower. Were it not for the dressing on his shoulder wound, no one would have ever suspected that just a few short days ago he appeared to have been close to death.

She studied him for a moment. He almost seemed to be more chameleon than man, changing appearance and personality easily. Somewhere under it all was the real man, and she was determined to find out exactly who that was.

For the first time since realizing she had a special ability, she wished she had a firm control of it rather than wanting it to go away. Then maybe she could help Kyle solve his case.

His handsome features, each and every chiseled line of his exposed chest, his hard athletic body stretched out on the couch—everything about him reached out and grabbed her. His kisses had heated her desire for more of him. She wanted him physically and emotionally. She wanted him in every way possible. The intensity on his face as he studied the notebook echoed the seriousness of the task he had set for himself—a task that had nearly cost him his life.

She tried to sound casual in an attempt to cover her concern for his safety. "Did you find something important?"

He looked up from his reading. Every time he saw her his thoughts tried to wander away from his assignment and toward his personal desire to pull her into bed with him and spend the night making love to her. He had been on plenty of assignments that were tougher, more dangerous, but none that taxed his personal resolve the way this one did. He swung his long legs around and sat up.

"I'm not sure. This seems to be some sort of a surveillance schedule—times, dates, names, places—with several seemingly unrelated notations scattered throughout. I'm sure of one thing, though. It involves Frank Brewster, his auto parts warehouse and the lighthouse." He reached for the two plastic evidence bags he had placed on the end table. "Here, what do you make of these?"

She looked at the two items for a moment, not sure what she was supposed to be seeing. "They're both the same brand of cigarette."

"Yes...but there's more. First, it's not a very common brand."

"Where did they come from?"

"The one marked B came from an ashtray in Billy Washburn's bedroom. I found the other one between the planks of the lamp housing deck of the lighthouse my first night here. It was fresh—the drizzle hadn't gotten to it yet."

Her brow wrinkled in confusion. "You mean that Billy had somehow managed to get to the top of the lighthouse tower?" An unmistakable hint of excitement crept into her voice. "Can you send the cigarettes to a lab and get a DNA match to prove that both of them were smoked by Billy?"

"Sorry, it doesn't work that way. Saliva contains virtually no cells, therefore no DNA. However, the lab boys tell me all body fluids contain antigens that indicate the blood type for that person. So, if the cigarette butts were sufficiently wetted with saliva the lab can determine if they were smoked by someone with the same blood type."

"You seem to know a lot about this type of thing."

"It's the kind of stuff you pick up along the way."

"I still don't understand why Billy would be interested in the lighthouse." As if to punctuate her statement she scrunched up her mouth and knitted her brow into a frown.

"He was apparently keeping track of something I think is connected to what I'm after. The main question is whether he was working with them or spying on them. One thing is for sure, whatever he was doing got him killed."

"Killed?"

He saw her eyes widen in shock.

"You mean Billy's death wasn't an accident? I knew you were suspicious of the circumstances, but I had no idea it might have been murder. Why do you think so? Just because of that notebook and a couple of cigarette butts?"

"Partly. The clincher was an insulin kit belonging to Billy. I found it in a locked drawer of the nightstand in his bedroom."

"Insulin? You mean Billy was diabetic?" She shook her head in confusion as if trying to make sense of the words. "But this is a small town. Something like that would be difficult to hide."

"Which explains why he went to see a doctor in Springfield and had the insulin prescription filled at a pharmacy there. He obviously wanted to hide the knowledge from people here."

"But why would he do that? What difference would it make?"

"Who knows? Maybe it was embarrassment over what he perceived as a weakness. Maybe for fear it would cost him his job. Could be any number of reasons for it."

She plopped down on the couch next to him, her total astonishment covering her like a blanket. She turned in his direction and stared at him for a moment, then the light of recognition came into her eyes. Her words came out in an excited rush. "But most diabetics can't handle alcohol. If Billy was diabetic, then the chances are that he couldn't drink. And that means—"

"Exactly. It also explains why Sam was so angry about the report that Billy had been drinking and ran his car into a ditch."

"I wonder if that had anything to do with what Sam said about the county not releasing the body until they had done some tests. I assumed he was referring to a routine autopsy." She studied Kyle as she turned the thought over in her mind. "Maybe there was more to it than that. What do you think?"

A smile of admiration spread across his face. "I think that's a very astute observation." Kyle picked up the notebook again. "But we need a lot more than that." There were still a few pages of notes that he had not looked at yet. He scanned the pages, frowned, turned back and reread a couple of pages. He closed the notebook and leaned back. It had been a long day, and he was not one hundred percent recovered.

"Tired?" She took the notebook from his hand and set it on the end table.

"A little." He put his left arm around her shoulder and drew her to him. It felt very comfortable, perhaps *too* comfortable. He nuzzled the side of her neck. She smelled good. He leaned his face into hers, pausing to nibble softly at the corner of her mouth before capturing it full on with a seductive kiss. She tasted good, too. It was an addictive taste, the kind that made him want more and more. His mouth lingered against hers, almost breaking contact then taking possession again as if he could not force himself to let go.

Her fingertips caressed his cheek. No one had ever touched the depth of her desires with mere kisses...until now. She welcomed the texture of his tongue brushing against hers. She knew they would make love. It would not be now. It would not be that night. She could feel the tension inside him in spite of the heated passion he conveyed. He was a man of many complexities and many passions.

It was Kyle who finally broke the kiss. He continued to hold her body next to his. His words were soft, even though they returned the atmosphere and conversation to the seriousness of his job. "Tell me about the Washburn family and Jeremy MacDonald, everything you can think of including MacDonald's death."

"Do you think there's a connection?" A tingle of excitement ran through her body as he gently brushed his thumb against her cheek, a body not yet totally recovered from the heat of his kiss.

"I'm not sure. I can almost see it, but I can't quite reach out and touch it...not yet. I have lots of pieces, but I can't fit them together."

"What I know is mostly hearsay, and it's kind of sketchy. Your best source of information would be the newspaper archives."

He inhaled the alluring scent of the jasmine woven into her hair. It seduced his senses just as it had the first day they met. There was too much of a comfortable familiarity between them. It was far more than what he felt was safe, but not near as much as he wanted. "I'll check that, too. But for now, tell me what you know...the way things were locally perceived when it happened."

"That was before my time, but as I understand it Jeremy MacDonald fell—" she pursed her lips in thought "—or was pushed to his death from the top landing of the lighthouse. Henry Washburn became an immediate suspect because of the fight they had gotten into earlier that day."

"What was the fight about?"

"Apparently Henry had accused Jeremy of paying unwanted attentions to his wife, which Jeremy had vehemently denied. Whether it was true or not is anyone's guess. Jeremy was a bachelor with a reputation of having an eye for a pretty woman regardless of her marital status. On the other hand, Henry Washburn was overly possessive and inordinately jealous where his wife was concerned. But, either way, the two men had come to blows in front of the hotel that afternoon. The next morning Jeremy's body was found at the base of the lighthouse tower. The time of death was estimated at somewhere between ten at night and two o'clock in the morning.

"Henry was their first and only suspect, but he had an

ironclad alibi. He had been in an all-night poker game, which was verified by four other people. With no real proof of foul play and the one and only suspect out of the running, the case was quietly closed. Unfortunately for Henry, that did not stop the rumors and innuendos. Gossip persisted in spite of his airtight alibi until he took his family and moved away. His son, Sam Washburn, returned to Sea Grove as an adult with his new bride. They had a son and led a quiet life, but the feelings of resentment apparently still lingered with some of the older residents in spite of the intervening years. I'm not sure exactly why—''

Kyle's body stiffened and his head jerked toward the side door. He abruptly moved Lauren away from him and reached behind his back to the clip-on holster attached to his jeans. He quickly withdrew the pistol and clicked off the safety. He motioned for her to turn off the lamp and go to the bedroom.

She hesitated, her stare fixed on the gun he held. He did not have time for this. He growled, ''Move…now!''

Her head jerked up to the point where she regained eye contact with him.

''Now!'' He watched as she snapped off the lamp then hurried to the bedroom and closed the door. He moved silently through the darkened room.

He stood next to the side door with his back pressed against the wall. He did not move for a full five minutes, then he heard it again. He reached for the doorknob. He eased the door open just enough for it to clear the edge of the frame and give him a crack to peek through.

The rush of cold air collided with his bare skin where his shirt hung open. He could see the faint illumination from the light at the garage door. Then he saw something move, something in the shadows at the back of the building. Kyle crouched close to the ground, slowly swung the door open, then darted silently into the cold night air. The ground moisture soaked through his socks. There had been no time to think about shoes.

A loud clatter of trash cans and lids wiped out the prevailing silence. A swift movement in the shadows presented itself in the dim lighting. He expelled a whoosh of relief as he straightened up. One, two...a family of three raccoons scampered across the grass. He turned to find Lauren standing just inside the open door.

"What happened?" Her words were anxious, her voice nervous. "Is everything okay? Are you all right?"

He heard her concern and saw it mirrored on her face, but at that moment it was secondary to the justified anger building inside him. He clenched his jaw in a tight line as he shoved the gun into the holster. He brushed silently past her, then closed and locked the door before switching on the lamp. He grasped her shoulders in a firm grip and fixed her with a harsh stare.

His irritation was immediate and emphatic. "I told you when this all began that you had to obey my orders without question and without hesitation. Both our lives depend on that. The amount of time it took for you to question what I was doing and for me to repeat instructions was enough time for one or both of us to have ended up very dead."

She totally ignored what he was saying, instead focusing on her own concerns. "Why do you find it necessary to carry a gun inside my home? Isn't it enough that you have the thing here? Do you also need to carry it on your person?"

"You've just witnessed why it's necessary. That could just as easily have been someone carrying a gun of his own."

"But it wasn't." She stood her ground. "It was just some raccoons looking for a free meal."

"Yes, and it could also have been a raccoon I heard the second before I turned and took a slug in the shoulder...but it wasn't." He continued to hold her in a tight grip as his stare bored into her. "And while we're at it, no one told you to come out of your bedroom. Didn't it ever occur to you that you just might be walking into a dangerous situation?" He felt her body stiffen, saw her eyes widen with the realization.

"Yes, you told me, and I did agree to follow your instructions." She glanced at the floor, then looked at him again. He had expected to see guilt, remorse or at least an apologetic expression. Instead he saw an assertive woman who showed no signs of backing down. She was neither combative nor contrite. Her words were straightforward and to the point. Her attitude was all business, showing no personal reaction to his outburst. "It won't happen again."

His insides melted, and the hard edge left his voice. "I know my job, Lauren, and I'm very good at it. This isn't a question of testing one will against another. It's not a matter of being in charge or giving orders. It's a matter of survival." He brushed his lips across hers, lingering for a moment before letting her go. He steeled himself against the desire flooding through his body by abruptly turning away from her. He went to the kitchen to pour himself a cup of coffee.

When he returned to the living room he was all business. "Tell me about Frank Brewster."

"What do you want to know?" She tried to take his abrupt change in stride.

"Anything you can think of."

"Well...the Brewster family has lived here for generations, but it was the two brothers, Frank's uncle Ralph and his father, Wilton, who started the auto parts business and hardware store and made the money. Ralph Brewster was eight years older than Wilton. Ralph died about twenty years ago. He had never married. For a long time there were persistent rumors about his having an illegitimate son who was being raised by out-of-state relatives. Ralph never said anything about it one way or the other, and the rumors eventually faded into obscurity. Wilton died about three years ago, and Frank's mother died the following year. Frank never married, so he's the last of the family line to inherit the property and business—unless those rumors about Ralph's son turn out to be true."

"Inherit the business..." Kyle's features contorted into a strange expression. At first she thought he was staring at her, but then she realized he was not focused on her at all. He seemed to be staring right through her. It was a fascinating glimpse into his thinking process. She could almost see various pieces of the puzzle coming together in his mind to form the beginnings of a picture.

He spoke in a distracted manner, his vague words not really making any sense to her. "Hmm...three years ago...sweats too much...too many nervous habits. The weak link in the chain." A grin spread across his face, followed by a self-satisfied expression. "Of course! It fits...it makes sense." He paced up and down, his body a bundle of barely controlled energy. "It was about three years ago when we first picked up bits and pieces about a small smuggling ring operating somewhere in the Pacific Northwest. We assumed it was a fairly new operation, but it isn't. It's been going on for decades!"

He stopped pacing and stared at her. "This could turn out to be the longest-running smuggling ring in history. My God." He waved his arm in a sweeping gesture. "Do you realize the ramifications? This organization could have started with the smuggling of liquor in from Canada during Prohibition, and then the contraband simply changed over the years with the needs and demands of the times. It's small enough to not really attract a lot of attention. They haven't flooded the market with illicit goods. In fact, we never would have become aware of their activities if they hadn't turned their hand to electronic components and computer chips on the government's do not export list—"

He suddenly stopped talking, having already said more than he should have.

The words had flowed faster than Lauren was able to assimilate them. She followed the gist of what he was saying, but did not understand all of it. What was the connection between Jeremy MacDonald's death and Billy Washburn's apparent murder nearly half a century later? How did Frank Brewster fit in? Who or what was this weak link Kyle had referred to? And what was the chain?

"We have lots of work to do tomorrow." He grabbed her hand and pulled her to the dining table, where he wrote out a list and handed it to her. "First thing in the morning I want you to start by collecting this information for me."

She studied the piece of paper, her lips pursed and her brow knitted in concentration. "This is a pretty tall order. Some of this might be a little too—"

"A little too difficult?"

She heard the challenge in his voice. She answered with as much confidence as possible. "No. It won't be a problem. It will just take a little digging, but I can do it." She folded the list and stuck it in her pocket. "What will you be up to while I'm doing this?"

"I think, my pretty pen pal, that Shane Nolan will be visiting the newspaper office." He put his arm around her waist and guided her toward the kitchen. "Why don't we have a little glass of wine?"

"That would be very nice." She was beginning to gain some insight into his world. He was a man filled with secrets and cloaked in danger. A man who worked alone and traveled alone, depending on his wits, intelligence and abilities.

She poured them each a glass of wine, which they carried to the living room. They settled into the couch, his arm protectively around her shoulder.

Kyle took a sip from his glass then set it down. His mood had turned pensive. He did not look at her, instead

referring to stare at the far wall. "It's not too late, you
now. You can still pack up and leave for a couple of
weeks until this whole thing blows over, until it's safe for
ou to return."

She looked at him, at his strong profile. The set of his
aw, the intensity of his expression—she did not like the
ilent signals they sent out. She swallowed the quaver in
er voice. "Are you asking me to leave?"

"Perhaps I am." He refused to look at her. His words
vere hollow, his voice distant. "The people I'm up against
ave already proven their ruthlessness. It would be much
afer for you if you weren't here. Today was just a trial
in to see if everything flowed smoothly. Tomorrow is
rhen the work begins, when we will both be operating out
a the open where anyone and everyone can watch what
e're doing." Kyle Delaney was a man fighting inner con-
icts—duty, responsibility, need and desire.

Lauren took a calming breath. "I promised I'd leave
hen you told me to go. Are you? Are you *telling* me to
o?"

He finally turned to face her. "I should be."

Her words came out a whisper. "But are you?"

He cupped her chin in his hand and leaned his face to
ers. "I don't think so…at least not yet." His mouth cov-
ed hers for only a second. He had to stop himself from
aying something he would surely regret. Then the full
orce of his desires took hold. He pulled her body against
s, twined his fingers in her hair and took total possession
' her mouth. He nibbled at her soft lips, then sought the
weetness of her taste. His tongue caressed hers.

She responded with an equal level of passion, welcom-
g every intimate gesture. She ran her hand across his
are chest, shoving aside his unbuttoned shirt. She felt his
rong heartbeat and the rise and fall of his breathing. Her
ngers came in contact with the bandaging on his shoulder,

and she felt him flinch slightly, a not too subtle reminde
of the very real danger that surrounded him.

"WHAT THE HELL do you mean by that? Are you tellin
me Kyle Delaney was a government agent?" Frank's voic
vibrated a full octave above normal, pure panic controllin
his words and actions. "How do you know that? Who tol
you he was a government agent?"

"His van said so. That whole business with the leasin
agency. It all went through proper channels, the officia
inquiry about an impounded vehicle. But it still figures.'

"You mean you aren't even sure he was an agent?'
Frank's voice was an octave and a half above normal.

The words were snapped out in anger. "I'm sure!"

"You killed a man for no apparent reason—"

"I had my reasons."

"Oh, yeah…I'm sure they were great ones, too." Sar
casm dripped from Frank's words. "And now, after th
fact, you think he might have been a government agent?'

"Calm down, Frank. No one's gonna trace it to us."

Frank's panic did an abrupt turn into anger. "Right…n
one will ever figure that one out. An undercover agen
comes to town, obviously on an assignment, and a da
later he gets blown away and you just assume whoeve
sent him will shrug and say, 'Oh, well.' For Christ's sak
the least you could have done was weigh him down befor
dumping him into the ocean. Whose bright idea was it t
waste this guy? Was it another of your brilliant plans fo
handling trouble? Did you even bother to clear it this tim
before you did it?"

"I didn't dump him in the ocean, he fell off the clif
You know, I'm beginning to get a little worried about yo
Frank. You seem to be comin' apart on us. Are we gonn
have to do somethin' about you, too?" The threat wa
implicit, with no attempt to cover it in softer language.

Frank's voice quavered in spite of his effort to contr

it. "You know I'm with you all the way. I think we should proceed a little more cautiously, that's all. Maybe cool it for a while. Kind of shut down the operation until everything calms out a little. You know what I mean?"

"Sure, Frank. I understand what you're sayin'. Now don't you worry about nothin'."

Chapter Seven

Kyle stacked the blankets on the chair, then folded the pullout bed into a couch. He had insisted on sleeping on the sofa and returning Lauren's bedroom to her. He knew he could not spend another night in her bed, at least not alone. He also knew he could not do another fool thing like he had done last night. It had taken every bit of self-control he could muster to break off what had turned into a delicious seduction of the senses and the body.

He knocked softly on her bedroom door. "Are you about ready?"

"Yes." The door opened and she joined him in the living room. "I'm all set."

He checked his disguise one last time in the full-length mirror then turned toward her. "Well?"

"It looks perfect, *Mr. Nolan.*" She grinned at him, but the grin quickly faded when he refused to respond in kind.

"Then let's get going. We have a busy day."

His words were clipped, and his manner could best be described as brusque. Lauren was not sure what was going on inside him. The night before could have very easily ended up with them making love, a possibility she embraced. Then suddenly he had turned distant, and she did not know why. She watched as he exited the side door, not even waiting for her. She grabbed her large shoulder bag and hurried after him.

The drive to the *Sea Grove Gazette* elicited no more conversation than the morning had. A nervous tension jittered through the air. Lauren parked in front of the newspaper offices. Kyle seemed outwardly calm, whereas she had a stomach full of dancing butterflies.

Without looking at her, he reached over and ran the tip of his finger across the back of her hand then gave it a squeeze. Before she could respond, he was out of the car.

Kyle opened the front door to the newspaper office then stood aside to allow Lauren to enter ahead of him. She led the way to Tony Mallory's office.

"Good morning, Tony." She smiled pleasantly as he looked up from his desk. "I hope I'm not interrupting."

Tony rose to his feet, glanced curiously at Kyle, then returned her smile. "Of course not." He gave her an affectionate kiss on the cheek. "Please, sit down."

"I'd like you to meet Shane Nolan, my pen pal from Ireland."

The two men shook hands. "Pleasure to meet you, Shane. Saw the two of you at Billy's funeral, assumed that's who you were. Can't beat the small-town gossip circuit. Sometimes makes me wonder why I bother putting out a newspaper." He shook his head and chuckled at the thought, then returned his attention to his guests. "May I offer you some coffee?"

"Nothing for me, thanks." She turned toward Kyle. "How about you, Shane?"

"Not a thing. Thank you."

Tony reclaimed his chair. "Well, what can I do for the two of you this morning?"

Lauren took charge of the conversation. "I've been telling Shane all about the lighthouse, all the work the historical society did on the renovations and about the ghostly apparition that walks the tower." She chuckled in an effort to keep the conversation light. "He's very interested in the historical aspects of the renovations."

"Being an archaeologist I'm interested in all things historical. My field describes things historical as being much older than a mere hundred years, but I'd still like to know more about the lighthouse."

"Naturally Shane has seen the brochures we hand out to the visitors and the old photographs we used as a guide for the renovations. So—"

"I must confess 'tis I who pushed this lovely lady into asking a favor of you. I should really be speaking for myself rather than putting the burden on her." Kyle did not want to appear impatient, but she was taking too long to get to the point—giving more of an explanation than was necessary. Besides, she was wasting time that neither of them could spare.

"I would be ever in your debt if you would accord me the privilege of going through back issues of your fine newspaper so that I may read about the lighthouse from a local perspective. After all, archaeology is a study of past cultures, which is the interaction of people and places, not just ancient ruins." Kyle smiled pleasantly but kept a keen eye on Tony's reaction. He noted the way Tony's eyes narrowed, how he seemed to be studying him, not at all the evasive behavior the newsman had presented when they had originally met, under different circumstances.

Tony rose from his desk. "This is quite a coincidence...second time in about a week someone has wanted to check the archives for information on the lighthouse." His expression was friendly, but his words had been precise and specific in spite of his casual tone. His eyes showed the skeptical nature of the thoughts going through his head.

It was okay. Kyle had judged Tony to be a very competent newsman and knew his instincts would kick in and prevent him from accepting the story at face value. Kyle was prepared for it with a ploy he had not mentioned to Lauren, but first he had to get her out of the newspaper offices and on her way to the courthouse to take care of the list he had given her.

"I know Lauren has a busy morning of personal errands. So, if you don't mind, I can easily amuse myself here while she takes care of her business. My grandfather ran a small newspaper. It will be interesting to compare your older issues with the newspaper in his village." Kyle raised an eyebrow and looked questioningly at Tony, as if waiting for his permission.

"Of course. I'm always happy to extend professional courtesy to the relatives of fellow newsmen." Again, the words were polite but the edge to his voice said otherwise.

Kyle turned to Lauren. "Why don't we meet for lunch at that little pub down the road, the one overlooking the harbor?"

"Oh? I thought we would go back to the tearoom for lunch."

Kyle saw confusion cloud her eyes. He took her hand in his and gave it an affectionate pat. "Now how can I be the one treating you to a fine lunch if we eat at your establishment?"

Kyle hustled her out of Tony's office and onto what she needed to be doing, then turned his attention to Tony. He glanced around as if to make sure no one could hear him. "I must apologize for that little deception."

"Oh?" Tony's obvious curiosity was tempered with a hint of smugness that said he had not bought any of the story. "What *little deception* are you talking about?"

Kyle dropped his voice to a conspiratorial level and again glanced around. "That bit about the lighthouse...I'm naturally interested in Lauren's activities, but I didn't have the heart to tell her what I really wanted from your newspaper archives."

He saw Tony's body straighten to attention and saw the

keen light of interest come into his eyes. "What is it you really want?"

"It's Jim Franklin." Tony's interest turned to abject surprise. Kyle continued with his ploy. "I wanted to read the newspaper articles about my friend's death, whatever it is that you printed. You can understand why I didn't want to mention this to Lauren...to dredge up all those old memories and reopen the wounds."

"Of course, Shane. I understand."

He saw the mood shift in Tony's eyes, but Tony looked away before he could determine if the change was also acceptance of his story. Tony led him to a back room and showed him the cross-referenced files and where to find things, just as he had done previously for Kyle Delaney.

"You just help yourself. If you can't find something, give me a yell. Otherwise, you're on your own."

"Thank you, Tony. I certainly appreciate your understanding of the delicacy of the matter." He noticed it again, the way Tony seemed to be purposely avoiding eye contact with him. It was the same as Tony had done before. Did it mean something, or was he just letting his imagination run away with him?

LAUREN FINALLY MOVED to the head of the line at the hall of records in the county office building. It seemed as if everyone in the county needed something that day.

"Next."

She presented her list to the clerk. "I need these records."

The clerk looked over the list then made some notations before handing it back, her attitude telling of the harried morning she had already been subjected to. "Your items number one, two and three are handled down the hall in room number one eleven. Item number four is on the second floor in room two seventeen. Item number five will be available to you here in about three hours. Come back then.''

The clerk did not wait for a response. She dismissed Lauren with a withering look, then shifted her gaze to the long line of people waiting for service. ''Next.''

Lauren glanced at her watch then headed down the hall, her progress interrupted by someone calling her name. She looked up and saw Irene Peyton hurrying toward her.

''Lauren, what a surprise.'' Irene looked around. ''Now, where's that handsome pen pal of yours? Surely you didn't leave him sitting home alone while you're taking care of business.''

''I, uh, was thinking about doing some remodeling at work so I thought I'd better check and find out what was required in the way of permits and that sort of thing.'' It was a feeble lie and she was not even sure why she felt the need to offer an explanation. She saw the puzzled look dance across Irene's face and the skepticism in her eyes.

''But Lauren, dear, isn't that the type of thing the contractor would take care of?''

''I suppose you're right.'' Lauren chuckled self-consciously, embarrassed at being caught in such a ridiculous mistake. ''I didn't think of that. I guess I hadn't given it enough serious thought to be considering a contractor yet. It was just something I had been mulling over in my mind. Uh…Shane and I were talking about it last night.''

''Which brings me back to my question. What have you done with that charming young man?''

''He's at the newspaper office. We'll be meeting at the Bayview Inn later for lunch.''

''Oh? The newspaper office?''

''Yes…'' She drew on the fabrication Kyle had created while they were in Tony's office. ''His grandfather ran a small newspaper in Ireland and he was interested in doing a comparison between that and a small-town newspaper here.''

Irene extended a friendly smile. ''Well, I must be running. I have an entire day of errands planned. I'll see you later. You say hello to Shane for me.''

Lauren returned the smile. ''I will.'' She watched as Irene pushed the button for the elevator. The older woman seemed to be everywhere at once and was involved in everything. Lauren recalled Milly telling her about the money Irene's parents left her. It seemed that everyone in town had referred to it as *substantial,* but no one seemed to know how much that was. Lauren allowed a brief thought about being as active and healthy when she reached Irene's age, then she hurried down the hall. She had her own business to take care of, hers and Kyle's.

The morning passed very slowly. She felt as if she spent most of the time waiting in various lines, but she finally managed to accumulate everything Kyle wanted. She picked up the last remaining documents, the ones that required the three-hour wait. She was to meet him in fifteen minutes. She hurried toward the building door, almost colliding with someone as she came around the corner of the hallway.

''Irene.'' She could not stop the surprise in her voice. She quickly shoved the documents she had just obtained into her shoulder bag. ''It seems that our paths are running parallel today.'' Lauren noted Irene's curious expression as the older woman pointedly stared at the papers protruding from the top of her bag.

''Yes, it certainly does.''

The two women exited the building, Lauren turning toward the harbor and Irene going the other way.

THE SOUND of someone opening the door to the newspaper office caused the clerk to look up from her desk. She stepped to the counter and extended a smile to the customer. "Hello, Irene. It's nice to see you. May I help you with something?"

Irene returned the smile. "Yes, you can, Trudy. I found a poor bedraggled-looking puppy sitting on my front porch this morning. She has a collar so she must belong to someone. Unfortunately, there was no tag. I'd like to place an ad in the lost and found column. I'm sure some little boy or girl really misses the cute little thing and is worried sick."

"Of course." The clerk reached for a form and handed it to Irene. "Just fill out this form." She handed Irene a pen. "What kind of a dog is it?"

"She's a little beagle puppy, looks to be about two months old. I fed her and fixed her a warm bed. I'll be leaving in a few days to visit my niece in Seattle so I need to find the puppy's owner before I go."

"Gosh, it seems like you just got back from visiting your niece. Is everything okay with her?"

"Yes, she's just fine. I have so few family members left, I like to visit them as often as possible." Irene filled out the ad form, then handed it to the clerk. While Trudy processed the paperwork, Irene glanced around the room.

Kyle made one final copy on the duplicating machine, then returned the last of the back issues to the shelf where he had found them. He looked up and saw Irene Peyton staring intently at him from the other side of the front counter. He waved when he spotted her, flashed his best smile and turned on the charm. "Top o' the morning to you, Irene. And what a joyous surprise it is to see you again."

"Why, yes. This is a pleasant coincidence, running into you here, of all places. Are you enjoying your visit to Sea Grove?"

"Very much so. 'Tis a delightful little community you have here."

"Did you find everything you were looking for,

Shane?'' Tony Mallory bustled into the room, speaking before he realized Kyle was talking with Irene.

He stopped short. "Oh...pardon me, Irene. I didn't realize you were here. May I help you with something?''

"No, nothing at all. I was just placing an ad in the lost and found when I saw Shane.'' She turned her attention to the clerk, paid for the ad, then turned to the two men. "Well, I must be on my way. I have several errands yet and the day is getting away from me.'' She extended a pleasant smile then left the newspaper office.

Kyle acknowledged Tony's earlier question. "I found what I was looking for, thank you.''

"I really didn't know Jim Franklin very well. I met him a couple of times, but that was all. I only arrived in town a few months before...well, before it happened. And, of course, Jim lived in Springfield rather than here in Sea Grove.'' He paused for a moment, as if gathering his thoughts. "I understand the two of you had been close friends for many years. How did you meet?''

Kyle chose his words carefully, giving Tony the story Lauren had related to him. "Ah, you test my memory...it takes me back a couple of decades. As you probably know, Jim was a Rhodes scholar and spent two years at Oxford. During that time he made several trips to Ireland. I think it was on his second visit that we met. It was in a pub. Here was this young American carefully counting his money to see if he could afford a second drink and trying to make sense of the bartender's thick brogue.'' He chuckled softly, giving the impression of recalling the incident.

For a moment Kyle felt as if he was being interrogated rather than engaging in simple conversation. He allowed once again that it was probably his imagination, but it was better to err on the side of caution than to be caught off guard. As if on cue, a twinge of pain tugged at his shoulder to remind him of the last time he had permitted a lapse.

Kyle shook hands with Tony. "I must be off. I'm to

meet Lauren at the pub for lunch, and I don't want to keep such a lovely lady waiting, especially on such a fine day." He hurried off, his mind analytically sorting and classifying the information he had been able to dig out of the back issues of the newspaper. Something nagged at his consciousness, something he had seen but had not really looked at—something that did not seem to be part of what he had been searching for, yet seemed to fit. He shoved the thought away. For the moment it did not apply to his case.

Of a much more personal concern was what he had read about Jim Franklin. Lauren's fiancé had been shot with his own gun in his home during a robbery attempt. She had been the one to discover his body. It certainly explained her dislike for guns in general and her adverse reaction to the fact that he carried one as part of his job. It also put yet another question mark into the practicality of his growing emotional involvement with her. It was an issue that did not seem to have any compromise to it. This was what he did for a living and he had no plans to change careers.

Kyle entered the Bayview Inn and proceeded to the dining room. Lauren had taken a table by the window overlooking the small harbor. "Sorry to have kept you waiting." The Irish accent flowed with ease and perfection. "I paused for a bit of conversation with Irene just as I was leaving the newspaper."

"Really? I bumped into her this morning, too—twice, in fact." A soft chuckle enveloped her words, followed by a thoughtful furrowing of her brow. "That woman certainly gets around."

Kyle scanned the menu. "I feel like I should order corned beef and cabbage out of respect for Shane Nolan."

"You won't be disappointed. In fact, all the food here is good."

He reached across the table and lightly brushed a wayward lock of her hair, allowing his fingertips to linger against her cheek. It was an innocent-appearing gesture, but also an extremely intimate one telling of the closeness between them. "But I don't like corned beef and cabbage."

To anyone watching them, it would seem they had eyes only for each other. She frequently touched his arm. On several occasions he reached across the table and squeezed her hand. There was the familiarity of sampling food from each other's plate. While they were playing out the scenario for any onlookers Kyle still managed to keep a sharp eye on everything that was going on around them—both in the restaurant and outside on the waterfront walkway and dock.

Several things caught his attention, not the least of which was Frank Brewster apparently readying a sleek cabin cruiser to put out to sea. He also noted Max Culhane get out of his squad car and do a leisurely foot patrol along the waterfront, pausing to exchange a few words with Frank, then continue on. Kyle glanced toward the parking lot. A second squad car had pulled into the lot. The glare on the windshield prevented him from seeing who sat in the driver's seat.

Kyle and Lauren finished their lunch and left the restaurant. "Let's go home—" He had not meant for it to come out that way. It was not *home*, at least not his home. "Let's go back to your place. I want to get a look at what you collected and see if I can put it together with what I already have." The image of Frank Brewster and the boat refused to leave his mind. Something would be happening very soon, possibly even that night. This did not fit into Kyle's projected pattern at all. "Besides, this damn beard is about to drive me nuts." He shot a sly grin Lauren's way. "What do you think would happen if Shane Nolan shaved off his beard?"

"I think he'd look a little too much like Kyle Delaney."

He frowned at her. "Spoilsport!" He grabbed her hand

and started down the street at a fast pace. "Come on, let's go."

"Yes." She hurried to keep up with his long-legged stride. "I should be checking in with Milly, too. I've been shamefully neglectful of my business the past few days."

THE DOCUMENTS Lauren had obtained, combined with several things Kyle had located in the newspaper archives, were spread across her dining table. She watched him as he studied the information. He occasionally made notes on a small pad. She tried to see what he was writing. It appeared to be some kind of personal shorthand or code and did not make any sense to her.

She was able to sneak a peek at a couple of the items he had copied at the newspaper office. There was a quarter page newspaper ad from the 1930s and another from the 1940s. There were copies of articles ranging from the early 1930s to the present, but they were stacked under the newspaper ads and she could only make out the dates at the top of each page.

The hours ticked away without Kyle saying a word to her. She did her best not to disturb his concentration. He seemed to be totally absorbed in a world of his own, one she did not understand, one he had only allowed her a glimpse of—a world of shadows, deceptions, danger...and guns.

He finally leaned back in his chair, his hands clasped behind his head and a satisfied smile on his face. His eyes reflected his excitement. "Well, I think that about does it."

"You look very pleased with yourself. The newspaper archives must have yielded some helpful information."

"They did, indeed." He leaned forward again, his expression serious. "Tell me about Tony Mallory."

"Well...he's thirty-eight years old and has a degree in journalism. He interned in Chicago and worked for a while as an investigative reporter. He showed up in Sea Grove almost eight years ago and went to work on our weekly newspaper. The owner had just had a heart attack. Apparently Tony's wife didn't want any part of small-town life and refused to leave Chicago. They ended up getting a divorce. At least that's Tony's version of what happened.

"Four years ago the owner died and Tony bought the newspaper from the family and has been running it ever since. I don't know what prompted him to leave Chicago and the fast-paced career of an investigative reporter to come to our small town."

"So he has no history here prior to eight years ago?"

"That's right." She wrinkled her brow in confusion. "Is there something important about that? Why did you want to know?"

"Just curiosity. He appears to be very organized." He shot her a questioning look. "You seem to know quite a bit about him."

"We…" Lauren felt a hint of embarrassment rise inside her. "We had dinner a few times, went to the movies. We're friends."

She looked for a diversion and finally settled on pouring two glasses of wine. She handed one of them to Kyle.

He refused her offer. "None for me. I have to go out."

"You're going out?" She could not hide her surprise, nor her displeasure at this unexpected turn of events. "But you've already taken off your disguise. Do you think it's wise to go out without it?"

"It's dark out, and I'm not going far."

"But—"

He put his fingers against her lips, stopping her protest. His voice was forceful without being harsh. "I have things to do that require my full faculties. I don't think I'll be gone long. We can have that glass of wine when I get back."

She made an attempt to be every bit as forceful as he was. "I'm going with you."

"No, you're not." It was a simple statement of fact that closed off any attempt at rebuttal. As if to reinforce that fact, he turned and walked into the bedroom. He reappeared a minute later wearing his jacket and carrying a bag slung over his shoulder.

"Kyle—"

"No!" He leaned over and placed a soft kiss on her lips, as much in an effort to stop her words as for the brief moment of pleasure it provided him. "I'll be back soon." He slipped the shoulder strap over his head so the bag fit snugly against his body, then he disappeared out the side door into the darkness of night.

Kyle quickly covered the short distance across the bluff. He had plenty of breath and ran at an easy pace, but each time his foot hit the ground he felt the thud in his shoulder. After carefully checking the grounds, he let himself into the keeper's cottage and went straight to the tower door. A couple of turns of the lock pick and he stood inside the dark cylinder, his head tilted as he stared through the darkness, listening for anything that did not belong.

He ascended the circular staircase, finally arriving at the top landing. The cold breeze off the ocean ruffled his hair and nipped at his cheeks and nose. He reached into the satchel and withdrew a pair of night vision binoculars, then scanned the water starting at the harbor entrance. It took only a couple of minutes for him to spot what he was searching for—Frank Brewster's cabin cruiser headed past the breakwater.

He continued to watch the boat. A few minutes out from the harbor the engines shut down, leaving the cruiser to bob with the natural movement of the ocean. The boat appeared to be dead in the water. It seemed to be a waiting game with Frank biding his time. A quick once-over of the area did not reveal any other ships. He continued to watch for several minutes, then the engines started up and the cruiser swung around to head toward the harbor. Kyle frowned. Odd...very odd, indeed.

He returned the binoculars to the pouch and went down the staircase, through the cottage and into the cellar. He wanted to check out the small side room.

He spread out the plans he had obtained from the government archives showing the original construction, then unrolled the blueprints Lauren had procured for him showing the structural reinforcement work done ten years ago. To his disappointment neither set of plans revealed anything unusual or out of place. Billy Washburn had managed to get to the top of the tower without going through the connecting door from the kitchen. Even though Billy's notebook had yielded some very interesting information, he had not made any notes about how he had gotten inside the tower. Another entrance existed, and Kyle had to find it.

He shined the flashlight around the small room, carefully checking the floor, ceiling and walls. The concrete floor seemed solid, as did the ceiling. Three of the walls appeared to be solid, but the fourth wall was another story. He had noted the patched area on his original visit to the cellar. Now he gave it close scrutiny. It had to be a door, and there had to be a way of opening it. He hoped it was some kind of release button or switch rather than an infrared remote control device or an electronic code.

He carefully checked the support timbers across the ceiling. A smile of satisfaction turned the corners of his mouth when his fingers came to rest on the small button hidden in a recessed area of one of the ceiling timbers. He was about to push the button when he heard the faint creak of the floorboards and the sound of footsteps above his head. Someone was in the cottage.

Kyle snapped off his flashlight. He reached for the gun nestled in the clip-on holster at the small of his back as

he ducked underneath the stairwell. The open spaces between the steps allowed him a clear view of anyone de-
scending. A moment later the door at the top opened and
a beam of light spread its glow down the stairs, followed
closely by someone wearing white sneakers and worn
jeans. The intruder paused for a moment when the one
squeaky step gave up its plaintive cry.

Kyle remained hidden, hoping that a confrontation
would not be necessary but ready should it become un-
avoidable.

Chapter Eight

As soon as Kyle saw the interloper he shook his head with a combination of relief and irritation. He paused long enough to holster the pistol before stepping out to confront his unwelcome visitor. His words held an unmistakably sharp edge. "What the hell do you think you're doing?"

Lauren's heart momentarily lodged in her throat, then dropped to her chest where it continued to pound in double time. She tried to gulp in a couple of deep breaths before she turned to face her accuser. She forced her voice into a calm she did not feel. "Kyle...you startled me."

"This is the second time I've caught you sneaking into the lighthouse late at night. What's your excuse this time? What are you looking for?"

"I was looking for you." She could almost feel his angry eyes on her, a feeling that sent a little shiver up her spine.

"What made you think I'd be here?"

"It's the only place close enough for you to go on foot and not risk being seen without your disguise. Besides, it's been your all-consuming interest ever since your arrival."

"Didn't it occur to you that this just might be a very foolish and dangerous thing for you to be doing? I was sure we already had this discussion, but apparently you've forgotten about it."

She did not know whether he felt concern or displeasure, but it had come out of his voice as mild anger. She lashed out in reaction to his accusation. "I'm not the one who was facedown in the mud with a bullet through my shoulder. I'm not the one someone tried to kill."

His voice took on a forced calm. He wanted to drive home his point without having it lost to any unwanted emotional outbursts. "That's only because you weren't the one threatening their livelihood and freedom...at least not until now." He saw her eyes widen in surprise. He knew he had captured her attention.

"Just what precautions did you take when you crossed the bluff on your way to the lighthouse? I mean, you didn't just casually saunter over here as if you didn't have a care in the world...did you?" He paused before continuing. "Hasn't it crossed your mind that *you* just might be under surveillance...your actions and movements watched by person or persons unknown?"

She tried to rationalize her actions, but it became more difficult with each of his verbal challenges. "Well, then, whoever is watching me won't find anything out of the ordinary. It's common knowledge that I often take walks in the evening, and the lighthouse is a favorite destination of mine."

He spoke quickly. "That was then and this is now." His voice softened a little, but not too much. "The difference is that they somehow found out Kyle Delaney was not who he purported to be and decided to do away with him." He allowed a moment of reflection. "I personally think it was much too drastic a step for them to take so early in my investigation. It shows either desperation or lack of cohesive leadership and planning."

The edge crept into his voice. "But, whatever the reason, it tells us they are on alert and everything and everyone comes under suspicion. This identity you've provided me is a good one, but it links a new person in town with you. It puts both of us in the spotlight if for no other reason than idle curiosity."

She spoke, making no attempt to hide her anger. "Don't patronize me, Kyle. Don't you dare treat me like some ditzy little airhead! I most certainly did not casually stroll across the bluff wearing a large flashing neon sign saying Follow Me—I Can Lead You To The Government Agent You Thought You Killed!"

He felt the sting of her well-aimed barbs. Even with the beam of her flashlight pointed toward the ground, he could see the heat of anger in her cheeks and the emerald fire in her eyes. This was neither the time nor the place to engage in an argument. He needed to defuse the situation so he could get on with his work.

"Okay, you were careful." He folded his arms across his chest and appraised her with a critical eye. "So maybe you can be just as careful on your way back?"

"I'm not going until you do. You were shot because you didn't have anyone to watch your back. I can do that. You look for whatever it is you're looking for and I'll watch out for you. I have excellent hearing, and my night vision is superior."

"No way! I refuse to let you get in any deeper than you already are. There's no way I'd allow you to be in the line of fire."

"You've already said I'm probably on their list, and now you're saying that you don't want me involved." She touched her fingertips to his cheek, then rested her hand against his chest. His solid heartbeat resonated to her palm, filling her with a sense of his confidence, determination and strength. "You can't have it both ways, Kyle. If I'm on their list then I'm already involved. If I'm not involved, then I'm not on their list and they're not watching me."

He took a calming breath, then let it out with a loud whoosh. "Well, it seems I've been hoisted on my own petard." He sought her eyes. He wanted her to know that his words did not come from arrogance or a sense of superiority. "I can't be worried about your safety and do my job at the same time. We've been over this ground before, and it just won't work."

She took a step backward. Her words were soft, but her voice was filled with resolve. "You do your job and I'll take care of myself. Now, we're wasting time. What is it you're looking for here? Anything other than some sort of secret entrance?"

"You think you have it all figured out, don't you?" His sigh of resignation was loud and unhappy, but it said he had decided to acquiesce rather than waste any more time. "Come on."

They returned to the small room and Kyle shined his light on the recessed button he had found. He motioned Lauren to one side. "Stand back and keep quiet. I don't know what we're going to find behind this wall." He snapped off his flashlight, plunging the cellar into darkness. Then he pushed the button. The wall swung open to reveal more darkness.

Kyle cautiously stepped through the opening into a hidden room. He stood perfectly still and listened but heard only the sound of crashing waves and the whistle of the wind coming from somewhere beyond. He felt the movement of air and the drop in temperature. He turned on his flashlight and shined the beam around the room, pausing each time it lit on something of interest.

"Well, well, well...look at what we have here." A shortwave radio sat on a shelf, its dial tuned to the marine frequency. A table had been shoved up against the wall. On the table was a lamp and by it an ashtray. He collected the two cigar butts from the ashtray and put them into a plastic evidence bag. He shined the flashlight on a small hole in the wall with a couple of wires running through it. "That's where they tapped into the cottage's electricity."

He poked around the empty crates stacked in the corner.

The original shipping labels were still intact. "Counterfeits."

"Counterfeits?" Lauren could not hide her surprise. "Do you mean these boxes contained counterfeit money?"

"No, not money. Counterfeit clothing...knockoffs of designer labels. This part of the country, the Pacific Northwest in general and here in Washington state specifically, is the gateway to the Far East. Anything and everything that's counterfeited in the Orient usually passes through this area, most often directly but occasionally via Canada. Clothes, nuts and bolts...you name it and someone is counterfeiting it and smuggling it in."

"Nuts and bolts? What is there about nuts and bolts that would make them something to counterfeit?"

Kyle continued to poke around as he answered her. "Nuts and bolts come in different quality designations. The ones used to hold airplanes together are made to much more exacting specifications. The counterfeits are labeled and sold to legitimate manufacturers as the genuine article, but they aren't."

"You mean a passenger plane could be flying up there right now with one of its wings or an engine held on by inferior nuts and bolts and the company that built it wouldn't know it?"

"That's exactly what I mean. The word *smuggling* doesn't apply just to drugs, although that's what people usually think of these days. In fact, this ring has been very scrupulous in avoiding all connection with drugs and guns." He rummaged through a large trash can, scrutinizing numerous sheets of paper then tossing them back into the receptacle.

"What are you looking for?"

"Whatever I can find. Anything that will tell me something I don't already know about what goes on here." He reached into his bag and withdrew a pair of tweezers, then used them to pick up several small items that had attracted his attention. He placed the items in another evidence envelope and put them in his bag.

"What is it?" Lauren had not been able to see what he had picked up. "What did you find?"

"Just some little pieces of cellophane."

More secrets, more hidden thoughts and feelings. She watched as he turned his attention toward the dark tunnel that led toward the sound of crashing waves. She felt the warmth of his hand clasp hers. His words were whispered. "Stay close to me and watch your footing."

He moved slowly and cautiously out of the hidden room and into the passage with Lauren closely behind him. Each step took them down, until the tunnel finally leveled out. In addition to the sounds of wind and waves, there was now the added sound of dripping water.

Kyle stopped and stood perfectly still. She could almost feel the tension running through his body in the way he held her hand. After what seemed like an eternity he slowly shined the beam of his flashlight around the interior of a large cavern.

"Oh, my God!" The words tumbled out of Lauren's mouth and echoed off the hard walls before she could stop them. "I never dreamed this existed."

"Pretty amazing, isn't it?"

"Did you know this was here?" She could not believe what she was seeing.

"Did I know? No. Did I suspect? Yes."

The moisture-laden salt air whistled through the large cave, dampening everything it came in contact with. Puddles of seawater filled the sunken spots in the rocky floor, a floor that sloped off into a large pool. He shined the light across the pool to the cavern wall on the other side. A spray of water crashed through the rocks then ran into the pool.

"Let's see where that water's coming from." Kyle led the way around the pool.

Another wave crashed into the cavern, showing the twists and turns in the rock wall that created a natural opening between the cave and the ocean.

"So that's it." Kyle sounded very pleased with his find. "This entrance would be completely under water at high tide." He kicked at a puddle, sending water splashing against a wall as he shined the beam of light toward the high ceiling. "The cavern would be partially flooded. Only at low tide could this cave be accessed from the open sea without the use of scuba gear." He looked around, shaking his head in amazement. "What a perfect setup." He turned toward Lauren. "The natural opening in the rocks is so well hidden by its twists and turns that I didn't spot it when I did a helicopter survey of the entire shoreline at both high and low tide...and I was looking for something like this."

"So, this is how the smugglers move their contraband in and out." She turned toward Kyle. "I've lived a stone's throw from here for most of my adult life, and I've been in and out of the lighthouse cottage untold numbers of times. I never knew any of this was here."

She stared at the natural opening in the rocks. "This doesn't look big enough for a large boat to pass through."

"I'd say you were right about that." The entrance was definitely not large enough for a boat the size of Frank Brewster's, especially with the twists and turns involved. "However, a dinghy making several trips between a fishing boat or cabin cruiser and the cave could haul quite a bit of stuff in a short period of time, and the boat itself would be commonplace enough so that it wouldn't attract any unwarranted attention. Once the merchandise is off the boat it would be easy to move it along the passage and out through the cottage cellar late at night. The entire procedure would work equally well in reverse. There's a huge trade in illicit liquor and cigarettes going from here to Canada these days because of the Canadian taxes."

Kyle skirted the large pool and started across the cavern toward the passage where they had entered. Lauren was about to follow him, but paused for a moment to take one last glance at the cave entrance.

"Kyle, look!"

The alarm in her voice telegraphed her sense of urgency to him, grabbing his full attention. He spun around and immediately spotted the flickering glimmer that grew brighter as it spread through the pool. He snapped off his flashlight and grabbed her arm, pulling her into a crouch with him. They watched from a tenuous cover of darkness as the scuba diver surfaced in the pool, the light coming from the diver's sea scooter.

Kyle tugged on Lauren's arm and they both ducked into a large crevice in the rocky wall. He moved her farther back so she was completely hidden by his body. It was not ideal concealment, but it was the best available. He reached for his pistol and clicked off the safety. He pressed his body as tightly against the rock wall as he could.

He clenched his jaw. His muscles tensed as the adrenaline pumped, leaving a sharp taste in the back of his mouth. The diver's intrusion into the cave represented only part of the danger. If the diver was meeting someone coming in through the cottage cellar, then a confrontation would be almost impossible to avoid.

The next thought that popped into his head was the distraction he had been worried about, the one he could not afford. How could he protect Lauren? Before he was able to speculate on the problem his attention was caught by a sharp sound that echoed through the cave.

The diver slapped his swim fins on the floor, then climbed out of the pool. He extracted a flashlight from the waterproof pouch attached to his weight belt and hurried to the far side of the cavern. Kyle watched as he shoved a rock aside high up on the wall, took something else from the pouch and placed it in the recess. He moved the rock into place. The diver returned to the pool, leaving the cavern as he had arrived.

Kyle and Lauren waited in the dark. His nervous system settled into a normal mode. After what he deemed to be a safe amount of time, he half turned toward her. "You wait here, I'm going to see what he hid." He started forward but was drawn to an abrupt halt.

Lauren continued to hold on to the back of his jacket, squeezing the material tightly in her fist just as she had the entire time they were hiding from the diver. Even though she found Kyle's calm manner to be a great comfort, her insides were still doing flip-flops. She knew if she tried to speak it would come out as a series of incoherent sputters. She forced her hand open and nodded her agreement.

She watched the trail his flashlight made as he crossed the cave to the makeshift wall safe and shoved aside the rock. He reached inside and withdrew a package wrapped in plastic. Her curiosity got the best of her. She went to see what he had found.

Kyle glanced at her then carefully peeled back the waterproof wrapping on the package. It contained a large roll of one-hundred-dollar bills. He heard her gasp in surprise as he counted them.

"I've never seen so much money all at one time in cash. How much is there?"

He continued counting. "Two hundred fifty thousand dollars."

"Is it real?"

"It sure is. It's obviously a payment of some sort, and this is the drop site." He reached for his little bag of tricks and brought out a special pen along with a pencil and notebook.

"What are you going to do?"

"I'm going to mark the bills then return them to their hiding place. It's always wise to follow the money trail."

The items in his bag captured her curiosity. "Do you always carry a special marking pen with you?"

"I carry a variety of items with me. You never know what kind of surprises you're going to find when you're out hunting." He handed her the notebook and pencil. "Here, you make a list of the serial numbers." They hurried to complete the task, working silently until everything was back the way they found it. Kyle led the way up the passage toward the cottage.

They both froze when the faint sound of muffled voices floated down from above. He did not need to issue any instructions. They turned and ran back to the cave. Every moment counted as Kyle made a quick assessment of their situation. He did not need to see the new arrivals. He was pretty sure who they were. What he did need to do was figure a way to get out of there. He grabbed his holster from the waist of his jeans, shoved it into his waterproof bag, then slung the shoulder strap over his head and across his body.

There was only one way out. He grabbed Lauren's hand and raced toward the pool. "I hope you know how to swim."

"I'm an excellent swimmer. I also know how to scuba dive."

Kyle let go of her hand and reached into his bag as they hurried across the cave floor. He withdrew an object about the size of a soft drink can, then zipped the satchel closed. "Here." He handed the strange object to her when they reached the edge of the pool. "This is a pressurized air canister with a diver's mouthpiece. It only contains about fifty breaths of oxygen, so don't gulp it all down at once." He slipped over the side and into the pool.

Lauren followed him into the dark ocean water. "What about you? Is this the only one you have?" She knew the tingle that ran across her skin was more than just the cold water. She felt the adrenaline pump through her body and the odd surge of excitement that accompanied it.

"I'll be okay." He took a couple of deep breaths.

The tide was low enough for them to make it out of the cave without having to swim underwater. Neither was sure what they would find on the other side of the wall—perhaps a boat with the diver who had been in the cave earlier. It was a chance they had to take, the lesser of two evils.

Kyle and Lauren floated with the retreating waves, the water tossing them about. She scraped her back on a jutting rock, but managed to hold the air canister and not cry out in pain. They finally made their way through the twisting passage and out to the open sea.

It was a long fifteen minutes from the time they entered the water until they tumbled onto the sandy beach in the small cove just down from the lighthouse. Even though she had the compact air canister, Lauren had still swallowed several big gulps of seawater. A coughing spasm racked her body as she gasped for air.

Kyle crawled over to her, scooping her into his arms. "Lauren…are you okay?" He held her tightly, crushing her body against his.

"Yeah, I think so—"

A wave splashed their bodies, shoving them down and dragging them through the wet sand. They groped their way across the beach until they were away from the water. The cold night air swirled around them. Lauren shivered as it hit her skin and whistled through her wet clothes. She tried to run her fingers through her wet hair to get it away from her face. It was matted with sand and bits of kelp.

Lauren's adrenaline level had never been as high as it had during the past half hour. The danger followed by the excitement of the escape had left her tingling with tension and raw energy that somehow had to get out. She did not know whether to laugh or cry. A moment later Kyle took the decision out of her hands. Her awareness of the pain caused by the scrape on her back vanished in a flash as he pressed his body against hers.

He cupped her chin in his hand and brushed a soft kiss on her lips. It tasted of salt water and sand...and it was wonderful. He wrapped her in his embrace and pulled her down to the sand with him. The excitement of events and the heat of the moment mixed together to form a powerful aphrodisiac—one that could not be ignored any longer. He claimed her mouth as his with every intention of possessing much more.

Then there was the sound—actually two separate noises—that jerked him to reality. One sound was a boat engine and the other an automobile. Perhaps they meant nothing, but that was a chance he could not afford to take. He had almost allowed his personal desires to overrule his good judgment. He quickly jumped to his feet, pulling her up with him. "Come on, we've got to get out of here."

THE TWO GLASSES of red wine still sat on the kitchen counter, just where she had placed them before Kyle left. She picked up both glasses and carried them into the living room, placing one on the end table next to the couch. She took a sip from the other glass, then held it in her hands while staring at the bedroom door.

She had dressed in a long robe and warm socks after showering. While Kyle showered and dressed, she stayed in the living room drying her hair. She could still taste the saltiness of his kiss. The tingle on her skin and the excitement that churned through her stomach had been a rush unlike anything she had experienced. Kyle frightening her in the cellar of the cottage, the unexpected appearance of the diver in the cave—harrowing encounters, to say the least, but they did not compare to their daring escape coupled with the brief moment of passion on the beach. She had heard about adrenaline junkies, but had never understood the concept until now.

Suddenly the rush turned to a shiver of trepidation when she recalled the gun Kyle held in his hand, ever at the ready should the diver have spotted them. He had been right about the danger. But she had also been correct in that he needed her help. Even he had admitted that the situation could have turned... She paused in her thoughts as she searched for the ridiculous word he had used in an effort to downplay the true danger. Awkward, that was the word. He had told her that things could have turned *slightly awkward* if she had not spotted the light from the diver's scooter, thus giving them time to hide.

The door opened and Kyle stepped out dressed in a sweatshirt and sweatpants. He vigorously rubbed a towel through his wet hair. "Well, I don't know about you but I sure feel a lot better now that I've had a shower." He flipped the towel off his head and ran his fingers through his damp hair.

Then he looked at Lauren. Her long copper-colored hair hung loose to her shoulders. She was a vision of beauty, sensuality and desire. Up until now he had been very careful to keep his desires in check. Those desires had wandered on numerous occasions, the most recent time less than an hour ago, but he had managed to rein them in before they completely got away.

She took a sip from her glass. "What happens now?"

"What do you mean?" Was she asking about their future, his intentions, the nature of their relationship? Had his discomfort over his growing emotional involvement with her made him jump to that conclusion? He did not know.

"How close are you to solving this case? Do you know who's behind it?" She took a calming breath before asking her next question. "Do you know who shot you?"

Kyle paused. He had no business sharing information with her, compromising his assignment and the case, but it felt so good to have someone to discuss it with. It was a luxury he had never before allowed himself. Besides, like it or not, she was totally involved. "I'm close. There's still some pieces missing, but I'm close. Lauren…" His voice was soft, the words difficult for him. "I want you to know how much I appreciate the help you've given me." He saw the combination of surprise and confusion in her eyes.

"You're talking as if everything's wrapped up. As if you plan to leave in the morning." Another wrinkle of confusion crossed her brow. "You're not…are you?"

"Not yet. I think I have most of it put together in my head, but that's not the same thing as proof. I can't take my suspicions into a court of law without something real to back them up, and right now what I have is circumstantial."

"Where do things—"

"Sorry, there's a closed sign on the business discussions for the rest of the night." He took a sip of his wine, then placed the glass on the end table. He cupped her chin in his hand and lifted her face as he leaned forward. Business, logic, rules, right and wrong be damned. One kiss would not be enough. A thousand kisses were not going to be enough.

His mouth came down on hers, consuming her in an explosion of passion. He darted his tongue between her lips—exploring the dark recesses, drinking in her sweetness, losing himself in her warmth and sensuality. He did not want to think about the future. He did not want to know what it held. All he cared about at that moment was Lauren and the way she felt in his arms. He reveled in the way she responded fully and openly, in the heat she conveyed to him—a heat that matched his own.

He deftly untied the sash at her waist and slipped his hand inside her robe. Her skin was soft, warm and silky smooth. He cupped her bare breast. His breathing quickened as the excitement spread through his body. She was everything he could ever ask for…and more. He eased her robe off her shoulders, then lowered his head until he was able to tease her nipple with his tongue. He gave a soft moan when her flesh instantly puckered in response to his stimulation. He slowly drew the hardened bud into his mouth and suckled for a moment before releasing the treat. He kissed the notch at the base of her throat, then nibbled seductively at her lower lip.

His words came out in a husky whisper. "Come to bed with me, Lauren. I want to make love to you so very much."

"Yes."

It was only one word, but it spoke volumes. The tenuous hold he had on what was left of his restraint vanished in a rapid heartbeat. Kyle rose to his feet and held out his hand to her. She placed her hand in his. The fires of passion he saw in her eyes matched the flame that burned deep inside him. He turned out the light and they walked hand in hand into the bedroom.

Lauren dropped her robe to the floor. She watched Kyle pull off his sweatshirt and toss it in the corner. Her hands met his as she reached to tug his sweatpants past his hips. It was not the frantic urgency of lust or youthful hormones. It was the intimate closeness of two people who cared for each other very much.

She was about to make love with this man who was destined to be the all-consuming passion of her life. Her entire body quivered in anticipation as they sank into the softness of the bed. Something caught her eye, a shadow moving across the window. Ty-Ty jumped off the dresser onto a chair. She dismissed the concern. It had been the cat, nothing more.

All her thoughts ceased. Nothing remained except the sensation of his fingers tickling her inner thigh and his mouth at her breast. She closed her eyes, moaning softly when his hand reached the moist heat of her sexual core.

Then she experienced a sharp intake of breath when he slipped a finger between her feminine folds.

She caressed his back, trying to remember to be careful of his injured shoulder. With each passing second it became more difficult for her to concentrate on anything other than the delicious sensations that coursed through her body. She trailed her fingers across the curve of his bottom, then across the taut muscles of his back. The feel of his bare skin sent tremors of delight through her body, but nothing matched the incendiary desires he stirred deep inside her. She reached for his manhood, wanting to give him as much pleasure as he was giving her. He shifted his weight, moving the lower half of his body away from her.

His words were a husky whisper. "Not yet, my lovely." He immediately captured her mouth with an added fervor. He wanted her so much that he knew her touch would destroy what hold he had on his control. He did not know what the future held, but he did know he wanted to shut out everything and make this night last as long as possible.

It would be difficult to say whose breathing was more labored or whose desires had been stretched closer to the ultimate. She welcomed the way he snuggled between her legs while covering her with kisses, starting at her throat and continuing down until he reached the moist heat of her womanhood. He bestowed the final kiss, igniting the convulsions deep inside her. She held him tightly while savoring each and every delicious sensation.

Kyle teased her nipple with the tip of his tongue then drew the succulent treat into his mouth. Everything about her excited him more than any other woman ever had— the feel of her skin, the heat of her response, the taste that was uniquely hers.

His hardened arousal probed gently, then he filled her with a smooth thrust. Her heat nearly took his breath away when she closed around him. He paused to enjoy the pure ecstasy of the moment before setting a rhythm that demanded more—a demand that each rushed to satisfy.

Chapter Nine

Kyle lay awake staring through the darkness as Lauren slept in his arms. He lightly touched the scrape mark on her back. He had not realized she had been injured in their escape from the cave until he saw the ugly red welt. A pang of guilt washed over him. If he had insisted that she return home rather than allowing her to stay with him, then she would not have been injured. She had assured him it was nothing serious, for him to put it out of his mind. He had shoved the image aside, but it had refused to completely leave.

He glanced at the clock on the nightstand. The glowing red numerals told him it would be daylight very soon. He kissed her on the forehead, wanting to hold her tighter but not wanting to wake her. Nothing in his life experience had prepared him for the internal upheaval their lovemaking had produced. He had never invested his emotions before, and the result had left him totally unnerved.

It was no good. He could not tell her what he felt. He had a job to do and then he would be moving on. That was the way it had to be. He had no options in the matter. He carefully disentangled himself and quietly left the warmth of her bed.

He made coffee, then stepped to the window and pulled back the edge of the drape. The first gray streaks of dawn

were beginning to lighten the morning sky. He released
the drape and retrieved one of his suitcases from the closet,
then spread his notes on the dining table. On a legal pad,
he made a chart listing people, places, dates, times and
events with an additional column for miscellaneous information he had not yet categorized.

"Good morning." Lauren's words were soft and thick
from sleep. She pulled her hair from her face, using a
ribbon to hold it at her nape as she wandered in from the
bedroom.

He smiled when he heard her. The sound of her voice
was all it took to bring the previous night's emotions rushing back full force. He twisted in his chair and held his
hand out to her. "Good morning, yourself. Did you sleep
well?"

She accepted his hand. The little squeeze he proffered
made her feel warm inside, that is if it was possible to feel
any warmer than she already did. No one had ever made
love to her the way Kyle Delaney had. No one had ever
made her feel the way he did. If there had been any lingering doubts in the back of her mind about his place in
her life, they had been incinerated by the heat of the passion between them.

"Never better." She returned the squeeze before with-
drawing her hand. "I smell fresh coffee." She went to the
kitchen, poured herself a cup and returned to the dining
room. She stood behind his chair, wrapped her arm around
his neck and rested her chin on his shoulder. "You look
like you're very busy. Have you been up long?"

Kyle took a deep breath. She smelled of sleep, clean
sheets, warmth and desire. He placed one hand on top of
hers and with the other he reached behind his chair. He
caught a piece of her robe and gathered it in his hand until
he had exposed her bare leg. He ran his fingertips along
the outer edge of her thigh. When his hand reached the

curve of her bottom, he abruptly stopped the gentle seduction he had initiated and allowed her robe to fall into place.

He had given in to his desire for Lauren once. He chuckled as he corrected the error. He had given in to his desires a total of three times before they finally went to sleep. But he could not compound the difficulty of the situation by giving in to those same desires again. As much as he tried to tell himself it was only physical and he could move on when the time came with no regrets or lingering attachments, he knew it was not so.

"I haven't been up too long. I'm putting together the facts I have so I can do a probability profile. It's a nifty little computer program that will do in minutes what it used to take me hours to do, and it's a lot more accurate."

Lauren straightened. "I'll stay out of your hair and let you work. I'm going to take a shower then go for a walk. I'll fix us some breakfast as soon as I get back."

Kyle watched as she went to the bedroom. A couple of minutes later he heard the shower go on. He stared at the list he had made. Something was missing. Milly. He had not included her name among those who could be involved. Not that he really suspected her of anything... He furrowed his brow as he recalled her saying something about a dinner date, then being picked up from work by someone in a squad car the evening he first met her.

He added her name to the others, a list that included Sheriff Max Culhane, two of his deputies, Joe Thurlow and Mitch O'Connor, the owner of the parts warehouse, Frank Brewster, self-appointed head of the Sea Grove social set and president of the historical society, Irene Peyton, real estate developer Harvey Sherwood, Mayor Dennis Kendrick; and the owner of the local newspaper, Tony Mallory. He began the task of putting the information into the computer. He was vaguely aware of the shower being turned off, but his attention remained focused on his work.

Lauren dressed then fixed her hair into a French braid.

She paused at the side door to tell Kyle she was leaving, but he appeared to be totally absorbed in his work, so she chose not to bother him. She stepped outside, closing the door behind her.

The nippy early-morning breeze stung her cheeks and nose. She stuffed her hands in her jacket pockets and headed across the bluff at a brisk pace. Mindful of Kyle's admonition of the night before, she made a conscious choice to not go to the lighthouse just in case someone was watching. She strolled along the edge of the bluff toward the place where it dipped down to the small cove—the point where she and Kyle had been able to crawl up on land after drifting out of the hidden cavern.

She scrambled down the narrow path to the small beach below, her sure footing taking her easily over the rocks. She walked along the sand for a few feet, her mind filled with the intense sensuality of Kyle Delaney. She picked up a stick and tossed it into the water, then watched as it washed on shore with the next wave.

A large clump of seaweed tumbled onto the sand along with the stick. Lauren bent to retrieve the stick then froze to the spot. An arm protruded from the tangled mass of seaweed. She closed her eyes for a moment as she gulped in the cold ocean air, then slowly exhaled.

Vivid images from seven years ago leaped to mind— the body of her fiancé sprawled on his living room floor, the gaping wound in his chest, the blood on the carpet. And then an image from not that many days ago—Kyle facedown and seemingly lifeless just beyond her side door. She shook away the disturbing thoughts. Now was not the time.

A sick uneasiness churned in the pit of her stomach as trepidation welled inside her. She took a couple of tentative steps toward the clump of seaweed, being careful where she stepped. She forced herself to concentrate on the surrounding area as she carefully scrutinized everything for any signs as to the body's identity. The kelp refused to give up any information beyond the fact that the arm belonged to a man. Another shudder ran up her spine, and the churning in her stomach increased. She swallowed several times in an attempt to lessen the lump in her throat.

The only thing she wanted at that moment was to get far away from that spot. With a trembling hand she reached out and pulled a small clump of seaweed over the exposed arm to hide it from sight.

Then she turned and ran. She ran as hard and as fast as the terrain allowed, not stopping until she got home.

She slammed through the door, totally out of breath. Kyle was not in the dining room where she had left him. In fact, he was nowhere in sight. Her voice conveyed the urgency and fear that consumed her. "Kyle...where are you?"

He immediately appeared from the bathroom, adjusting the last touches of his Shane Nolan disguise. "What's the matter, Lauren? What's wrong?"

She saw concern blanket his face as he responded to her outward stress. "Down on the beach...a body."

He rushed to her, grabbing her shoulders. "A body? Who? Where?"

She tried to catch her breath, to slow her erratic breathing.

"Calm down, Lauren. Do you want a drink of water?"

"Give me a moment." She took another calming breath before continuing. "I don't know who it is, but it's a man. He was tangled up in the seaweed in the cove and I couldn't see his face. No one else was around. I didn't touch anything, other than to cover up the arm that was sticking out." She looked into his eyes. "What do you think it means? Does it have something to do with the case?"

He scowled as he turned her words over in his mind.

His response was hesitant. "Well, I'm not sure. It could. So many people showing up dead all at once in such a small town, counting me among the dead, certainly defies the laws of probability."

"Do you want me to call the sheriff and report the body?"

"No. Let me take a look first before everyone else gets in there and disturbs any clues." He reached for his jacket. "Let's go."

A few minutes later they scrambled to the sandy beach in the cove. Lauren pointed out the tangle of seaweed that held the body.

Kyle scanned the horizon with his binoculars, then turned his attention to the surrounding bluff. It was still very early. There was no one in sight. "You stay here."

She looked around, a cross between amusement and irritation filling her response. "Stay where? You mean right here rather than fifteen feet over there where the body is? Why? Is it suddenly going to leap to life and grab me? Really!" She took a couple of steps toward the object of their discussion.

He grabbed her arm, stopping her from going any farther. It might have been his natural instinct to be in charge or possibly his desire to protect her that had directed his actions. He did not know. "I don't want you tromping all over the scene and possibly contaminating some of the evidence."

"No way. I was at the scene earlier this morning. I'm the one who found the body, remember? I didn't disturb anything then and I won't disturb anything now. Besides, it might be someone I can identify."

She was right. He pulled her to him, gave a playful little tug on her French braid, then kissed her forehead. "Okay, but watch where you step. I don't want the beach to look like it's been overrun by a platoon of soldiers on maneuvers when the sheriff gets here."

Kyle studied the beach between him and the body, then carefully made his way across the open sand to the clump of seaweed. Lauren followed in his steps, coming to a halt about three feet away. She watched as he knelt in the sand and lifted the tangled seaweed from the victim's head.

Her breath caught and her hands flew to her mouth as soon as she saw the face, but not in time to stop her gasp. "Oh, my God! It's Frank Brewster!"

"It certainly is." His words were very matter-of-fact, without emotion, not even surprise. He turned the body over, searching for a wound. He found none. He checked Frank's pockets and inspected his clothes. When he finished his cursory inspection, he rose to his feet.

She looked away from Frank's body, focusing her attention instead on the way Kyle clenched his jaw into a hard line. She saw the angry glint in his eyes as he stared out at the ocean. "You...you don't seem too surprised by this."

"I suppose I'm not. I wasn't expecting to see his body washed up on the beach this morning, but I figured he'd be next."

"You mean Frank is involved in all of this?"

"Right up to his neck, but he's not alone. I think Billy was killed because he was spying on Frank and saw things he wasn't supposed to. Only I don't think Frank killed him."

"But why would Billy Washburn be spying on Frank Brewster?"

"According to Billy's notebook, it was several things—mostly a desire to clear his grandfather's name in the death of the lighthouse keeper, Jeremy MacDonald. Billy's suspicions came from seeing some strange crates stored at the warehouse and late night movement of these crates. He started paying attention and keeping notes. He thinks Jeremy was killed because he stumbled onto the fact that the lighthouse was being used to smuggle contraband."

The information he was sharing was quite a revelation and definitely more than she had expected to hear. "But if that's true then it means—"

"It means they have been doing business for a very long time. A clever operation run over the years by smart people. Not so large as to garner immediate attention because of the volume of contraband it moved, leaving the setup free to continue operations for decades. If they hadn't turned to smuggling electronic components we probably still wouldn't know about them. I would guess that Frank was their weak link. From what I've been able to discern, he didn't have the backbone for murder or the brains to be in charge. I suspect he was about to become an embarrassment to someone, so he had to be dealt with. I don't know—"

"But, Kyle...Frank Brewster couldn't have been more than a baby, if that, when Jeremy died."

"You remember our discussion about inheriting the business? Well, there were his uncle and father. Three years ago is when his father died, almost three years ago is when we became aware of a small ring operating in this general area of the country—"

The bright flash only lasted for a fraction of a second, but it caught Kyle's eye. "Don't make any sudden moves. There's someone on the bluff watching us. The sun just glinted off something, probably a pair of binoculars. I want you to hurry to the house and call the sheriff to report finding a body. Tell him you and Shane were taking an early-morning walk and stumbled across it. I'll stay here."

Lauren instantly obeyed his instructions. As soon as she was out of sight, Kyle returned his attention to Frank's body. He didn't dare do anything other than a visual inspection of the area, not with some unknown person watching him. He stared at Frank's sneakers. They appeared to be his favorites, judging by what remained of the pattern on the well-worn soles. There was nothing unusual about the way he was dressed…jeans, a black sweat-shirt and a warm jacket with a water-repellent outer cov-ering. He had not found anything out of the ordinary in Frank's pockets, just a wallet containing money and credit cards and a set of keys—keys he had slipped into his own pocket without Lauren noticing.

He scanned the surrounding cliffs, to all outward ap-pearances only a casual glance. He could feel impatience building inside him. He did not have time to waste stand-ing around. He retreated to the bluff wall and leaned back in a crevice, ostensibly to wait but in reality to find some-place where he would be out of sight of the unknown person watching him.

He reached into his pocket and withdrew the keys. The car keys, both ignition and trunk, were obvious, as was the key to a safety-deposit box. He studied the other keys for a moment. The shape of the key and the manufacturer's name told him that five of them fit door locks—probably house, downtown office, warehouse, warehouse office and something else, like maybe the side door into a garage or some type of storage shed. He turned his attention to the three small keys on the ring. One he recognized as the type of key that usually fit an alarm system control box. Another was a padlock key, and the last one was the kind that fit either a desk drawer or a file cabinet, probably in Frank's warehouse office.

It appeared that Frank Brewster kept all his keys to-gether on one ring. Kyle knew that was certainly going to make life a lot easier for him when he searched Frank's office. It would save him the time and trouble of having to bypass a security system. Kyle wrinkled his brow into a momentary frown. Conspicuous in its absence was a key that would fit a boat ignition. Frank kept his bank safety-deposit key on that ring, so why not the boat key? Unless someone else had taken it off the ring—

"Down here, Max. Shane is standing guard to make sure

no one touches anything." Lauren's voice came from above him, louder than it needed to be, to alert him to their presence.

Kyle pocketed the keys and stepped into the open. He called to the top of the bluff. "Down here, Constable." He watched as Lauren scrambled down the path with Max following as fast as he dared. "This is a surprise. Is it typical here in the States for the chief constable to be the one responding to a phone call?"

Max shot Kyle a quick look. "I happened to be in the area when the call came in." He proceeded directly to the body. He started to kneel down, but instead whirled and glared at Kyle and Lauren. "This body's been moved."

"That it has, Constable. But I only turned him over to determine if he was still alive...if there was anything we could do." Kyle's expression was open and honest, his answer entirely plausible.

Lauren added her validation to what Kyle had said. "That's right, Max. I know CPR." She paused as she stared toward the body, a helpless expression clouding her face and a quaver coming into her voice. "But it was too late, he was already dead."

Kyle put his arm around her shoulder and gave it a comforting squeeze. Again, the Irish accent flowed smoothly. "I can see how upset you are, Lauren. Why don't you return to the house and brew us a cup of tea? I'll answer the constable's questions, then be along in a few minutes."

Lauren was not sure what Kyle was trying to do, but it was apparent he wanted her home rather than on the beach. "Of course, Shane." She hugged her arms to her body and hunched her shoulders against the early-morning dampness. "I'll see you shortly."

When she reached the top of the bluff she glanced around, noting the arrival of another patrol car. She could not see who was driving. Then she spotted Harvey Sher-

wood sitting in his car. She waved at him, but he did not
respond. He seemed to be concentrating on something else.
She hurried across the bluff toward her shop.

Max returned his attention to the body. He immediately
reached into Frank's pockets, pulled out the wallet and set
it aside. He continued to search. The frown that crossed
his face said he was not finding what he was looking for.

"You need any help down there, Sheriff?" The voice
came from the bluff.

The sheriff looked up at the new arrival. "Yeah, Mitch.
You can call the coroner."

"Have you identified the body yet?" Another new arrival on the scene made his presence known.

Kyle turned and looked up. He saw Tony Mallory walk
to the edge.

"Mallory!" Max Culhane's tone held irritation. "What
are you doing here?"

"I heard the call on my scanner while I was on my way
to the office, so here I am." Tony took a notepad and
pencil from his pocket. "Now, who is it and does it appear
to be foul play?" He started down the path to the beach.

"You stay up there, Mallory. This is a crime scene.
Only authorized personnel are permitted here until further
notice. I don't need a whole bunch of people messing up
the evidence."

"Crime scene? So it is foul play. Who's the victim?"

"Crime scene only refers to unknown circumstances,
that's all. Your press credentials don't make you authorized."

Tony pointed to Kyle standing off to one side. "Why
is Shane Nolan allowed at the crime scene? Professional
courtesy?"

"He and Lauren was the ones what found the body. He
was just standin' guard till I arrived—" Max turned a
harsh glare toward Kyle "—and now he's leavin'."

Kyle was barely aware of the sheriff's directive. Tony's

words were still ringing in his ears—*professional courtesy*
He had never quite shaken his uneasy feeling about Tony
about what he felt were suspicious and evasive actions o
the newsman's part. Was it just an idle expression or ha
Tony not been convinced Shane Nolan was who h
claimed to be?

"Didn't you hear me?" Max took a couple of step
toward Kyle. "I said you was just leavin'."

"Ah...and right you are, Constable. I'll be on my wa
back to Lauren. The poor girl was properly upset over a
this."

Kyle scrambled up the cliff, making sure he took a goo
look at everything and everyone gathered at the top of th
bluff. He noted a pair of binoculars on the dash of Mitc
O'Connor's patrol car. Mitch had arrived almost as quickl
as the sheriff. But when he glanced at Tony's car he sav
binoculars there, too. There was another car parked clos
by. He recognized Harvey Sherwood sitting behind th
wheel. He started to say something to him but remembere
it was Kyle Delaney Harvey had tried to bribe. Harvey ha
never met Shane Nolan.

He also spotted Joe Thurlow. The young deputy ha
positioned himself at the edge of the road to keep back th
few onlookers attracted by the flashing lights on the sher
iff's squad car. There was certainly an excessive numbe
of people responding to the call for such a small town.

"Shane!" Tony hurried over to Kyle. "Has the body
been identified? Do you know who it was? What can yo
tell me?"

"Hold up...give me a bit of a moment to catch my
breath."

"Sorry." Tony shot a look in Max's direction then re
turned his attention to Kyle. "The sheriff likes to keep
secrets from the press, even though he shares with his bud
dies."

"Well, you surely can't think I'm...I mean, I'm a

stranger in town, a foreigner enjoying a visit to your lovely country. Of course, this incident is a bit upsetting—an unpleasant memory for me to take back to Ireland." Kyle did not like the silent signals Tony's body language sent out or the edge to his questions. They left him with the possibility that Tony suspected the charade he was playing.

Tony sidestepped his comments. "So tell me, Shane, who is it down there wrapped up in the seaweed shroud?"

"Frank Brewster."

"Frank Brewster? Are you sure it's him?"

"Lauren said so." Kyle noted that Tony had just the right amount of surprise in his voice, the properly shocked expression.

Tony scribbled notes in his pad while continuing to ask questions. "Any signs of foul play—bullet holes, knife wounds, things like that? Anything unusual about the way the body looked? Did it wash up on shore or was it placed there? And—" he looked up at Kyle "—just how did you and Lauren happen to find it?"

"Well, now, it's a simple story." Kyle proceeded to give Tony the facts. When he finished, he excused himself, saying he needed to return to Lauren and see how she was doing. He did not like the way Tony's eyes narrowed and his jaw clenched and unclenched.

Kyle found Lauren nervously pacing up and down the kitchen with a cup of tea in her hand. She rushed to him as soon as he entered.

"I'm glad you're back. I found something you should see." She tugged at his hand. "It's behind the building, around back. I found it when I was taking out the trash a few minutes ago."

She showed him the spot outside the bedroom window. "These footprints shouldn't be here. There's no reason for anyone to have been standing outside my bedroom window."

She watched as he knelt and gave the area close inspection, then she continued. "Last night I thought I saw something move at the window, but when Ty-Ty jumped down from the dresser I just assumed it was him. However—" she felt a flush of embarrassment spread across her cheeks "—I wasn't exactly thinking clearly."

He rose to his feet and put his arm around her shoulder, drawing her to him. His voice was soft and sensual, sending little ripples of excitement through her body. "You mean last night—" he nuzzled the side of her neck "—while you were having your way with me…taking advantage of my naïveté…seducing my innocence—"

She took a step backward in an attempt to escape the magnetic hold he had on her senses. Was he purposely steering her away from the situation? Hiding the seriousness he attributed to her discovery? "Kyle, please…this is important. What do you think this means?"

He could not ignore the determination on her face. "Okay, you want to know, so here it is. I think it means Frank was alive and alone and standing outside your bedroom window at midnight. Then this morning about seven-thirty he washed up on the beach quite dead. Which leaves us with several unanswered questions."

Chapter Ten

Lauren had not been prepared for Kyle to unload that bombshell on her. "What makes you think it was Frank who was outside my bedroom window last night?"

"I got a good look at Frank's shoes when I was checking the body. The unique design on the bottom of his sneakers and the unusual wear pattern on the soles exactly match those prints. Since there are no other footprints around, he must have been alone." Kyle brought out the key ring he had taken from Frank's pockets. "It appears that all his keys are here...except for the key to his boat. Yet he was on his boat in the bay last night."

"How do you know he was on his boat and that the key is missing?" He had one surprising bit of information after another.

"I saw him from the lighthouse tower." He knitted his brow in a moment of concentration. "At least I saw him prepping the boat while we were having lunch and I saw his boat out on the bay—but I didn't actually see him take it out. As for the boat key, certain shapes and sizes of keys fit certain things. You know yourself that you can tell a car key from a door key just by looking at them. It's the same with a key that fits a boat ignition."

"But who would have taken out his boat if he didn't? And if it was Frank outside my bedroom window about midnight, then we know he was alive then. And the cave...who was it we heard coming in through the entrance in the cottage cellar? Would that have been Frank? And if so, then who was with him?'' She paused, biting nervously at her lower lip. ''And why did you take Frank's keys?''

''You seem to have more questions than I have answers.''

''You can answer about the keys, can't you? I mean, you must have had a reason for taking them.''

''It's much easier to break into a building when you have the keys that fit the locks.'' He pulled the key ring from his pocket again, holding it by an oddly shaped small key to add emphasis to his next words. ''And in this case, even the key to the security alarm.''

''So...'' A little grin played at the corners of her mouth. ''Are we going to break into Frank's warehouse, his downtown office, his house—or all of them?''

He took in a deep breath, held it for a moment, then expelled it slowly. He tried to choose his words carefully. ''Breaking and entering is illegal. I could get a court order that would allow me to go through everything, but it would put me in the spotlight before I'm ready for that to happen. I also believe that anything of value to my investigation would be gone by the time other agents arrived on the scene with the proper paperwork. I probably won't be able to use what I find in court, but it should give me what I need to get a proper search warrant. If I should be caught, then the manipulators behind the scenes would have me free in no time. You, on the other hand, wouldn't have that type of protection.''

He touched his fingertips to her cheek, then quickly withdrew. ''I don't want you going with me, Lauren.'' He took her in his arms and held her closely. ''If there's any trouble, I don't want you in the line of fire. Besides, I can work faster alone.''

She rested her head against his shoulder and slipped her arms around his waist. "We're in this together, Kyle. I'm going with you. When are we going to do it...tonight?"

He ran his fingers through her hair then kissed the top of her head. "Has anyone ever told you that you're incredibly stubborn?"

"I've heard it before...once or twice."

"I'll bet it was a lot more than that." He brushed a soft kiss against her lips. "You're also incredibly beautiful." He captured her mouth again, this time with a kiss of deep meaning—perhaps even more than he consciously wanted to show.

KYLE TURNED OFF the alarm system then tried the door keys until he found the one that unlocked the door of the Brewster auto parts warehouse. "I'm still not sure why I allowed you to talk me into this."

Lauren followed him inside then closed the door. "You know everything I said made sense, especially the part about saving you time because I've been here before and know the layout." She leaned close to him and pointed down the hallway. "Frank's office is the third door on the left."

They moved quickly and silently. Kyle used Frank's keys to unlock the office. He stood inside the door, shining his flashlight around the room. He moved swiftly toward the computer while giving orders to Lauren. "You keep an eye on the outside hall while you're checking his desk."

"I've never broken into an office before. What am I looking for?"

"Anything that doesn't seem to belong to an auto parts business, any records that don't seem to make sense. I'm particularly interested in bank records or shipping and receiving paperwork that doesn't seem to relate to any purchase orders or sales invoices. Make copies of anything you find." Kyle turned on the copy machine so it could warm up then turned on the computer and began a search of the myriad directories and their files.

They each worked quietly and efficiently. Lauren copied numerous pieces of paper and Kyle printed out several pages of information from the computer files. When he had finished, he turned off the computer and put the printouts into his pack. He picked up the wastepaper basket and rummaged through the contents. "I love offices with sloppy maintenance service. Usually wastebaskets are emptied on a daily basis." A smile of satisfaction was the response to what he found. He quickly placed several items in a small plastic evidence envelope, the same type of small folded pieces of cellophane he had found at the lighthouse—a definite tangible connection.

He turned his attention to cracking the wall safe. A moment later the safe door swung open. He reached for a rolled-up paper, took it out of the safe and studied it for a moment. "Bingo." He shoved the important find in his bag then took a look at the other papers in the safe. He also noticed an unusually large amount of cash. He quickly checked it and found the markings he had made on the money they had found in the cave. He left the money in the safe, but removed another item, then closed and locked the safe door. He reached for a piece of hard candy from the bowl on Frank's desk, unwrapped it and popped it into his mouth.

He turned toward Lauren. "How are you doing? Find anything interesting?"

She turned off her flashlight and set it on the desk. "Yes, I think I found a few suspicious things. There was an invoice for auto parts that showed—"

He jerked to attention. His voice whispered against her ear. "Shh...someone's out there." He felt her stiffen in response to his words. "Do you know where this other door goes?" He had noticed the door on the opposite side of the office, but had not checked it out. "And please don't tell me it's a closet or a bathroom."

"It goes directly into the warehouse." She shoved the copies she had made into her bag.

He took her hand and they quickly exited the office through the back door. The security lighting in the warehouse provided just enough light for them to make their way through the storage shelves and crates. They heard loud and angry voices, but they were not distinct enough to recognize the owners or the words.

The voices spilled over into the warehouse, the words clearly discernible. "Whoever it is must have gone this way. You take the right and I'll take the left."

Kyle pulled his gun from the holster. Again, his voice was barely above a whisper. "While they're making their way through the warehouse, we need to get into the office and out the front." He stood still and listened, determining the positions of the unwelcome intruders, deciding which route to take to the offices. He grabbed her hand. "This way."

They made a dash for the office, keeping low behind crates and shelves of boxes. They reached the relative safety of the office, then went into the hallway. That was when they heard the shout that sent a jolt of fear through Lauren.

"There! They just went into the office. Stop them!"

Kyle and Lauren ran down the hallway and out the front door. Kyle's words were urgent as he let go of her hand. "Run as fast as you can across the field, keep low and head for home. Don't stop for anything, no matter what you hear. Turn on the bathroom light and the shower, then turn on the television in the living room. If anyone comes to the door and asks, tell them I just got into the shower."

"Where will you be?" She was not sure what scared her more, the thought of some unknown men chasing her or Kyle staying behind to face them alone.

"Go!" The authority in his voice was absolute as he barked out the command.

She turned and ran. Her heart pounded violently in her chest with each step she took. Her mouth went dry, but she dared not stop for even a second. She reached her door just as she heard a sharp sound explode through the cold night air, followed by two more loud explosions. She stopped dead in her tracks. A cold foreboding jolted through her body. It had been the sound of a gun, no mistake about it. She whirled around, trying to peer through the darkness.

Indecision raced through her. She took a couple of steps toward the warehouse then stopped. No. She needed to follow Kyle's instructions to the letter. She opened the door and hurried inside. She went straight to the bathroom and turned on the shower as he had instructed her to do. She quickly changed clothes, putting on her long robe, then went to the living room, turned on the television and sat on the couch. She stared blankly at the screen without really seeing anything, her body and her nerves tensed as she waited for the unknown.

The sound of the bell in the shop startled her. It had only been fifteen minutes, but it seemed like forever since she had burst through the side door. She did not know what had happened to Kyle, but she could not ignore the door. She took her time turning on the lights in the shop and making her way to the front of the building. She opened the door louvers and peered outside. Max Culhane stood on the other side of the door. She unlocked and opened it, but did not step aside so he could come in.

"Max, this is a surprise. What brings you here so late at night? Is something wrong?" She did her best to keep her voice casual.

Max ignored her questions as he purposely shoved past her. He walked slowly through the shop, looking into the tearoom and into the bookstore. When he arrived at the entrance of her living quarters, she stepped in front of him to block his way. "Why are you here, Max?"

"I want to look around, Lauren." He chomped his cigar between his teeth and glared at her. "Now, step aside."

She looked at him questioningly as she cocked her head. "Look around for what? You don't have the right to barge in here and search my home without either my permission or a search warrant." She refused to move out of his way.

"Someone broke into Frank Brewster's warehouse, took a couple of shots at me when I came to investigate the security alarm."

She registered the appropriate amount of surprise. "Are you saying that you think it was me? Why would I do such a thing?"

"Didn't say that. I just want to make sure no one's hidin' here." Max tried to look past her into her private living quarters.

"Well, I can assure you there are no suspicious characters hiding in my closet."

"Where's your houseguest?"

"He's taking a shower." It took all her control to keep from turning to look toward the bedroom, hoping against hope that he would miraculously appear in the doorway.

"Is there something wrong out there, Lauren?" Kyle's voice came from the back, the Irish accent surrounding his words.

Lauren suppressed the audible sigh of relief that flooded through her when she heard him. "It's nothing, Shane. Just the sheriff. It seems that Frank's warehouse was broken into and he's looking for the culprit. He wants to know if we've seen anyone."

"A break-in, you say." Kyle made his appearance dressed in sweatshirt and sweatpants with a towel slung around his neck. His Shane Nolan disguise was in place, the wig wet as if he had just gotten out of the shower. "Well, Constable, this has certainly been a busy day for you. What type of disreputable person would break into an establishment immediately following such a tragedy as the accidental death of the proprietor?''

"You, uh, didn't see no one sneaking round—no strangers hanging about?''

"I just this minute stepped from the shower, Constable. But I certainly didn't see anyone earlier. We'd been watching television." Kyle turned toward Lauren. "Did you see anyone lurking about during the evening?''

"I didn't see anything out of the ordinary." Lauren turned from Kyle toward Max. Her expression was stern, showing her displeasure at his rude intrusion. "Was there anything else you wanted?''

The sheriff shuffled his feet in an awkward manner, then finally spoke. "Naw, I guess not." He shot Lauren a harsh look, then added one for Kyle. He turned to leave, then paused long enough to make one final comment before walking out the front door. "But if something else occurs to me I'll be back.''

Kyle and Lauren watched as the sheriff walked to his car, then she turned off the store lights and they quickly retreated to her living room. She threw her arms around his neck. Her words came rushing out, covered in the relief she felt. "When did you come in? I heard the shots just as I reached my door. Oh, Kyle...I was so scared. I almost turned around and went back to see if you were okay.''

He kissed her tenderly on the forehead. "You did the right thing. That fool sheriff was just shooting at shadows, that's all.''

"He said he had gone there in response to the alarm. I thought you turned it off.''

"I did. It wasn't an alarm that brought him there.''

"I was so afraid Max was going to force his way in here even though I told him he couldn't." She rested her head against his chest, taking comfort in the warmth of his embrace. "I...I don't think he believed me about not knowing anything."

"I'm sure he didn't believe you. He just didn't know what to do and had no legal grounds for pursuing things without creating a scene. You noticed the flashlight he had in his hand? It was yours. The one you set on the desk in Frank's office."

Lauren jerked her head back and stared at him, shock covering her face. "Oh, no! I forgot it. It'll have my fingerprints on it."

"There's nothing we can do about it now. If it comes up, just go to where you normally keep that flashlight as if you fully intended to find it in its proper place. Then be surprised that it's not there. Look around for it but offer no possible explanation as to what might have happened to it. The guilty are too eager to provide a plausible explanation in hopes of satisfying the suspicion and *proving* they're innocent. They usually end up overexplaining. If anyone asks, the flashlight simply disappeared and you don't know how, when or why. Don't try to explain it."

He took her hand and led her toward the bedroom. "Now, let's take a look at what you found in Frank's office."

MAX MAY HAVE LEFT Lauren's premises, but his squad car was still parked in front. He leaned against the side of the car as he talked to the man seated in the passenger side. "I didn't see nothin' out of the ordinary. She said she was watchin' television and then this Shane guy comes walkin' in from the shower."

"So what's the problem?"

"I got a hinky feeling in my gut. I don't think she was tellin' me the truth." Max glanced at the front of the building. "I ain't sure what Lauren's up to and I don't know about this Shane Nolan, but I'm sure she knows too much…maybe both of 'em knows too much.'' Max walked around the car to the driver's side and got in.

"Don't do anything rash, Max. We already have three suspicious deaths to smooth over—first Billy, then Kyle Delaney and now Frank. The last thing we need is for some big-city newspaper to pick up the story and produce a lot of sensational headlines about a serial killer. We don't need that type of national focus on our quiet community.''

Max chomped down on his cigar as he started the car. "Yeah, well…'' He put the car in gear and pulled away from the curb.

KYLE LAY IN BED staring up at the ceiling. He had been awake for almost an hour but had not wanted to disturb Lauren's sleep by getting out of bed. His mind worked quickly and efficiently, putting together all the bits and pieces they had found at Frank's office. But he needed the thread that connected all of it.

Frank had been so very obvious. He was also so very dead. The weak link had been eliminated, thus breaking the direct connection between the actual doing and the planning. He needed the paper trail that would reconnect the chain of command. It would take some more digging. It was the very top person he wanted to nail, and that was not going to be easy. All he had at the moment were his suspicions and some flimsy circumstantial evidence.

Lauren stirred in her sleep. He folded his arms around her, and she snuggled against him. She was warm. She was soft. Making love to her set his body on fire as well as his heart and soul. He thought he just might be falling in love, and the prospect frightened him more than any danger he had faced during his career.

She slowly opened her eyes then stretched out her legs. Her words were thick with sleep. "Mmm…good morning.''

"Good morning, yourself.'' He slid his hand over the

curve of her bottom, then rolled her body on top of his. His lips nibbled at her earlobe then he placed a soft kiss on her mouth. "Now this is how I'd like to spend the day."

"It sounds like an excellent idea, except for the fact that one of my employees has asked for the day off. I need to attend to my business since I'll be shorthanded and it's too much for Milly to cover by herself. After all, she's already doing some of my work in addition to her own."

"We both need to tend to business. The information we gathered in last night's raid on Frank's office pretty much nailed down the system for moving the contraband in and out. Frank would use phony shipping documents to move the crates, interspersing them with his legitimate deliveries so the drivers had no idea they were carrying contraband material."

"Can you make any arrests yet?"

He rolled her body off of his then sat up, swinging his legs off the side of the bed. "Proof, my dear. Proof." He ruffled his fingers through his tousled hair in an effort to smooth it. There was still a bit of tenderness to his shoulder, but it was no longer bothersome. "The courts can't convict just because I say I know something is so—they want to see hard evidence."

He stood and reached for his clothes. "We have some. There's the money delivered to the cave, part of which ended up in Frank's safe. There are the delivery work orders you found showing unusually large shipments of auto parts to various locations on the same dates as Billy Washburn's journal shows the mysterious crates being moved—and there's no sales invoices to correspond with those deliveries. I have computer records showing a botched attempt to delete files connected with those shipments and a computer date and time stamp saying those particular files had been accessed the same night Frank was outside your bedroom window. In fact, it was probably just a couple of hours before he was killed.''

Kyle quickly dressed, but did not bother with his Shane Nolan disguise. ''I found two bank accounts under other names showing large cash deposits. I have a safety-deposit box key with no record of the box. I have two murders that have been made to look like accidents. I have an attempt on my life in spite of my cover identity.''

Lauren pulled on her robe. ''That sounds like a lot to me. What else do you need?''

''I need proof obtained through legal means.''

She headed for the kitchen to make some coffee. ''What about Billy Washburn's journal? I'm sure Sam would say he provided it to you in an effort to prove that Billy's death was not due to his having an accident while under the influence. It has all that information he gathered while keeping an eye on Frank's movements.''

''The journal is evidence, but Billy is dead, so we don't have him to attest that he actually saw what was recorded. Frank Brewster is dead, which eliminates any testimony from him as to how and why the money made its way to his safe. It also eliminates any possibility of his turning witness against the others involved. I suspect it was that concern that got him killed.''

Lauren started the coffee then returned to the bedroom. She paused for a moment, her stomach muscles tightening and the tension hitting her when she saw him check his gun then clip the holster to the back of his jeans. The ever-present weapon. It remained always at the ready. Even as they made love it rested on the nightstand within easy reach. Would she ever be able to see it and accept it without that horrible feeling in the pit of her stomach?

''Who else is involved? Do you know yet?'' Lauren took her clothes from the closet and laid them out on the bed.

''There's Max, of course.''

"Max Culhane? You believe he is actually part of the smuggling operation?" Her voice was filled with surprise.

Kyle stared at her for a moment. "Certainly he's involved. He didn't just happen to show up at Frank's warehouse last night. My guess is that he came for the money. That story about responding to an alarm was pure fiction. He's been involved for years, even way before he became sheriff."

"Are you sure?"

"You didn't suspect that? After all, his construction company did the structural reinforcement of the lighthouse. There's no way he could have done that and not known about the hidden room off the cellar. And the rolled-up plans I found in Frank's safe show the secret entrance into the tower I've been looking for...the entrance Billy used to spy on Frank's movements. There's no way Max wouldn't have known about that, either."

Lauren sat on the edge of the bed. "It all makes perfect sense when I hear you say it. I guess living here makes me see these people in a different way than an outsider would. I've never particularly liked Max, but that's about all the thought I've given him."

She looked at Kyle. The gravity covering his face and the intensity in his eyes sent a little shiver up her spine. He was right. This was no game. "Is Max the leader? Is he the one behind everything?" She swallowed to ease the discomfort building inside her. "Even the murders?"

She squeezed her eyes shut and her words came out in an anguished gasp. "If only I had some kind of control over my psyhic abilities instead of just getting visions I don't understand and feelings I can't accurately interpret. Then I could tell you..." Her voice trailed off. All the *what if*s weren't going to change things.

His words were soft and caring. "Don't do that, Lauren. Don't put that kind of pressure and stress on yourself. The good guys are going to win and the bad guys are going to

jail." He brushed a soft kiss against her lips and gave her
hand a little squeeze of comfort.

She accepted his words and the accompanying comfort.
"You, uh, you were saying about the murders?"

"I believe Max is responsible for Billy and Frank, but
as far as being in charge of the smuggling ring—no way.
The planning and execution takes someone with a sharp
mind, nerves of steel and a lot of cunning. None of those
attributes apply to Max Culhane. Like Frank, he's just not
smart enough to have pulled off this successful an operation." He paused, more for dramatic impact than to gather
his thoughts. "Did you know that Max used to be in business with Frank Brewster's father and uncle many years
ago, before Max started his construction company?" He
saw the surprise on her face.

"No, I didn't. How did you find that out?"

"I saw a couple of advertisements for their business in
the newspaper while I was going through the old back
issues. Frank just didn't have the backbone for any of this.
According to the obituaries, his uncle Ralph died twenty
years ago and his father, Wilton Brewster, died three years
ago. Max and Wilton Brewster continued in legitimate
business for a little while following Ralph's death. I think
Max was involved in the smuggling long before that. I
think it was Ralph, Wilton and Max. Max probably inherited Frank in the business when Wilton Brewster died, and
Max and Frank were probably nothing more than hired
help. It's really amazing what you can find out in small-
town newspapers—" The vision exploded in his mind.
The little bit of something that had been nagging at him
finally materialized. He could not stop the big grin from
spreading across his face.

"Kyle? What is it? What's wrong?"

"I just remembered something, that's all. It was another
photograph I saw in an old issue of the newspaper, some-

thing on the society page about the high school prom."
He leaned over and kissed the tip of her nose.

"Something that will lead you to the person in charge?"

"Well, it's certainly given me another direction for my
search and it also fits in with other little bits I've been
picking up." He took her hand. "Now, you have your
business to take care of and I have a disguise to put on."

She pulled on his hand before he could turn away.
"You're keeping something from me." She felt his muscles tense before he withdrew his hand from her grasp.

"Well, now...if I told you everything all at once then
there wouldn't be any mystery left and you'd soon become
bored with me." He flashed a practiced smile, but she saw
the seriousness in his eyes and it scared her. He was a man
of too many secrets. She was intimately involved with him
and his case, yet at times she felt like a complete outsider.

KYLE WALKED into the newspaper office and immediately
spotted Tony Mallory. "And a good morning to you,
Tony. A fine day it is, the sun shining and the sky as blue
as can be."

"Good morning, Shane." Tony glanced past him for a
second. "Lauren's not with you?"

"No. The poor girl was shorthanded at her shop and
had to fill in so I'm on my own today. I thought you might
have some more information about Frank Brewster's
death."

"Oh?" Tony's body visibly stiffened. "Any reason
why?"

"Well, now." Kyle heard the suspicion in Tony's voice.
"It's not every day that a man and woman are out for an
early-morning walk and come across a dead body on the
beach. Naturally, I'm curious. What do the officials think
happened?"

"I'm sure it will be accidental death by drowning."

"You sound as if you might have other thoughts about it."

Tony picked up a sheet of paper from his desk and studied it for a second before answering. "Is there any reason I should?"

"I guess not." Tony seemed anxious to end the discussion. Kyle decided to move on rather than arouse undue suspicion. "There is something else I was wondering. Do you suppose it would be possible for me to look at a few more of your old copies? I thought it might be interesting to see how a small-town American newspaper handled the society section. You know—coming-out parties, engagements and weddings, the various social functions of the city's prominent families."

"You know where everything is, so just help yourself. I'll be in my office if you need anything."

Kyle quickly located the photograph he remembered glimpsing. He checked several subsequent issues of the paper and found another extremely interesting tidbit of information about graduating students who were going away to college. He had several things to follow up through official records. He also had a list of people he needed to have background checks run on. He replaced the back issues of the newspaper, waved thanks to Tony, then continued on his way.

His next stop was the sheriff's office at the county office building. "Good morning, Constable. You know, you had Lauren quite upset with your unexpected visit last night. I thought I'd stop by to see if you were able to apprehend your culprit. Do you have any news that I could relay to her? Something to ease her concerns?"

"No, we didn't find nobody *else* in the area." His words were pointed and his tone accusatory as he rose from behind his desk in a menacing display of body language.

Chapter Eleven

As soon as Kyle left the sheriff's office, Max grabbed the phone and hastily dialed a number. "Yeah, it's me. This is the first chance I've had to give you a call. We went to the warehouse last night, but when we got there someone else was inside. Two of 'em, I think. Don't know who—they gave us the slip. I found a flashlight on Frank's desk, might belong to one of the people what broke in. Other than that, there ain't nothin' to go on."

"Do you have any thoughts on this? Do you think it might have been nothing more than a common thief taking advantage of Frank's sudden demise?"

"Yeah, I suppose it coulda been...but I don't think so. If that was the case, they would've broken into his house instead of the business. The copy machine was on, and I think someone was usin' the computer. That don't sound like no common thief to me. Whoever it was took off across the bluff. I stopped at Lauren's place to see if she'd seen anyone and she was mighty nervous. Even refused to let me in the back rooms. Told me I needed a search warrant if I wanted to take a look around. Then this Shane guy comes strollin' out saying he was in the shower...I don't know. Something 'bout him just don't sit right with me. Lauren, too. The two of 'em find Frank's body, and now this."

"Just stay calm, Max. I don't want you doing anything rash...*again.* I'll handle this in my own way."

"Yeah, sure. Whatever you say." Max pulled a cigar from his shirt pocket and lit it.

As soon as Max hung up the phone, the recipient of his call dialed a number and waited until someone answered. "I just heard from Max about last night's break-in at the warehouse. What do you think about it?"

"Frank was scared. He was about to cut and run. Wouldn't have surprised me if he had gone straight to the feds and tried to cut a deal for himself. The only thing that kept him from doing it the night before last was the fact that he hadn't gotten to the safety-deposit box yet. He needed to wait until the bank opened the next morning. Unfortunately, Max got to him before I did." The male voice showed no emotion.

"I suppose you're right. It's a shame that Frank somehow missed out on his father's and his uncle's finer qualities—the keen mind, sharp instincts and iron nerves. Both Ralph and Wilton would have been very disappointed to see him as the weakling he was. Perhaps if Ralph had lived he could have done more with him than his father was able to accomplish."

"He had to be taken care of, but it should have been handled differently. Max was sloppy. He has been sloppy about several things lately."

"Yes, you're right. It's a situation that will have to be dealt with, especially in light of that other matter we discussed."

The telephone conversation was terminated as both parties hung up the phone.

LAUREN CHECKED the cash register tape for the second time. "This is one of the best days we've done in quite a while."

Milly chuckled good-naturedly. "I guess being shorthanded on help and having an unusually sunny day following several days of drizzle and gloom are ways of guaranteeing extra customers."

"I love seeing these kinds of totals, but I'm sure glad this day is over. All I want to do is kick off my shoes, change into something very comfortable and not move for the rest of the evening."

"That's exactly what I'm going to do." Milly gathered her purse and jacket. "Is there anything else you need before I go?"

"Not a thing, Milly. I'll see you in the morning. Good night."

"Good night, Lauren."

Milly reached the front door just as it opened and Kyle entered the store. "Milly, 'tis a pleasure to see you again. Are you through for the day?" He checked his watch. "Oh, I didn't realize it was so late. You have a nice evening."

"I'm bushed. I'm going to go straight home and soak in a hot tub." Milly went out the door as Kyle held it open for her. He continued to watch as she hurried to the corner. It appeared as if she was waiting for someone. Then a squad car pulled up to the curb and the passenger door opened. This time Kyle was able to recognize the driver. It was Max Culhane. Kyle slowly closed the door. Milly's words about being tired and going straight home were still fresh in his mind. He did his best to hide his troubled thoughts from Lauren.

Lauren locked the door, turned out the lights, and the two of them disappeared into the back. As soon as they were closed away from the business part of the building, he pulled her into his arms and slowly, sensually and very thoroughly explored every bit of her mouth with a long, hot kiss. When he finally released her, he was fully aroused, and her face was flushed with excitement and her breathing had become ragged.

It took Lauren a moment to catch her breath. "Well, if that was the appetizer, then the main course ought to be really spectacular."

He shot her a decidedly wicked grin. "And you're going to go absolutely crazy over the dessert."

She reached her arms around his waist, every thought and fiber of her consciousness focused on the pleasures yet to come...until her hand touched the holster nestled in the small of his back. She stiffened to attention and took a step backward. Once again the necessity of his carrying a gun brought reality to the situation.

"How was your day?" Her voice was nervous, her movements awkward. "Did you uncover anything new while I was tending to my own business?"

She did not need to tell him what had caused her change of attitude. He knew. As soon as he felt the pressure against his back from her hand touching the holster, he knew. What he did not know was what to do about it.

He also took a step back, putting additional distance between them. "I picked up some very interesting information at the newspaper office and did some follow-up checking on the prom photograph. I've also requested background traces on a few people. If what I suspect turns out to be true, then this case will be taking a very interesting twist off into left field."

"What does that mean? What do you think you'll find?"

"I think I'll find illicit love, an illegitimate son and decades of secrets." He flashed her a teasing grin. "You know, the kind of stuff you'd find in a steamy novel about the inhabitants of a small town and their hidden secrets." He dropped the grin and once again turned serious. "So far it's pure speculation on my part, not much more than a gut hunch based on some very skimpy circumstantial evidence."

"Does that mean you aren't going to tell me?"

He took a steadying breath. He had already shared far more of his personal speculations and thoughts than he should have, especially for a case still under investigation. "It wouldn't be fair to others if I mentioned certain suspicions and then had them end up not being true. No matter what happens, those thoughts would not leave your mind. It's like telling a jury to ignore something they've heard in court. That bit of information, whether it's true or not, remains as part of their thoughts. They can't simply forget it just because someone told them to."

She searched his expression and saw the concern in his eyes. "You're trying to protect me from something, aren't you?"

He kissed her on the forehead. "I think I'd better get rid of this disguise before this beard drives me nuts."

She accepted his abrupt change for what it was. He did not want her asking him any more questions about whom he suspected. "If you're putting Shane Nolan away, does that mean you won't be venturing out tonight?"

"Well, I do want to go to the lighthouse again. I want to verify the entrance to the tower that's marked on the plans Frank had. I also want to take another look at the cave."

Lauren reached for her jeans and sweater. "Just give me a minute to change clothes. I'm going with you."

Kyle made no objection to her decision. In ten minutes they were on their way across the bluff toward the cottage. Everything was just as it appeared on the plans. He found the hidden entrance to the tower without difficulty, noting that he would have found it on his own had he applied himself to looking for it. Then they went down into the cave again.

"Kyle...look at all of this!" She turned toward him, her eyes wide with surprise. "Where did all this come from?"

He shined his flashlight around the interior of the cavern. Several small crates and boxes were stacked neatly above the high tide line toward the entrance between the cellar and the cave. "This is a little unexpected, but I guess it probably fits in with that large cash payment we saw...part of the money in Frank's safe." He gave a visual inspection of one of the crates without opening it. "I wonder if this is incoming or outgoing. Whichever it is, it probably won't be here for long. Even without Frank, the operation still needs to continue on schedule."

"Look at this. This one is damaged, the edge is broken. It's almost open."

"Don't touch it!" Kyle looked over her shoulder at the broken crate. He gave the box a thorough visual inspection, then carefully pried the broken lid open enough to see inside. "Cartons of cigarettes...must be on its way to Canada." He took his special marking pen and put his initials on as many cartons as he could get to without taking the crate apart. He reattached the lid, took another quick look around the various boxes and crates, then tugged on Lauren's hand. "Come on, let's go."

An hour after they had left, they returned to Lauren's. Kyle removed his disguise then set up his portable computer and cellular phone to make the connection to download the information he had requested.

Lauren came up behind his chair and put her arms around his neck. "You can use my phone for that. I don't mind."

He immediately turned off the computer screen so she could not see what was happening. "Can't risk having the phone company's record of my long-distance calls showing up on your phone bill and falling into someone else's hands."

He scooted his chair from the table and pulled her into his lap. "Do you suppose I could talk you into fixing us something to eat while I finish this?"

She let out a purposefully audible sigh of resignation as she rose to her feet. "In other words, you don't want me to know what you're doing so you're sending me out of the room. You know, Kyle Delaney, you're almost giving me the feeling that you don't trust me.''

She may have said it with a teasing grin, but he definitely caught the undercurrent of uncertainty that suddenly filled the room. ''My life is in your hands—literally. How much more trust can there be than that?'' Secrecy was part of his job. Sharing was not something that came naturally to him, nor was he comfortable with it in spite of the fact that he had already broken almost every rule in the book where Lauren Jamison was concerned.

A long moment of silence hung between them before he spoke again. ''Why don't you get started on that dinner while I finish up here?'' He tried to extend a smile that said everything was going to be all right. He was not sure he succeeded. He watched as she went into the kitchen, then he returned his attention to the information feeding into his computer.

The cat jumped up on the table and stared at him, its tail twitching back and forth in an agitated manner. ''Well, Ty-Ty. Are you here to give me a bad time, too? Are you trying to make me feel guilty?'' He reached out and stroked the cat's head. ''Well, it's not going to work. It's been tried by people far more adept than you.'' He frowned at the cat for a moment, then gave it another affectionate stroke on the head. He was irritated with his own thoughts as he returned to his work. Ty-Ty took it as a sign that his presence was not required. He jumped down and scampered across the room.

Kyle leaned back in his chair, his hands behind his head. He closed his eyes for a minute. The material he downloaded pretty much confirmed his suspicions, which had been formulated through a combination of little things that did not belong and the information he had gathered from the newspaper archives. But that's all it had done...confirmed his suspicions. He did not yet have the type of hard proof needed to make arrests. That would take more work and, from what he had seen of things so far, a lot of luck.

The Bureau had provided him with more information than he had requested, facts the chief thought he needed. Someone had made an Interpol request for information about Shane Nolan. The identity of the person requesting the check, which included current whereabouts, was unknown. Normally that type of request would need to originate with a law enforcement agency, but not necessarily. This added a new problem for him to deal with.

There was something else he had found interesting. There had been only one phone call to the number on Kyle Delaney's business card and only one inquiry to the Coast Guard about the body reportedly found in the ocean—both from Tony Mallory, who stated that it was a follow-up for the next issue of the paper.

"Dinner's ready." Lauren's voice came from the kitchen, followed by her carrying a tray. "It's nothing fancy, but it's probably edible." Her tone was upbeat, in contrast to the worried expression on her face. She set the tray on the dining room table.

"Looks good." He finished putting his work tools away—the notebook computer, cellular phone and scrambling device. "Smells great, too." He helped her take the things off the tray, then held out a chair for her.

Lauren sat down, but Kyle remained standing. He awkwardly shifted his weight from one foot to the other, paused as if he was about to say something, then changed his mind.

"What's the matter? You seem particularly edgy tonight."

"It's nothing." The case was drawing to a close. He would soon be moving on. It was a thought that did not please him. "I guess I'm just a little restless. Things have been strange for me on this case. I'm not accustomed to being cooped up, not being able to be seen in public without a disguise. Even on cases where disguises are involved, I haven't had the necessity of hiding my real face from everyone the way I have here.'' He tried to muster a teasing grin, but was not too successful. "I haven't had to play *dead* before.''

Lauren watched him as he ate. She knew him intimately yet did not know him at all. He was troubled by something…something he did not want her to know about. She felt unsettled, both about Kyle and the future. In spite of her absolute certainty that he was the one great love of her life, she had no idea what their future held, or for that matter if they would even spend it together. She forced the distasteful thought away. She refused to accept that eventuality.

"What's your next step?'' Lauren took a bite of salad. "What do you plan to do about the cartons of cigarettes in the cave?''

"I plan to wait until someone moves them. I imagine that should happen some time very soon. I don't think they would want to keep the contraband where it is for too long. I'm surprised they moved any merchandise at all. Their pattern has been to wait until the darkness of the new moon. They must have an anxious customer to be doing business now, with clear nights and bright moonlight.''

They continued with their meal, making small talk that did not seem to relate to the case.

"The monthly meeting of the historical society is scheduled for tomorrow. It's my turn to host it. It will be at three o'clock, right after we finish serving lunch in the tearoom.''

"Give the society my regards. I can find plenty to do to keep me busy. I still have several loose ends to deal with.'' Several loose ends, indeed. The information he had downloaded had provided him with some answers but had left him with a whole new set of questions.

There had to be a key—one element, one missing factor that would bridge the gap between what he *knew* and what he could prove. He had to find the link that would connect the smuggling with the person he suspected to be the brains behind the operation. He also needed to track down the money trail.

The evening proceeded as they continued their superficial conversation and watched the late news on television. Lauren felt the tension that surrounded Kyle and did not know what to do about it. Even as they lay in bed later she was still very much aware of his tensed muscles. He did not seem to be able to relax. He was distracted, and she did not understand why. They did not make love. He seemed to be content to merely hold her in his arms, to know that she was there beside him. She had asked him if something was wrong, but his only response had been a distracted kiss on the forehead.

Lauren finally fell into a troubled sleep. Warnings appeared to her in the form of dreams. They were more a feeling than a vision, a sense of foreboding that she could not clearly define. She knew only that they warned of life-threatening danger, but she did not know who was involved. She knew that the warning related to Kyle's complicated life, yet it did not have the same feel as her original vision of the man hurtling off the cliff into the ocean.

MILLY EXITED the small restaurant about ten miles up the coast. She stood just outside the door and waited. A moment later Max Culhane joined her.

"That was a delicious dinner, Max. We'll have to do this again."

He patted her on the fanny with a familiarity that said it was not the first time. "I think we have things to talk about, Milly. Let's go to my house."

LAUREN WATCHED as Kyle put the finishing touches of his disguise in place. He took a step from the mirror, stared at his image and frowned.

"What's the matter?" She reached out and touched his arm. "You look like you're unhappy about something. Anything I can do?"

He took her hand and raised it to his lips, placing a soft kiss on her palm. "No, nothing. I'm anxious to be rid of this disguise, that's all. It's very limiting. I have half a dozen sets of identification—driver's license, credit cards and so forth—for half a dozen different identities and disguises—but not for this one. And here I am, supposedly a foreigner in this country, and I don't have a passport to show. I can't risk being seen driving a car." He frowned at his image in the mirror once again. "What if your erstwhile sheriff or one of his deputies decided to pull me over for a routine traffic violation?"

"Is there somewhere you need to go? All you have to do is say so and I'll drive you."

"No, nowhere in particular at this moment." He offered her a reassuring smile. "Besides, you have a business to run and your historical society meeting. I think I'm going to see if I can rent a small fishing boat and putt-putt around the harbor and out into the bay."

Their conversation was interrupted by the sound of the doorbell. They looked at each other, neither one verbalizing the obvious—who would be at the door so early? And why?

"You'd better go answer it." Kyle gave her a reassuring smile. "Maybe it's just a delivery of some sort."

"You're probably right, nothing to worry about." She headed toward the front of the shop.

Tony Mallory picked up the morning newspaper from the porch and handed it to her as she opened the door. "Good morning, Lauren."

She could not hide her surprise. "Good morning,

Tony.'' She tried to project an upbeat, friendly manner. ''Are you now delivering the newspapers as well as publishing them?''

''No, but I am here on business.''

She did not invite him in. ''Business?''

''May I come in?''

She hesitated for a moment, then stepped aside as she offered him a friendly smile. ''Of course.'' She closed the door behind him. ''Now, what may I do for you?''

''Actually, it's Shane I came to see. Is he here?''

''Did I hear my name being mentioned in vain?'' Kyle appeared from the back, projecting good cheer and total affability. ''And a good morning to you, Tony. This is, indeed, a pleasant surprise. What is it I can be doing for you?''

Tony approached him and the two men shook hands. ''I'd like to interview you for the newspaper.''

Kyle's surprise was genuine. ''Me? What possible interest could I be to your readers?''

''Noted archaeologist, author of two books, international traveler—I'd say there was quite a bit there that would be of interest to my readers. I realize you're here on vacation and to visit friends—'' he acknowledged Lauren with a nod and a smile ''—but we don't often have someone of your background in our little community.''

Kyle maintained his composure and resisted the impulse to shoot a quick look in Lauren's direction. Tony's use of the word *background* had captured his attention and set his senses on full alert. Could Tony have been the one requesting the Interpol check on Shane Nolan? An interesting possibility.

''My goodness, Tony. It seems that you've been checking up on me. I'm flattered, of course, but I wouldn't have thought two obscure volumes about archaeology would have been that widely known. Are you a student of archaeology, perchance?''

"I'm a newspaperman. I'm a student of many things, and right now archaeology is on that list."

Kyle turned toward Lauren and offered her a confident smile. "Perhaps an interview would be an enjoyable way for me to pass some time today since you have a busy schedule of your own."

"But I thought you had planned to do some fishing today."

He saw the anxiety in her eyes and understood her concern. It was a concern that he did not share, however. He had once used the guise of an archaeologist as a cover for an assignment. He felt confident he could handle any of Tony's interview questions.

Tony looked from Kyle to Lauren then back to Kyle. "Oh? You had other plans for the day? I certainly don't want to interfere..."

Something about the way Tony let his voice trail off did not sit well with Kyle. He was not sure whether or not he was reading something into the situation that was not there. He addressed his comments to Lauren. "No problem at all. I can challenge your fish to a test of wills at another time." He turned to Tony. "Where would you like to conduct this *interrogation?*" He smiled innocently, but had chosen his words with specific care.

"Well, perhaps we can talk while we take a little stroll along the bluffs." Tony paused. "That is, if you don't mind the walk."

"Not at all. I'm accustomed to taking brisk daily walks." Kyle turned to Lauren again. "See you later." He gave her hand a quick squeeze that told her not to worry.

The two men left by the front door and walked at a leisurely pace toward the bluffs.

"Well, now. What would you like to know that would enlighten the readers of your fair community?"

"You don't mind if I record our interview, do you? I

find it much easier and a great deal more accurate than taking notes."

"Not at all. You go right ahead."

Tony turned on the handheld recorder. "Let's start with some basics. Is this your first trip to the States?"

It was an innocent enough question, but one Kyle did not know the answer to. All he could do was improvise based on the information he had. Shane's letters had spoken of times he had spent with Jim Franklin in Ireland, of the fact that they had met there, but had not mentioned any trips Shane had made to the States. "Yes, it is. And a lovely country you have. I never realized how large it was. Other than that unfortunate incident about finding the body on the beach it's been a grand trip, a grand trip, indeed."

"Pardon me for saying, but I find it a little odd that you didn't come for Jim Franklin's funeral, especially in light of what close friends you apparently were." It was a pointed statement accompanied by a clearly purposeful look meant as a definite challenge.

Kyle leveled a curious look at Tony, containing just a hint of a challenge of his own. "Are you suggesting that I should have presented myself at the door of a grieving fiancée whom I had never met and thrown a good old-fashioned Irish wake to be attended by people who were complete strangers to me and might possibly be offended by my country's traditions and customs?"

He saw a look flash through Tony's eyes for just a second then disappear. It was capitulation, and it told him he had hit his target. For Tony to have pursued that particular line of questioning would have been far beyond the scope of an innocent interview for the newspaper. If he was suspicious of Shane Nolan, then he would have to find a different way to prove out his theories. Kyle had to admire Tony's quick recovery when the newsman continued without missing a beat.

"Tell me a little bit about your educational background."

Kyle fielded all of Tony's questions with confidence and skill. He was relieved that there were no more attempts to trip him up. They returned to Lauren's a couple of hours later, where Tony said his goodbyes and left.

Kyle entered the store. Lauren and Milly were deep in conversation. He caught Lauren's eye then went into the back. She followed a couple of minutes later.

"What was all that about?" Her question had a hushed urgency about it that matched the expression on her face.

Kyle furrowed his brow in a thoughtful manner. "I'm not quite sure. There was no question that he was pumping me, but I don't know exactly what his intentions were or what triggered his suspicions about Shane Nolan."

"Be careful, Kyle." A cold shiver moved through her body. "Something is wrong. There's danger out there. I don't know what it is, but I can feel it."

He cupped her chin in his hand. "I'll be careful." He leaned forward and placed a light kiss on her lips. "You be careful, too. If Tony is questioning Shane Nolan's identity, then you can bet he's also taking a hard look at you and what your role in all of this might be."

"Do you think Tony's involved in the smuggling?" She took a breath to calm the anxiety building inside her. Was this what Kyle was trying to keep from her? There had already been so many surprises about the people who lived in Sea Grove, including the fact that one of them had shot Kyle. It was a possibility she did not like, but one she knew she must face. "And in the murders?"

He placed his hands on her shoulders. He saw the uncertainty in her eyes and the distress that covered her face. "There are so many twists and turns to this case. Every time I get something neatly boxed and wrapped, something new shows up." He drew her into his embrace. He threaded his fingers through her hair and cradled her head against his shoulder. "Everything is going to be okay. Tony seems to be very good at his job. His newsman's instincts tell him there's a story, and he's trying to sniff it out."

"Are you sure? Do you really think that's all it is?"

Kyle paused before responding. "I hope so."

Chapter Twelve

Kyle walked the few blocks to the downtown harbor, leaving Lauren to tend to her business concerns and prepare for the meeting of the historical society. He casually strolled along the dock, stopping occasionally to admire different boats. He paused for a long time in front of Frank's boat, then looked around for the harbormaster's office.

Kyle knocked softly on the jamb of the open door. "Excuse me."

The man who was bent over the desk looked up from his work. "Can I help you?"

"I hope so. I was wondering...Frank Brewster's boat. I don't mean to sound crass by following on the heels of the tragic accident, but do you know if the family intends to sell it?"

"The boat never did belong to Frank. It's owned by some big-city corporation out of Seattle, something called Triangle Associates. They pay the mooring expenses, all maintenance and upkeep. They list Frank as the primary user of the vessel, but he's not the owner."

"Oh, I see." Among Kyle's many accomplishments was the ability to read upside down. The man was going over the harbor log, which clearly showed Frank's boat going out twice on the night in question—once when Kyle spotted it from the lighthouse tower and again several hours later. The second run lasted only fifteen minutes, and the log showed that Frank checked out but did not check in upon his return to the dock. Obviously someone else had brought the boat back and moored it. But who?

The man eyed Kyle for a moment. "Anything else you want?"

To make his query seem innocent, Kyle followed with another request for information. "Do you know of any other boat of the same general type and size that might be for sale?"

"I'm not a yacht broker. Go try Sea Grove Marine Sales at the other end of the harbor. That's what they do...they sell boats." With that, the man returned to his paperwork signaling that his part of the conversation was at an end.

Big-city corporation...Triangle Associates. The words played over in his mind as he slowly made his way along the dock, pausing every few yards so anyone watching would see him looking over several other boats. It was an important new piece to the puzzle. Finding out who owned Triangle Associates was at the top of his list.

He returned to Lauren's, entering through the side door so no one would see him. He sent a coded fax requesting a rush on all information about Triangle Associates. He should have the information that day.

He glanced at his watch. It was almost four-thirty. Surely the historical society meeting would be over by now. He ventured into the bookstore and immediately noticed Harvey Sherwood talking with Milly.

Kyle stood back and watched for a moment. Harvey seemed nervous, but then he had seemed jittery every time their paths had crossed. After a couple of minutes Harvey hurried out the door. Kyle went to the bookstore section, glanced at some of the magazines, then wandered toward the tearoom. The sound of several voices, all seemingly speaking at once, reached his ears.

"Hello, Shane." Milly gestured toward the sound of the voices as she gave him a friendly smile. "I think they're just finishing up now."

Kyle peered around the corner into the tearoom. He immediately spotted Lauren and Irene. He counted five other people, three men and two women. Everyone was standing, preparing to leave. He caught Lauren's eye and she gave him a quick smile indicating she would be through in a moment. He stepped over to the counter where Milly was ringing up a sale. He watched as the historical society members left. Irene and Lauren were the last to exit the tearoom.

"I'm very excited about your plan for the old railroad station." Lauren's enthusiasm was obvious. "Do you think there will be any problems in raising the necessary funds?"

"Now don't you worry yourself about that, Lauren. That's my area. Everything will work out just fine. I have a sizable pledge from a corporation to help with the restoration of the railroad station and the creation of a local history museum. The rest of it should all fall into place without any problems."

"I'm going to have to go with you to Seattle on one of your arm-twisting trips so I can see how you do it."

Irene chuckled good-naturedly. "Well, I do seem to have a knack for fund-raising."

"Good afternoon, ladies." The postman came through the front door, his mail pouch slung over his shoulder and a stack of envelopes in his hand. "Nice day today, isn't it?"

"Mr. Erskine, what a pleasure to see you." Irene smiled as she stopped to greet him.

"You look lovely today, Irene." He turned his attention to Milly, who was standing patiently waiting for him to give her the mail. "Sorry I'm late. Mail truck from Springfield had motor trouble this morning and didn't get here until after eight o'clock.''

He handed her the magazines and letters he held in his hand. "Several pieces for you today, Milly." On top of the stack, glaringly apparent to anyone standing there, was an envelope with an Irish stamp, a Dublin postmark and a return address showing Shane Nolan as the sender.

The breath froze in Lauren's lungs. A letter from Shane—it was totally unexpected and certainly the last thing she and Kyle needed. Should she say something? Make an attempt to explain the letter? She quickly scanned the expressions of the people present. Irene did not register any reaction, but Milly seemed perplexed. She glanced at Mr. Erskine. He had an odd expression on his face, or at least she thought he did. Maybe she was allowing her anxiety to drive her imagination.

Lauren quickly turned toward Kyle. She hoped she had been successful at hiding the apprehension that suddenly shot through her body. His expression remained unchanged. She could not tell if he was aware of the situation.

"Goodbye, Lauren." Irene's voice broke into her thoughts. "I'll check with you in a few days about the next phase of the railroad station restoration, as soon as I return from visiting my niece."

"That'll be fine." Lauren did not know if the quaver was really in her voice or if she just thought it was. Either way, the uneasiness churned inside her.

"Milly, you be sure and give my best to your family." After saying her goodbyes to Milly, Irene turned her attention to Kyle. "Have you been enjoying your stay in Sea Grove, Shane?"

Kyle's smile was gracious, his manner open and friendly. "Ah, delightful little town you have here. I'm enjoying my holiday ever so much. I'm only sorry I will have to be leaving soon, but duty calls me back in Dublin.

I've agreed to instruct an archaeology class at the college for the upcoming session, and I must prepare my lectures.''

"Lauren never mentioned that you also taught. That must give you quite a feeling of satisfaction, to be able to share your knowledge and profession with eager young students.''

"Well, I must admit to a touch of concern. This is the first time I've ever attempted this type of thing. I was quite flattered when I was approached. I hope I justify their faith in me.''

Irene extended a confident smile. "I'm sure you'll do just fine, young man.'' She turned toward the door, then paused. "You make sure you stop by before you leave. I don't want you slipping out of town without saying good-bye.''

"Oh, that I will. You can bet on it, Irene.'' Kyle gave a friendly wave and smile as Irene left the building.

Lauren turned her attention to Milly while surreptitiously concealing the letter in her pocket. "We had another busy day today, Milly. Would you mind closing by yourself this evening?''

"No problem, Lauren. You run along. I'll lock up the front of the building when I leave.''

"Good night, Milly.'' Lauren and Kyle retreated to her private living quarters at the back of the building.

As soon as the door was closed she withdrew the letter from her pocket and turned to Kyle. "Did you notice this?'' She held it up for him to see. "I think Mr. Erskine was a little confused by it, and Milly seemed to be staring at it. I don't know if Irene saw it or not.''

"Oh, I'm sure Irene noticed it. There isn't much she misses.''

Her voice was filled with alarm. "I didn't know whether to say something or not. Should I have tried to cover it up by saying something like, 'Oh, look…here's that letter you mailed three weeks ago—it finally got here'? Did I do the right thing?''

"You did the right thing by doing nothing. It's always good in this type of situation to keep as low a profile as possible. It's the same thing as offering explanations that aren't requested when answering questions. Your saying something would have drawn unnecessary attention to the letter.''

"What do we do now?''

"Why don't you open the letter and see what it's all about?'' Kyle shared her concern but knew he could not let her see it. The appearance of the letter cast a whole new set of rules over the situation. If there had been any doubt before, it was erased. Her life was at stake every bit as much as his.

Her fingers trembled as she opened the envelope and withdrew the single sheet of paper. She unfolded it and quickly scanned the page then handed it to Kyle without saying a word. He took it from her and read the letter. It said Shane had broken his leg and as a result had not been able to participate in the archaeological dig. He had decided to drop her a quick note to let her know.

Kyle returned the letter to her. The stern expression on his face said as much as his words. "That's it! I've got to wrap this up very quickly.'' He stared at her for a moment, then turned away. "I'm going to put you in protective custody until this thing is over.''

"Me? Is that really necessary?''

He turned to her, placing his hands on her shoulders then drawing her to him. "There's no way anyone could be convinced you're nothing more than an innocent victim of circumstances.'' He leaned forward and placed a soft kiss on her lips. "I'm so sorry...I wish there was something else I could do, but it's too late. I should have sent you away a long time ago. I never should have allowed you to become involved.''

She tried to swallow the hard lump that had formed in her throat, but it refused to go away. She spoke softly, her words tentative and surrounded by uncertainty. "Maybe no one noticed. Just because a letter was delivered doesn't mean that anyone paid attention to it."

"You know as well as I do that your postman noticed. There was no way he could have missed the Irish postmark and stamp when he was sorting the mail for delivery. You told me Mr. Erskine spreads the news faster than he delivers the mail. So, even if Irene and Milly weren't aware it's still a sure bet they and everyone else in town will have the information very quickly." He expelled a heavy sigh as he dropped his hands from her shoulders. "There's a lot to do and it has to be done tonight."

"Right." Lauren squared her shoulders and clenched her jaw in determination. "What do we do first?"

"We?"

"You bet *we!* You've already said that there's no way I can claim ignorance, so there's no reason for you to shut me out." She headed for the bedroom. "I'm going to change clothes, I'll be right back." She disappeared into the other room.

As soon as she was out of sight, Kyle grabbed his cellular phone and made a call. His conversation was quick and to the point. "What do you have for me on Triangle Associates?"

"You've got a good one here. Triangle Associates is based in Seattle and is hidden behind miles of paperwork designed to conceal ownership from prying eyes."

"What about bank accounts? Who signs the checks for Triangle Associates and who are those checks sent to? And what about deposits? Who does Triangle Associates receive money from?"

"Deposits to the account are made every few days, and a lot of it is in cash with each deposit just a few dollars short of the amount the bank would be required to report as an excessive cash transaction. The total amount of money deposited over the course of a month adds up to considerable. The checks are signed by an accountant who simply disburses funds per written instructions. Now, here's something you'll really like. Triangle Associates has an account in each of five different banks, all of them showing the same type of deposits. I can tell you what I think, but I don't have a definite paper trail for you yet."

"Just give it to me…and I'll bet it matches up with what my gut is telling me." Kyle listened intently, assimilating everything and adding the pieces to his puzzle. "That's great work, Gus. It won't do for court, but it confirms my theory."

Kyle mentally shifted to a new topic. "There's been an unexpected complication here. I have reason to believe that my cover has been blown…again. This base of operation is no longer safe. You're going to have to flush out that paper trail. I think you're going to need it to prosecute this case." He listened for a moment, then hung up.

Kyle quickly placed another call. "I need a team immediately." As soon as he finished with the second call, he wandered into the business part of the building. Milly was just gathering her things to leave for the day. "Good night, Milly. Have a pleasant evening." He walked her to the front door.

"Good night, Shane."

After locking the door, he walked into the tearoom. He stood for a moment, staring at the table where the historical society had had their meeting. A slight smile turned the corners of his mouth. Stacked on the table in front of Irene's chair were the neatly folded candy wrappers from what was obviously her favorite type of candy, just as he had seen at her house.

Lauren appeared from the back room dressed in jeans and a dark sweater. "I'm all ready. Now, what do we need to do?"

"Nothing for a few hours yet. It's still too early in the evening to be sneaking around. And I'll be going alone." She started to say something, but he quickly hushed her words by placing his fingertips against her lips. "No argument."

"OUR PROBLEM has escalated. We have a serious situation with Lauren and her houseguest." The words had an edge of controlled anger.

"What do you want me to do about it?" The voice at the other end of the telephone conveyed exasperation. "First Billy, then Kyle Delaney and finally Frank. I don't think the public is going to believe two more *accidental* deaths in such a short time."

"There are ways. Perhaps we can take care of *all* our problems with one solution."

"*All* our problems? Do you mean—"

"Yes, that's exactly what I mean."

KYLE CHECKED his watch. "Lauren, I want you to stay here. I'm going to the cave to check on a few things, just some last-minute details. I won't be gone long."

"But—"

"I promise not to become enmeshed in any death-defying antics or perform any heroics without you. It's just a simple little routine matter. As soon as I get back we'll talk about what's next. Okay?"

She hesitated, weighing his words, then managed to produce a feeble smile. "Okay. But don't you be gone very long or else I'll have to come looking for you."

"No! Under no circumstances do I want you to come looking for me." He saw the objection forming on her lips and cut her off before she could say anything. Things were critical and time was important. "Here." He wrote a phone number on a piece of paper. "If I'm gone more than two hours call this number, identify yourself to whoever answers and they'll take it from there." She took the slip of paper, stared at it for a moment, then looked at him. He kissed her cheek in an attempt to reassure her.

Kyle headed for the door, pausing to check the ammunition clip in his gun. He did not need to look at her. He could feel the censure in her eyes and the disapproval that covered her face. He replaced the pistol in the holster at the small of his back and opened the side door.

The feeling slapped her in the face without warning, a cold feeling of dread that caused her to visibly shiver. "Kyle...don't—" She was not sure exactly what to say. "Don't go...maybe later...maybe I should go with you—"

"What's the matter?" He quickly crossed the room to her. He saw the stark reality of her fears in the way she hunched her shoulders and the apprehension in her eyes.

"It's out there, Kyle. Something or someone. There's danger out there. Please don't go."

He took her hands in his. "I have to." He gave them a reassuring squeeze. "I'll be careful." He turned and disappeared out the side door, moving stealthily into the dark.

His words did nothing to calm her nerves. The other impression had been so vivid, the man lurching off the cliff. This one was different. She could not get a clear vision to go with the feeling. She only knew that it was life-threatening danger and it was out there in the dark, waiting for an opportunity to strike.

She tried to settle her thoughts on other matters, to busy herself so she would not stare at the clock. She ran a load of laundry through the washing machine, then transferred it to the dryer. She did the dishes, swept the kitchen floor and thought about rearranging the cupboards. She was desperate to find little chores that would occupy her time while he was gone, but it was no good.

She could not shake the feeling of danger that stuck to

her every thought and action. She nervously paced through the kitchen, into the living room, around the bedroom and back to the kitchen.

LAUREN MIGHT HAVE been anxiety-ridden and nervous, but Kyle was just plain angry. He knew he was cutting his time close, pushing against that two-hour limit he had given her, but he had not considered the possibility of having both exits from the lighthouse cottage cut off. He did not know what the occasion was, but several cars and a group of teenagers had descended on his location. Trying to leave without being seen would be next to impossible.

Then snatches of conversation floated his way. "Get out of here...over by the breakwater...build a bonfire on the beach..."

Kyle watched from the cottage window as the teenagers piled into the cars and left. He glanced at his watch. He was already a few minutes beyond the time limit he had given Lauren.

He cautiously slipped out of the cottage, but remained close to the building as he hugged the shadows. He had to be sure everyone had left before he started across the bluff.

Lauren had her gaze riveted to her living room clock. She could not stomach any more of the stress that jittered through her body. Kyle had been gone for two hours, and that was too long. Her insides twisted into knots that pulled tighter with each passing minute. She could not handle the waiting and not knowing for one more moment.

She grabbed her jacket and a flashlight, prepared to go out to look for him. She opened the side door, then paused. His instructions had been very specific. She was to call the phone number. She hurried to the kitchen, retrieved the piece of paper he had given her and lifted the telephone receiver.

The feeling came flying at her from out of nowhere, stopping her in her tracks. She kept getting mixed signals, feelings of eminent danger interspersed with a sense of calm. Panic consumed her. Was Kyle in danger again?

"Well, well…looky who we got here."

The gruff voice slashed through the still air and continued to the core of her consciousness. Her heart skipped a beat then gave a heavy thud in her chest. She slammed down the phone receiver, whirled around and found herself face-to-face with Max Culhane. She tried to catch her breath and project a calm manner. She looked past him and realized she had left the side door open when she had returned to the kitchen.

"Oh…Max. You scared the breath out of me. I didn't hear you come up behind me." She tried to muster a casual smile. "What are you doing here, especially so late at night? Is something wrong?"

His eyes were hard, and his features were set in a scowl. "I reckon I might ask you the same thing—your door standin' open and you dressed to go out with a flashlight at the ready."

"I was about to take my evening walk." Kyle's words rushed back to her. *Don't overexplain. Don't say more than required. Don't offer explanations for something that hasn't been asked.*

"Looked like you was in some kind of a hurry. Now, just where was you headed?"

The uneasiness did not build slowly, it erupted full-blown. She was alone in her kitchen with a man who was becoming more menacing by the second.

Lauren backed away from Max, hoping to put some distance between them while edging closer to the open door. "You didn't tell me what brought you here at this time of night. I'm afraid I'm busy now, so if it's not important I'll have to ask you to leave."

"Not so fast." Max grabbed Lauren's arm in an iron grip. "Where's your friend? Were you on your way out to meet him? You know, Lauren, you really should've stayed outta things. You really should of."

"I don't know what you're talking about. Please, Max—" She tried to pry his fingers loose from her arm. "You're hurting me." She knew her anxiety showed in her voice, but she could not stop it. "I don't understand what's going on here. Let go of me."

"Answer me, Lauren." The sheriff's tone was mean. "Where's your friend?" He unholstered his revolver and forcefully moved her along in front of him. "Let's go find him."

The realization was crystal clear, and so was the meaning of her premonition. The danger was not directed toward Kyle, the danger was hers—a very real danger. Max shoved her through the side door and across the bluff toward the lighthouse. She stumbled on the uneven ground. He jerked her upright and shoved her forward. "No tricks, Lauren. I'd hate to have to shoot you right here and now."

They had almost reached the lighthouse parking lot when Max brought their procession to a halt. "I'm asking you one more time, Lauren. Where's your friend?"

"I told you, Max. I don't know where he is."

"I'm right here, Constable." Kyle's voice was firm and steady, showing not a hint of fear or weakness. He had rounded the corner of the building and was about to dash across the bluff toward Lauren's when he heard the voices. He had come to an abrupt halt, quickly sizing up the situation. He did not know if she had dialed the emergency number, but he guessed she had not. It looked as if Max had gotten to her first. "I must insist that you unhand the lady."

The sound of Max's angry words and Lauren's less than firm reply still lingered in his mind. He had waited too long to get her to safety. Now he would have to do something, and do it quickly. He took a calming breath, unholstered his gun and held it behind his back as he stepped from the corner of the cottage.

Max whirled at the sound of Kyle's voice. He did not move any closer to the edge of the bluff. He continued to grasp Lauren's arm in his strong fingers. "So...you just out for your nightly walk, too? Seems to me the two of you would be walkin' together."

"Turn loose of her, Max." Gone was the Irish accent and the affable attitude. Gone was any pretense of innocence. "If she's not out of your reach by the time I count to three, I'm coming after you." Kyle paused for half a second then spoke again. "One..."

Max pulled Lauren in front of him, using her as a shield. He raised his revolver toward her head. "I'd stop countin' if I was you, or I'll drop her on the spot."

The sound of Kyle's voice had produced a wonderful feeling of relief in Lauren, but her euphoria was short-lived. She felt Max's raspy breath wheeze against her nape and his chest heave up and down against her back as he nervously gulped in as much oxygen as he could. She had never been as frightened as she was at that moment. Her mouth felt as dry as cotton balls. She was aware of Max's fingers digging into her arm, but was numb to the pain. She feared her heart would either pound its way out of her chest or stop beating altogether.

Focus. She knew she had to concentrate on Kyle, on what he said and did. She closed her eyes for a brief moment as she forced a calm through her body and pumped her energy. She also knew she needed to be totally attuned to what Max was doing, to even the slightest movement or change on his part. She recalled Kyle's words about a fraction of a second making a difference.

Max waved the gun toward Kyle, a gesture clearly visible in the moonlight. "You get out here in the open where I can see you better. All of us, we're gonna take a little walk together."

Kyle moved slowly, never taking his eyes off Max and Lauren. "Why don't you turn her loose? I'm a far more valuable hostage. My family has money. I can wire Dublin and have money here in twenty-four hours—"

"Cut the bull. You sure ain't nobody named Shane No-lan. And if you think I'm gonna turn her loose just because you say so then you're dumber than you look. Now, move over here…nice and easy."

Kyle moved slowly, his gun still in his hand behind his back. One thought raced through his mind—one thought that overshadowed everything else. Could he take out Max without hitting Lauren? He was at a bad angle and was confident that Max would not allow him to maneuver into a position where he could get a better shot. Everything depended on Lauren and her ability to move quickly and decisively.

The opportune moment presented itself. Kyle made the most subtle of movements, hoping it was enough for Lauren to notice…praying she was not too frightened to realize what he wanted her to do. In response to his silent instruction, she forcefully jammed the elbow of her free arm into Max's solar plexus. He let out a loud grunt and doubled over in pain. Lauren dived to one side, hitting the ground with a thud.

A split second later the shot rang out, sounding more like the explosion of a cannon than a handgun. Lauren's scream followed so closely that there was not room for even a breath between the two sounds. Kyle's pulse jumped and his heart pounded in his throat as the cold fear swept over him.

Chapter Thirteen

"Kyle?" Lauren's voice was so soft he could barely hear it above the roar of the blood rushing in his ears.

He bolted across the open ground that separated them, any semblance of caution thrown to the wind. "Lauren?" He knelt next to her, helping her as she tried to sit up. "Are you all right?"

"Yes, I think so."

"Were you hit? Can you stand and walk?" A bit of a calm began to settle over him.

Her voice became stronger, more in control. "I'm fine."

His words came quickly and with extreme urgency. "Come on, we've got to get some cover."

Lauren's reaction was slow and confused as she stumbled to her feet. "Cover? I don't understand."

It was Max who did not move. The moonlight made the blood look more black than red as it oozed from the gaping wound on the side of his head. It ran down the sheriff's neck then spread a dark stain across his shirt.

Kyle did not hesitate. He grabbed Max's gun, shoved it into his jacket pocket, then took Lauren's hand and turned toward the cottage—the closest available shelter. "It's far from over. I'm not the one who fired that shot!"

Lauren's eyes went wide with shock. "What? Then who did?"

"Is everyone all right?" The shout came from the direction of the parking lot followed by the sound of some-one moving through the tall grass at the edge of the bluff. "Lauren, are you okay? Who else is with you?"

Kyle quickly dropped to the ground, pulling Lauren down next to him. "Don't answer...don't move. Let him show himself first. Did you call that phone number I left you?"

"No. I'm sorry, Kyle. I had the phone in my hand and was about to dial when Max grabbed me."

"It's okay, don't worry about it. It just means that we're on our own for the time being."

Kyle peered through the darkness. It seemed like an eternity before he saw a shadowy figure moving in their direction. He remained still. The unknown man continued toward them, growing closer with each step.

The stranger paused when he reached Max's body, bending down to check, then straightening up. He looked around again. The moonlight glinted off the barrel of a rifle with a night sniper scope cradled in the crook of his arm. He called out again. "It's safe now, Lauren. You can come out."

An involuntary gasp escaped her throat as she clamped Kyle's hand in a hard squeeze. Her words came out in a breathless rush. "It's Mitch O'Connor."

Kyle jerked his head in her direction. "Are you sure?"

"Positive."

The soft Irish accent again surrounded the words as Kyle called to the shadowy figure. "Who's there? Is it safe to come out?"

"It's Deputy O'Connor. Is that Shane Nolan? Is Lauren with you? Are the two of you all right?"

"'Tis I, Constable. And the lovely lady in question is here with me. She's a bit shaken, but quite unharmed." Kyle tugged on Lauren's hand when she attempted to stand up, pulling her back to the ground. "What happened out there? Why would the sheriff threaten Lauren like that and why would someone shoot him? Are you sure the danger has passed?''

"The area's secure." Mitch swung the strap of the high-powered rifle over his shoulder to free his hands, then removed his gloves. "There's nothing to worry about."

Lauren was very confused. She understood why the sheriff had grabbed her. If Max was involved, then his information that Shane Nolan was an impostor and she had been harboring him certainly made her a target. But what was Mitch doing here and why had he shot Max?

"Mitch? What's going on?" Lauren's voice did not reveal the fear and anxiety that filled every corner of her consciousness.

"Glad to hear your voice, Lauren. I'd like to get your statements. Do you suppose we could talk somewhere else? Somewhere warm and light? I've already called for an ambulance."

As if on cue, Kyle saw the headlights of a squad car pull into the lighthouse parking lot, followed by another vehicle. He reached into his jacket pocket and took out Max's gun. He held it out toward Lauren. "Here, take this. I want you to have—"

"No!" It was emphatic, sharp and absolute. "I refuse to touch a gun. Don't ask me to."

Kyle saw the hard determination that covered her face. It was obvious there was no possibility of changing her mind or even having a discussion of the matter at some future date. He could see that for Lauren it was an unequivocally closed subject. He put Max's gun back in his pocket.

"If you're sure it's safe, Constable..." Kyle turned to Lauren and lowered his voice to a whisper. "Come on, let's find out what's going on. I think it's okay, but keep close to me and stay alert."

Kyle holstered his pistol, slowly rose to his full height,

then looked around at the people moving across the bluff toward Max's body. When he was satisfied everything was all right he indicated that Lauren should stand up. He clasped her hand in his. "Come on." They walked the short distance to where Mitch O'Connor was waiting.

"Well, Constable, that mean-looking weapon slung over your shoulder would lead me to believe that it was you who shot Sheriff Culhane." Kyle paused, obviously waiting for Mitch to answer the verbal challenge he had tossed at the deputy.

Mitch did not pause, did not even bat an eye to indicate a moment of apprehension. "And you'd be correct in that assumption." He turned and started across the bluff toward Lauren's place, indicating that they should follow him.

A few minutes later they were settled around Lauren's dining room table. Kyle was once again the perfect persona of Shane Nolan. It was possible the sheriff had not conveyed the information about Shane. He would leave it up to Mitch O'Connor to determine that Shane was a fraud. "So, Constable, now that we have the lights turned on and we're all warm, suppose you explain to us why the sheriff would have tried to abduct Lauren—" Kyle leveled a cool gaze at Mitch "—and why you felt it necessary to kill him without giving him the opportunity to surrender."

Mitch took a swallow from his coffee mug then placed it on the table with a deliberately slow movement. "I've been watching Max for quite a while now. Both he and Frank Brewster have been up to no good for a long time. I was never quite sure what they were doing. They were real careful about covering their tracks, but then things started to fall apart for them. I think Billy Washburn stumbled onto something and Frank did away with him."

"Really? What could the young lad have known that would have cost him his life?"

"I really don't know, but he worked for Frank. Maybe he overheard a conversation or saw something he wasn't supposed to see. Maybe he tried to blackmail Frank. I just don't know. I am convinced that he was somehow a threat and it cost him his life." Mitch took another sip of his coffee.

"But I still don't understand. Why would you have shot the sheriff?"

"I felt I had no option. I think it's obvious that Lauren's life was in imminent danger, and I knew Max was more than capable of killing her. After all, he killed Frank Brewster."

"Frank was murdered?" Lauren blurted out the question. Even though she and Kyle had discussed it and she knew it was true, she was surprised to hear Mitch say it in such a matter-of-fact way. "And you think Max did it? But from what you've said, Max and Frank were partners. Why would Max kill his partner? Do you have any proof of these crazy theories of yours?"

Mitch O'Connor turned in his chair toward Lauren. His face was expressionless as he addressed her questions. "I have my own personal observation that he had a gun to your head. Do you deny that he threatened your life? Do you deny that you honestly believed your life was in danger?"

"Well—" She looked at Kyle, not at all sure how to answer Mitch.

"I think, Constable, that we certainly owe you our gratitude. He most assuredly would have killed Lauren, and I'm sure he would not have dealt too kindly with me, either. What I don't understand is why? What possible threat could Lauren have been to him, even in light of his apparent criminal activity?"

"Well." Mitch shifted his weight in the chair. "Lauren lives within a stone's throw of Brewster's warehouse, and she found his body on the beach. I don't know if she was actually a threat to Max or whether he simply imagined that she was. Either way, it's immaterial. He apparently thought she knew something or had seen something that would incriminate him." He stared at Lauren. "Did you see anything that I should know about?"

The motion of Kyle's head was so slight as to be almost unnoticeable, but Lauren caught his guidance and followed his silent instructions to the letter. "No, Mitch. I'm not aware of anything unusual going on and I haven't seen anything suspicious."

Mitch directed his attention toward Kyle. "How about you, Mr. Nolan? You see anything suspicious?"

"Nary a thing, Constable. But then, being a stranger to your country there might be something you would consider suspicious that I would not give a second thought...or even the other way around."

The banter continued for another half hour. Both Kyle and Lauren held firmly to their stories. Finally Mitch carried his coffee cup to the kitchen sink, then turned to them. "I guess the only thing left is to ask if either of you picked up the sheriff's handgun. It wasn't with his body."

Kyle forced a startled expression, then he jumped to his feet. "I'm glad you mentioned that, Constable. It completely slipped my mind. I picked it up as a precaution when I went to get Lauren." He reached for his jacket. "I have it here in my pocket." He produced the weapon and handed it to Mitch.

The deputy took the revolver and slipped it into his jacket pocket. His expression gave no hint as to whether he believed Kyle's story. "I'll expect both of you at the sheriff's station tomorrow morning to make an official statement."

Kyle rose to his feet. "Of course, Constable. We'll be there."

Mitch left and Lauren quickly locked the door behind him then closed the drapes. She ran to Kyle, who wrapped his arms around her and held her body close to his.

"You're safe now, Lauren. Everything's all right." He wished he had more confidence in what he was saying.

"I was so frightened. Max was like a total stranger rather than someone I'd known for years." She continued to draw the comfort he provided. She felt the even rhythm of his heartbeat, the strength it conveyed to her.

"I know. I'm sorry you had to go through that." This was a definite setback. With the shooting of Max Culhane, the two suspects against which he had a case were now dead. His other suspicions were still valid, but he was once again left with only bits and pieces of circumstantial evidence. It was not enough.

He held Lauren tighter when he felt a slight tremor work its way through her body. He did not know what to do to stop it. She had displayed courage, a quick mind and a cool head under pressure. He should never have allowed her to be in a position where her mettle would be tested like that. She could have been killed and he would have been responsible just as surely as if he had pulled the trigger himself. It was too late to get her to safety, to move her out of harm's way. Her life was in his hands. For the first time in his career he questioned whether he was capable of completing an assignment.

"I SEE that our problem with Max has been resolved. A fitting conclusion to our business arrangement." A brief pause sent a moment of silence along the phone line. "You know, in light of recent developments I've been giving serious consideration to folding things up for a while. It's been a long and profitable run, but perhaps we shouldn't tempt fate any further."

"It's up to you. I do agree that we need to cool things for a while. Thanks to Frank's panic and Max's heavy-handed bungling there's too much attention being directed this way. And now there will have to be an investigation into Max's untimely demise—even if it's nothing more than simply going through the motions to satisfy the public demand for answers. We'll have to make sure all suspicions stop with Max and everyone considers the case closed.''

LAUREN GRADUALLY STIRRED to wakefulness. She reached to the other side of the bed. Not only was Kyle not there, the sheets showed no lingering hint of any body heat. She opened her eyes and looked around. It was only five-thirty in the morning. Except for Ty-Ty curled up on the foot of the bed, she was alone. She slipped out of bed and put on her robe.

The rest of her living quarters were as deserted as her bedroom. She turned up the heat to take the morning chill out of the air. She checked next to the phone, the refrigerator door, the bathroom mirror and the nightstand. There was not even a hastily scribbled note saying where he had gone or when he would return.

She took a quick shower and dressed. They were supposed to go to the sheriff's station and give Mitch O'Connor their official statement about what had happened. Surely Kyle would not skip that. To do so would put a glaring spotlight on him. She made herself some tea, hoping it would calm the uneasiness inside her.

KYLE BUSIED HIMSELF with the finishing touches to his new plan of attack.

He had lain awake long after they had gone to bed, his mind filled with the options available to him. The plan he had settled on did not totally please him, but it seemed the lesser of several evils. But first he needed to gather some more information, and he needed to do it away from Lauren. It was going to be risky, and he did not want her knowing and anticipating what might happen in the next twenty-four hours.

He picked the lock on the side door of Max Culhane's

house and quietly entered through the laundry room. He moved swiftly through the house, pausing to peer into each room to get his bearings. After giving everything a quick once-over, he slowed down and began a more thorough search.

His first target was the desk. He paused to study the framed photograph—a picture of Max and Milly on a boat. He pulled open a drawer and found some bank statements. He stuck them in his bag. Then he found the telephone bills and a key to a safety-deposit box. He added it to the bank statements. He scanned the contents of a file cabinet drawer. He moved confidently through the small house, checking some things and skipping over others.

He paused in the living room, noting a half-empty coffee cup and an empty beer bottle on the coffee table. He bent over and sniffed the contents of the cup, being careful not to spoil any possible fingerprints. He stuck his finger in the coffee then put it in his mouth to get a taste. A slight smile tugged at the corners of his mouth. It was exactly what he had expected.

Since the kitchen was clean, he surmised that Max's visitor must have been there late in the evening after the dinner dishes had been washed and put away—shortly before Max had gone to Lauren's...or was *sent* to her place.

He hesitated, then reached into the candy dish and took a couple of pieces. He unwrapped one and popped it into his mouth, then stuck the other one in his pocket for later. Satisfied that he had gotten everything he could from his search, he left through the back door. He looked up and noticed the first gray streaks of dawn stretching across the eastern sky. He needed to get off the streets before sunrise brought the light of day and curious onlookers.

He hurried to Lauren's and entered silently through her side door. He went directly toward the bedroom. He had things to do and very little time.

Lauren met him at the doorway between the living room and bedroom. "I was worried."

"I had a few things I needed to take care of." He gave her a soft kiss on the cheek as he slung his bag off his shoulder and tossed it toward the bed.

"What kind of things? I thought Max's death put an end to your investigation. You have Frank and Max, you have a shipment of cigarettes in the cave, you witnessed the man placing the money in the cave and then found the same bills in Frank's safe. You have Mitch O'Connor's testimony about watching Max and Frank. You even have a link between Billy Washburn and Frank in the form of Billy's journal, something Mitch apparently doesn't know about. Other than the paperwork, what's left?"

"It's not all that easy, Lauren."

A look of confusion clouded her face. "Are you saying that the investigation is still in progress? That you're still in danger?"

"You don't find all of this just a little too convenient? Do you really think the person who did such a sloppy job of grabbing you and who was most likely the one who bungled the attempt on my life could really be the brains behind such a successful smuggling ring? A ring that I believe started by smuggling liquor in from Canada during the final year of Prohibition and now, in an ironic twist of fate, has come full circle by smuggling liquor and cigarettes into Canada? That's decades of clever planning and a keen sense of how to change with the times. That sure as hell isn't Max Culhane!"

"But if not Max, then who?"

"The pieces are still falling into place. For now it's best to let them believe they've outsmarted everyone."

"Do you know who is involved?"

He studied her, then finally answered her question. "Yes, I think so. I just don't have enough proof to act. My bits and pieces of circumstantial evidence will just get our case laughed out of court. I need something substantial and conclusive.''

''Like what?''

He shot her a teasing grin. ''Well, a full confession from all parties involved would certainly go a long way toward making my case.'' He turned to the coffeepot, indicating that he did not want to answer any more questions.

And to make sure she did not pursue it, he changed the subject as he poured himself a cup of coffee. ''I'm sorry about what happened to your fiancé.'' He turned and saw the expression on her face. He was not sure exactly what it was, but it definitely was not friendly. He felt a pang of guilt stab at his conscience.

Her voice was flat, almost a monotone. ''How do you know what happened to Jim? It wasn't in any of Shane's letters.''

He set the mug on the kitchen counter and placed his hands on her shoulders. ''I'm sorry. I had no business blurting that out. It's just…well, I came across an article about his death in the newspaper while going through back issues. It came as quite a surprise to me, since you hadn't mentioned any of it and none of Shane's letters had mentioned specifically how he had died.''

He knew what was happening, and he did not seem to be able to stop it. He was distancing himself from her in preparation for the time when he would be moving on. It was not going to be easy. In fact, it just might be the most difficult task he had ever performed. He knew there would be a place inside him that would die when he had to finally say goodbye.

An odd-sounding ring reached his ears. It was his cellular phone. He retrieved it from his bag in the other room, along with the scrambling device. ''Yes?'' He listened, then responded.

Lauren was only able to hear his side of the conversation…and it made no sense to her.

"You can trace back ten years and it's a blank prior to that? Does it match up from the other end? What about military records, do you have the files on both of them?" He listened. "Okay, good. Now, what about the other one? My feeling is that it's okay, but what do you show? Any information on that Interpol trace yet? I know it hasn't been that long, but—" A smile spread across Kyle's face as he took in the information.

"Good. You'll make contact and take care of the necessary arrangements?" He listened for another minute then disconnected from the phone call.

He put the cellular phone in his bag. He took his time returning to Lauren. For the entire duration of his phone conversation he felt her eyes on his back. He owed her his life but he knew that as much as he wanted it to be so, he would not be able to share that life with her. He began gathering his belongings in preparation for his departure, the disguise kit being first. There was no more need for Shane Nolan.

The insistent buzzing of the doorbell interrupted Kyle's activities. Lauren hurried to answer it while he hung back, not wanting to show his face prematurely.

Tony Mallory shoved past Lauren as soon as she opened the door. He glanced around the parlor and into the tearoom. "Where's Shane Nolan?" His voice was angry, his words abrupt.

"Tony! What's the meaning of this? You come barging in here at six o'clock in the morning and you don't even have the courtesy to say hello before making demands?"

"This is important, Lauren. I've just come into possession of some very important and incriminating information."

"Incriminating information? What about?" She was not sure whether to be apprehensive or angry. "You're not making any sense. Now, slow down and tell me what this is all about."

"It's this." He handed her a piece of paper. It was a fax from London, and it showed a copy of the back of a book cover—a book written by Dr. Shane Nolan, noted archaeologist and lecturer. The back cover contained a photograph of the *real* Shane Nolan. "I don't know what this guy staying with you has been telling you or what he's up to, but he's an impostor. I contacted a buddy who's on assignment in London, and this is what he found. I want you to come with me right now, get out of here before something happens. We'll report this to the authorities—"

"That won't be necessary, Tony." Kyle stood in the doorway.

A thousand words would have been woefully inadequate to describe the expression on Tony Mallory's face. His eyes widened in shock, and his mouth fell open. He stared at Kyle for what seemed like a full minute before he was able to speak.

"You! I thought you were dead!"

Kyle walked casually across the room toward Tony. "Did you?"

"The Coast Guard report about the body, your van impounded, your belongings boxed up from the motel..." Tony shook his head to clear the confusion from his mind. "I tried to verify your identity with the Coast Guard. When I couldn't get a straight answer from them, I called the phone number on your business card. All I got was an answering service that said they would take my name and phone number and refer the message."

"You'll be happy to know that your message was efficiently relayed to me." Kyle tried to sound casual while remaining alert to Tony's every move and intonation.

"Damn!" Tony's frustration exploded. "I feel like I've been run around the block then dumped on my own front porch so I could contemplate what a stupid fool I am." He looked at Kyle. "I'm a newsman, a trained investigative reporter, and I couldn't come up with anything other than a newsman's curiosity."

"Not true. You came up with conclusive proof that the person you knew as Shane Nolan was a fraud. And given more time, I'm sure you would have turned your suspicions about Kyle Delaney into a first-class investigation. Tell me, just for future reference, what piqued your curiosity about Shane Nolan?"

"It was the photographs from Billy Washburn's funeral. Every time I pointed a camera in your direction you managed to turn your back to me. I can understand that occasionally happening in the natural course of things, but not every time. It seemed to me as if you were purposely avoiding my camera. Then, I wasn't completely happy with your responses to my interview questions."

Kyle extended his hand toward Tony. "I want to thank you, not only for your concern for Lauren but for the fact that you acted on your suspicions on her behalf."

Tony accepted Kyle's handshake, his suspicion tempered with confusion about the unexpected turn of events. "Lauren and I have been friends ever since I arrived in Sea Grove. I'm...I'm very fond of her."

Tony did not need to say more. Kyle sensed a history between them.

Lauren started to say something, but before any words could escape her mouth she froze.

A man with a grim expression and dressed entirely in black had suddenly appeared behind Kyle. The intruder had moved silently across her kitchen until he had reached his position, the gun in his hand poised.

"Everything okay here, Kyle?"

Without turning or showing any surprise at the interruption, Kyle answered the man standing behind him. "Yeah, Wayne. Everything's under control." He glanced over his shoulder and shot the newcomer a teasing grin. "You're going to have to work on that...I heard you come in."

Chapter Fourteen

Lauren looked questioningly at Kyle. "You know this man?"

"Sure do. He's part of my backup team, along with Steve..." Kyle nodded toward the other man who had just made an appearance through the front door. "I called them in. They've been here for a couple of hours." He turned to Tony. "Your arrival and obviously agitated condition did not go unnoticed."

Tony plopped down in Lauren's favorite chair in front of the fireplace, the remnants of suspicion now replaced by confusion. His words were uttered in a plaintive voice. "Will someone please tell me what the hell is going on here?" His gaze went from Kyle to Wayne, who had stepped through the connecting door to join them, and finally to Steve, who was still by the front door.

Tony returned his attention to Kyle. "The word *backup* denotes some kind of law enforcement activity." He knitted his brow into a deep furrow as he stared intently at Kyle. "Is this some sort of an undercover operation?" His eyes widened as the full impact of the situation settled over him. "You're a government agent of some sort who's on assignment!" He made a quick grab inside his jacket.

Steve moved swiftly and silently behind Tony and

grabbed his wrist. "Real easy now, Mr. Mallory. Slowly bring your hand out in the open where I can see it."

Tony did exactly as instructed, bringing his notepad and pencil into view. "I just wanted to take notes."

Steve took the pad and pencil from Tony and set them on the table. "That's not advisable at this time, Mr. Mallory. I'm afraid this isn't a press conference. There will be an official statement made at the conclusion of this matter."

Confusion continued to cloud Tony's features as he looked questioningly at Steve. "How do you know my name?"

"We have a file on everyone involved—"

"Sorry, Tony." Kyle cut off Steve's words as he crossed the room toward the newsman. Wayne hung back in a position that allowed him to keep an eye on the side door.

Tony looked from Steve to Kyle. "Why would you have a file on me?" His voice and manner grew irritable. "Just what the hell am I suspected of doing?"

"No one's accusing you of anything, Tony, but you kind of walked in on this and now you're going to have to stay put for a little while." Kyle turned away from Tony, indicating that he was through answering questions.

He extended a warm smile toward Lauren, his eyes telling her not to worry. "Would you mind making some fresh coffee? I have a feeling it's going to be a long morning."

Lauren offered a feeble smile and reluctantly went to the kitchen, her mind in a whirl of bewilderment. Two more agents on the scene could only mean that Kyle expected trouble.

Tony remained in the chair. A scowl, tempered with an obvious curiosity and a hint of anxiety, covered his features. Kyle drew Wayne and Steve into the far corner where they held a quick conversation, then the two agents departed.

"Come on." Kyle approached Tony. "Let's move all this into the back where we can't be seen." Kyle escorted Tony into Lauren's living quarters, closing the door behind them.

Tony had recovered from his shock and had become antagonistic. "I know my rights. You can't hold me here against my will." His look was defiant, almost adversarial. "You either have to arrest me or let me go."

Kyle leveled a hard, cold stare at Tony. Several seconds passed in silence, during which time Tony's resolve noticeably crumbled and was replaced by a nervous uncertainty. Finally Kyle spoke, his words slow and carefully measured. "No one is holding you here. I'm simply *requesting* that you remain for the next few hours. We're into critical timing on the wrap-up of this operation. It would seem to me that as a newspaperman you would be grateful for the opportunity to have a firsthand account of a major smuggling bust."

Tony nervously shifted his weight. "Smuggling, huh? That makes you a customs agent. Well, a scoop that the wire services and the major newspapers could pick up—"

Kyle turned his back on Tony and addressed his comments to Lauren. "I'll be back in a little bit."

He turned toward Tony again. "Like I said, I'd appreciate it if you'd stay here for a while." It may have been a request, but the tone of voice and stern expression made it an order.

Kyle disappeared into the bedroom. When he reappeared a few minutes later, he had changed clothes and was again wearing his shoulder holster. He also had the clip-on holster securely snugged into the small of his back. He shrugged into his jacket, gave a quick wink of confidence to Lauren and left by the side door.

Lauren's stomach had been doing flip-flops for the past hour. So much was happening, but she was not sure exactly what. Of particular concern to her had been the fact that Kyle was carrying two guns when he left. He obviously was expecting trouble—serious trouble—and he did not want her anywhere near it.

She turned her attention to Tony in time to see him retrieve his notebook from the front parlor, then return to the kitchen and pour himself some coffee. She tried to make casual conversation when he returned.

"I'm sorry about this, Tony. Everything just sort of happened. One minute life was normal, then all of a sudden a whirling dervish named Kyle Delaney descended on Sea Grove and turned everything inside out."

Tony sat down and flipped open his notebook. "If I'm going to be stuck here, then I might as well make good use of my time. Start at the beginning and tell me everything."

Lauren was not really listening to him. She had gone to the window and pulled back the drapes just enough to peek out. She saw Kyle talking to a man she had never seen before. Steve and Wayne were nowhere in sight. Kyle and the other man disappeared around the corner of the building.

A hand reached past her and pulled the drape into place. "Lauren?" Tony's voice came from directly behind her. She turned to face him. His expression was somber. There was an intensity about him she had never noticed before. A slight shiver ran up her back.

He stared at her for a moment, then put his arm around her shoulder and led her away from the window. "You know I've always cared about you a great deal. Things didn't work out between us, but I thought we had remained good friends."

She offered him a weak smile. "Of course we're friends, Tony."

His attitude became more upbeat. "Then let's pass the time by you filling me in on everything."

"I can't do that. Any information will have to come

from Kyle.'' She shot him a teasing grin. ''But then, as a newsman trained in investigative reporting, I'm sure you already knew that.''

He returned her grin. ''Yeah, you're right. I knew that.''

KYLE LEANED against the wall of the secret room off the cottage cellar. He felt confident that no one would be checking on the contraband during daylight hours. He watched as the technician did a video scan of the radio, lamp, table and any other surface that might hold an image the computer could convert into a binary code for a fingerprint match.

He had already turned over the cigar remains he had taken from the ashtray. The bite mark match against dental records would clearly point to Max Culhane's involvement. He had also turned over the cigarette butts that tied Billy's death in with the lighthouse. But the little scraps of cellophane...he had held back one of them from each location, handing the rest to the lab technicians.

''How's it coming, Henry?'' Kyle walked to the technician who was putting his equipment away. ''Do we have anything we can find a match for?''

''Can't say for sure until I run them through the computer and check them against our known suspects. I should have something for you real soon.''

''Could you rush it?'' Kyle did not like the waiting, but he knew he needed the fingerprint evidence to get his arrest warrants. So, like it or not, he would wait.

Ten minutes later the two men left the cottage. Kyle checked his watch then headed toward Frank Brewster's warehouse to meet the team arriving with the search warrant. When Kyle gave them the go-ahead they would move through the warehouse to inspect each and every box, verify the inventory against legitimate invoices and confiscate any suspicious materials. They would also impound various computer records.

Other search warrants had been issued for houses and offices, bank records and safety-deposit boxes. As soon as the fingerprint match was confirmed, the two arrest warrants would be issued. The Canadian authorities had been briefed. The Coast Guard had been alerted to the cave entrance and the shipment of cigarettes waiting to be moved. Any activity at sea would be monitored, and those involved would be intercepted and arrested. Kyle felt an anxious tingle in the pit of his stomach. Everything was in place. As soon as he gave the word, the final phase would be set in motion.

The waiting…Kyle hated the waiting. Too many things could go wrong at the last minute. His cellular phone rang. He took it from his pocket and flipped it open. "Delaney here."

"Kyle, we have the report back from Interpol. The request for verification of Shane Nolan's whereabouts came from the sheriff's office. The person doing the asking was Mitch O'Connor. They were about to send the requested information when we contacted them."

"Well, that doesn't surprise me. What about Joe Thurlow? Are you all set with him?"

"Everything's a go. Just waiting on word from you."

"Where are you now, Wayne?"

"One block due south of the sheriff's station. Mitch O'Connor, Joe Thurlow and two other deputies are in the building, along with the normal shift personnel. There doesn't seem to be any unusual activity at the moment."

"Stay put. I'll be there in a few minutes." Kyle terminated his phone conversation, then picked up the agency car Steve had provided for him.

Everything about this case had been out of the ordinary. At the moment he felt particularly restricted by not having an established base of operation. He had been able to function out of Lauren's place when it was only him and his face could not be shown to anyone else, but he certainly would not be able to lead a strike team while sidestepping her employees and customers.

He returned to Lauren's, parking on the far side of the lot. He started to get out of the car but stopped himself at the last moment. It was no good. He needed to get used to the idea of not seeing her whenever the desire struck him.

A few minutes later he picked up Wayne and parked with a view of the sheriff's station. Kyle nervously drummed his fingers against the steering wheel. He set the cellular phone on the dashboard and stared at it, his brow knitted into an impatient furrow. "Ring, dammit!"

The phone rang, almost as if the order had been heard and acted upon. Kyle grabbed it, listened for a moment, then pushed the button to disconnect the call and get a dial tone. "We have a fingerprint match on both suspects. The arrest warrants are being signed at this moment." He shoved the phone at Wayne and snapped out his words. "Make your call."

Wayne looked at him, a quizzical expression covering his face. "What's the matter with you, Kyle? I've never seen you so uptight about a case before. Everything's going according to plan, isn't it?"

"Yeah, everything's moving along like clockwork—couldn't be better." He knew the words sounded as sarcastic to Wayne as they did to his own ears. He took a deep breath, held it for a minute, then let it out. He forced calm into his voice. "It's nothing. Just a personal matter I need to deal with." A personal matter, indeed. Each passing minute brought him closer to the time when he would have to say goodbye to Lauren, and it was tearing him up inside.

Wayne made the phone call. A couple of minutes later Joe Thurlow and Mitch O'Connor walked out of the sheriff's station, got in Joe's patrol car and drove down the street. As soon as they pulled into the parking lot of the Brewster warehouse, three members of Kyle's team met them and proceeded inside to serve their warrant and begin their search.

While Mitch O'Connor was involved at the warehouse, Kyle and Wayne served a warrant on his landlord granting them permission to search his house. In the case of Frank Brewster and Max Culhane both suspects had been murdered, so Kyle acted on his belief that crucial evidence was in danger of being removed and exercised his field judgment to go inside without a warrant.

They began a methodical search of Mitch's premises, paying particular attention to bank statements and telephone bills.

"Look at this!" A big grin spread across Wayne's face as he held up a key. "Found it hidden in a pair of socks buried in the back of a drawer. Looks like it belongs to a boat."

A knowing smile lit Kyle's face. "And there's no record of Mitch O'Connor owning a boat." He took the key from Wayne. "Want to bet whether or not it fits Frank's boat?"

"Bet with *you?*" Wayne made an overly exaggerated show of rushing to the mirror and staring at his reflection. "Did someone write the word *sucker* all over my face when I wasn't looking?"

The ringing of Kyle's cellular phone interrupted things. He pulled it from his pocket and flipped it open. "Delaney here."

Steve's voice came through. "Our other suspect is on the move, I think headed in your direction and looking mighty agitated. Amazing how fast word got around town about the search of Brewster's warehouse."

"Have they turned up anything yet?"

"Oh, yes. So far it's a large stash of liquor packed to travel outbound, and the incoming consists of a shipment of knockoff designer jeans. Interestingly, the jeans were packed inside counterfeit designer luggage. They were certainly making maximum use of the storage space."

"Great. Are they about through with their search?"

"They figure another hour or so."

"We're through here. Put someone outside this house and report any activity to me." Kyle disconnected from the call, then turned toward Wayne. "Let's make tracks out the back, but first take an impression of the boat key then put it back. Wipe down that entire dresser, including the handle, and also the bedroom doorknob. Make sure the bedroom door is closed. I want to be able to pull fresh prints and testify as to when they were made."

The two men took care of last-minute details then headed for the back door. As they moved down the hallway, something caught Kyle's eye. Sitting on a small table was a double frame containing two photographs. He paused for a moment. He had seen one of the photographs before, a young teenage boy and girl with an older boy. He took the photos with him as he ducked out the back.

Kyle glanced at his watch. "The other warrants should be arriving any minute. Let's go make the first of our arrests."

They drove to Lauren's. Kyle parked his car next to her garage but did not go inside the building. He saw Tony Mallory at the window watching what was going on. Things were far enough along now that Tony could not inadvertently spoil the sequence of events. The sound of a helicopter landing on the bluff signaled the arrival of his warrants. He motioned toward the window for Tony to come outside and join him.

Kyle gestured in the direction of the warehouse as he and Tony walked across the bluff. "If you stroll along in that direction you just might find a story big enough to be picked up by the wire services and the major metropolitan newspapers. Tell whoever tries to stop you that I said it was all right."

The two men stared at each other for a moment. "I, uh…" Tony was having difficulty with his words.

"You'd better hurry." Kyle saved him the embarrassment of having to show gratitude for the break on the news story.

"Thanks." Tony started across the bluff at a fast walk that quickly turned into a run.

Kyle looked over the two arrest warrants and handed one of them to Wayne. "Here, you take care of this." He put the other warrant in his pocket.

The two men went directly to the warehouse where Joe Thurlow and Mitch O'Connor watched as the customs agents impounded crate after crate of contraband. Several warehouse employees were standing at the front door, talking excitedly as the proceedings unfolded in front of them.

Kyle and Wayne approached the two deputies. It was Kyle who spoke while Wayne moved closer to Mitch. "Gentlemen, if you could step over here…" Kyle gestured toward an area out of hearing range from everyone else.

Joe Thurlow's face remained impassive, showing absolutely no reaction to the sudden resurrection of Kyle Delaney. But then he had met with Kyle and Wayne early that morning, before Kyle went to Max Culhane's house.

"You…I thought you were dead!" Mitch registered disbelief at seeing Kyle standing in front of him.

Kyle smiled knowingly. "Did you?"

The nervousness, the anxiety, the wariness…it all showed on Mitch's face and in his body language. He moved uneasily, edging toward the car.

The smile disappeared from Kyle's face. "I suggest that you not attempt to go anywhere." He nodded toward Joe, then took a step back so the young deputy could take over.

"Mitch O'Connor, I arrest you for the murder of Max Culhane. Please turn over your weapon and your badge."

"What the hell are you talking about?" Mitch's voice was indignant, but his hand moved toward the butt of the gun protruding from his holster.

Joe drew his gun and took a step back. "Don't try it,

Mitch. Real easy now, take that gun out and give it to me.''

Mitch handed his weapon to Joe Thurlow. Kyle noticed the way Mitch's gaze furtively darted around, taking in everything and everyone. In a movement so subtle as to go easily unnoticed, Kyle reached inside his jacket to his shoulder holster and wrapped his hand around the grip of his pistol.

Wayne took over. "And I have a federal warrant here for the arrest of the person calling himself Mitch O'Connor. This warrant will fall in line in a secondary position with the federal government deferring to prosecution on the state charge of first degree murder."

Joe Thurlow jerked his head in Wayne's direction. "*Calling* himself Mitch O'Connor? I don't understand—"

Joe's lapse of attention was all Mitch needed. He dropped to the ground and rolled as he reached for an ankle holster and pulled out a small .25 caliber semiautomatic pistol. He managed to squeeze off one shot, grazing Wayne's arm.

Before he could get off a second shot, Kyle leveled his aim at Mitch and fired.

The pistol flew from Mitch's hand. His cry of pain filled the air, then his body lay still. The dark stain spread across the chest of his uniform shirt. Kyle turned to Joe Thurlow and snapped out an order. "Call the paramedics." He kicked the pistol away from the body, then bent down and placed his fingertips against the side of Mitch's neck to feel for a pulse.

The curious warehouse workers had scattered for cover at the first shot. Joe dashed to his squad car and grabbed the radio to call for help. Kyle took a deep breath, then slowly let it out. He looked at Wayne, his expression solemn as he shook his head to indicate that it was too late for help.

Kyle holstered his gun and stood up. "You okay? It looks like he nicked you."

Wayne examined the rip in his jacket sleeve, his hand coming away with a smear of blood across his palm. "Just a flesh wound."

"Have the paramedics look at your arm when they get here."

"It's no big deal. A bandage should do the trick." Wayne carefully removed his jacket and inspected the rip in the sleeve. "Looks like he ruined my favorite jacket, though."

Kyle glanced at Mitch's body. "Well, I guess that takes care of the state's murder case. I'm convinced that Max Culhane and Mitch O'Connor arranged Billy Washburn's death and then Max killed Frank Brewster. Mitch did away with Max, and now Mitch is gone."

Wayne surveyed the impound activity that had only slowed for a moment then resumed as if nothing had happened. "So, where does that leave us?"

"The state's murder case against Mitch O'Connor is closed, but there's still the possibility of a conspiracy to commit murder case for the state and, of course, our other federal warrant that hasn't been served yet." Kyle turned away from the scene and looked into the distance. "Get Steve over here to keep an eye on things while you're getting your arm patched up." He walked away, not waiting for Wayne's response.

Joe Thurlow returned from the squad car. He glanced toward Mitch's body, then turned to Wayne. "I still don't understand. What did you mean when you said *the person calling himself Mitch O'Connor?*"

Wayne gave one last look at Kyle's retreating form, then turned his attention to the young deputy. "When we ran a background check we could only go back ten years. Prior to that time, Mitch O'Connor did not exist."

STRONG FINGERS tightened their grip on the binoculars trained on Wayne and Joe as they talked. The line of sight slowly panned to Kyle and followed him as he proceeded toward Lauren's place, then swung to the scene in front of the warehouse, lingering for a moment on Mitch O'Connor's body. The paramedics were there, and the coroner's wagon was just pulling into the parking lot. The unnoticed observer put the binoculars in the case, then turned and walked away.

Chapter Fifteen

Lauren felt it and then she saw it. The danger was far from over. It was very real and it was very near. Once again, she saw a gun, and it was pointing at Kyle. Once again a gun threatened violence and the possibility of death. She closed her eyes as the shudder jolted through her body. She had heard the two shots, but that was not it. Whatever danger existed was still very real and was yet to come.

She heard the side door open. She whirled and saw Kyle framed in the doorway. She ran to him as soon as he stepped inside the room. She threw her arms around his neck. "Are you okay? I've been so worried. I heard shots—"

He had not planned to, in fact he told himself that he would not do it, but he could not stop himself. He enfolded her in his arms and held her tightly against his body. He threaded his fingers through her hair, then he covered her mouth with a kiss of love and caring.

Her voice trembled with a combination of fear and relief. "Thank God you're all right. I heard the shots...I didn't know what to do." An awkward, uncomfortable chuckle jumped out of her throat. "It's funny, isn't it? The things that go through a person's mind in times of stress? I heard the shots and I actually said I was glad it was too early for any of my employees to be at work yet."

He held her head against his shoulder, resting his cheek against her hair. How was he going to be able to face the rest of his life without Lauren? He slowly took in a breath and just as slowly expelled it. He released her, his movements and words carefully calculated. "Stress does funny things to people, both emotionally and physically."

Kyle removed the holster from the back of his jeans as he walked across the living room. He set it on the end table, then took off his jacket and tossed it across the arm of the couch, the sleeve falling over the holster. He turned to face Lauren, who had followed him and seemed to be watching his every move. He tried to muster a casual smile. "Do you have any coffee left over?"

She hesitated. "Aren't you going to tell me about the shooting? You seem to be all right." She waited, making no effort to get any coffee.

"It was nothing for you to worry about. Just a little trouble when we were making an arrest, that's all." He jammed his hands into his front pockets, took them out, ran his fingers through his hair, then walked to the window and peered out. He turned toward her and offered a weak smile. "I could sure use that coffee."

She did not move, did not respond to his request. "What's the matter, Kyle? You seem to be a bundle of pure nerves."

"It's nothing...just the natural letdown following a major bust."

"Everything's over? You've made your arrests? What was the shooting about?" She could see it on his face and hear it in his voice. He was holding back something, and it frightened her.

He took a calming breath. "It was Mitch O'Connor." He stared at her, his face the impassive mask he had perfected. "He's dead."

"Dead?" The quaver in her voice increased as she continued to speak. "Why? What happened?"

"Joe Thurlow had just arrested him for the murder of Max Culhane. Wayne was in the process of reading him the federal warrant covering his involvement in the smuggling operation when Mitch got off a shot, nicking Wayne in the arm. We had no choice. We, uh, *I* had to take him out."

She thought she had accepted the fact that Kyle's job involved a gun. But she did not know how she would be able to cope with the direct knowledge that he had killed someone as part of that job. She intellectually understood the concept of shooting in self-defense, kill or be killed, but she did not know if she would ever be able to reconcile those two extremes.

The bell at the front of the building interrupted their conversation. Lauren went to answer it and found Irene Peyton standing there.

"Irene." Her surprise was genuine. She glanced at her watch. "We won't be open for another hour yet."

Irene stepped inside, even though Lauren had not invited her. "I just wanted to check on you. I worry about you out here all by yourself, so isolated from everything. I saw all the activity, that terrible shooting. Are you all right, dear?"

"Why, yes. I'm just fine." Lauren stayed by the front door, hoping Irene would take the hint and leave. "It was nice of you to stop by to check on me."

Irene continued toward the back. "I hope I'm not intruding, but I could sure use a cup of nice hot tea to soothe my nerves. Oh, dear. I'm afraid that shooting just has me so upset."

Lauren called after her, trying to prevent Irene from going into the living quarters. "Why don't we have our tea out here?"

"That's all right, Lauren." Kyle opened the door. "I think we can invite Irene in for some tea."

Irene's eyes widened in surprise as she stared at Kyle.

Lauren joined her, and the two women went into the living room.

Kyle turned to Irene. "Would you like to sit down?"

"Oh, my, yes. I think I'd better sit down. I'm just at such a loss. We all thought you were dead…that Coast Guard report, your not coming back to your motel room, abandoning your van…" Irene chose a comfortable chair.

Lauren shot a curious look in Kyle's direction. Something about Irene's manner did not seem right. But that did not bother her nearly as much as Kyle's strange behavior. There was an unusual edge to his voice, something she could not define. She made no move to fix tea, and Irene did not pursue the request.

Lauren seated herself on the couch. She did not understand what was happening but knew it would not be wise to intrude into what was taking place. She reached for the jacket Kyle had tossed across the arm of the couch. She held on to the collar, squeezing it tightly in her hand in hopes of drawing some comfort.

Irene smiled at Kyle in a solicitous manner though her eyes were hard and cold. "That was very naughty of you to have deceived us like that, young man. We were all so worried."

"Worried? What would you have been worried about?"

A look of umbrage covered her face, and her eyes narrowed almost to slits. "I don't believe I understand what you mean and I certainly don't care for your attitude, young man. You seem to be accusing me of something."

Irene turned to Lauren. "And you, harboring him… knowing full well that he was safe and not sharing that information with me."

Lauren looked at Irene curiously. The conversation between Irene and Kyle had been openly adversarial. And now this woman who she thought was her friend seemed to be attacking her. This was not the Irene Peyton Lauren knew.

Her words were hesitant. "Irene…why would you say that I was *harboring* Kyle? Why would you assume he had been here at all, let alone hiding out here, which is what harboring implies? And even if it was true, why would it upset you so much?"

Irene fumbled in her purse while Kyle kept a watchful eye on her movements, his shoulder holster and pistol very evident. She produced one of her hard candies, a cinnamon ball. She unwrapped it, put it in her mouth, then folded the cellophane wrapper in that peculiar way of hers.

"That's certainly an odd little habit of yours, the way you fold those candy wrappers." Kyle's voice was calm and he presented a relaxed demeanor as he leaned against the doorjamb. "I noticed it at your house that first day. I also noticed the little stack of candy wrappers you left by your place at the table in the tearoom at the historical society meeting."

Irene stared at the folded wrapper for a moment. "I must do it out of habit. I wasn't aware I'd even done it."

"That's kind of what I figured. I've never seen anyone do that before." Kyle picked up his bag from the corner of the room and set it on the coffee table. "But you know what, Irene? I also found those folded candy wrappers in the wastebasket at Frank Brewster's office the day after he died and on the table in Max Culhane's house, right next to a cup of cold coffee that had been placed there a matter of a few short hours before he died. I even tasted that coffee, and it definitely had cinnamon candy dissolved in it. Both of those men were involved in a smuggling ring and both of them were murdered. How do you explain that?"

"Kyle Delaney, just what are you accusing me of?" Irene became indignant, almost hostile. "And why shouldn't my candy wrappers be at those places when I've been there several times for various reasons? Frank has been very generous in his contributions to the society's various projects. And it's certainly no secret that I've had to request assistance from the sheriff on various occasions. We've had vandals painting graffiti on some of the Victorian houses that are in the process of being restored. I've had to ask if his deputies could keep a more watchful eye on them."

"That still leaves me with a problem, Irene. What were you doing in the hidden room off the cellar of the lighthouse keeper's cottage? You know, that little room that leads into the cave in the cliff below the lighthouse. The route used to smuggle goods in and out of the country, a route that's been in use for decades."

"I have absolutely no idea what cave you're talking about, young man. I don't know anything about any smuggling, and I certainly am not familiar with any hidden room in the cellar of the cottage."

Kyle reached into the bag and withdrew two of the oddly folded pieces of cellophane. "I found these in that little hidden room. Do they look familiar?"

"I don't see what some folded candy wrappers prove. Anyone could have folded those." Irene rose to her feet. "Now, I'm afraid I must insist that you stop this silly interrogation immediately."

Kyle watched Irene. She stared straight ahead, her face pinched into a tightly set mask, her lips pursed. "We've been able to lift your fingerprints from some of the candy wrappers. Do you still claim that you don't know anything about that cave or about the movement of contraband?"

Irene picked up her purse. "I refuse to listen to any more of this nonsense." She held one glove and looked around. "My other glove...what did I do with it?" She opened her purse and rummaged for a moment, then suddenly pulled out a small handgun identical to the one Mitch O'Connor had carried in his ankle holster.

"Irene!" Lauren's senses jumped to attention. Her voice

cut through the air, filled with alarm. "I don't understand—"

"Hush up, Lauren." The words were harsh. The pillar
of the community had vanished. "I don't want to hurt
you." Irene turned her attention to Kyle. She waved the
gun at him, motioning him to sit on the couch with Lauren.

Kyle remained outwardly unruffled. He slowly reached
over and squeezed Lauren's hand in an attempt to calm
her fears, then leaned back in the far corner of the couch
in an effort to put as much distance between Lauren and
himself as possible. "Now what, Irene? Do you plan to
shoot both of us? It's over. I have an arrest warrant with
your name on it. Your participation in all of this is already
fully documented. Just how far do you think you'll get?"

He saw the desperation in her eyes. What he did not see
was any confusion or hesitation. There was a hardness that
had not been visible before, a steel edge that seemed to
encompass all of her. It was surprising, yet it was not. She
had always projected the proper society matron persona,
but Kyle's investigation had led him to believe that she
was the calculating brains behind the decades old smuggling ring—a person so ruthless she had coldly ordered the
murder of one of her own cohorts while condoning two
other murders within her organization. She had just proven
him correct. She was not to be taken lightly, nor was she
to be underestimated.

"I'll have to deal with you, just like I did the others."
Irene waved the gun erratically. Her eyes had taken on the
look of a trapped animal fighting for survival. She paid
watchful attention to Lauren, but the primary object of her
vituperative attack continued to be Kyle. "Things were
just fine until you showed up. You've caused me untold
problems and personal loss. Some of it didn't really matter
because our operation needed to be streamlined. The ranks
needed to be weeded out, the dead wood chopped off."

Irene paced up and down, her actions becoming more erratic with each passing minute—including her nervous habit of gesturing with the handgun clutched tightly in her grip. She talked incessantly, as if she was compelled to tell it all. It was obvious that her world was unraveling in front of her eyes.

"Frank was a weakling. He lacked the nerve of his father and the brilliant mind of his uncle." Irene allowed a cold, heartless chuckle as she stopped pacing and stared at Kyle. "You should have heard him when he realized you were alive. He saw you through Lauren's window and ran straight to his office and started pulling together things to leave town."

She paused, taking on a quizzical look as if a thought had just occurred to her. "I never did figure out just what he was doing outside your window. I thought he was going to have a stroke the way he was carrying on about it over the phone. Just kept saying it was time to get out, that he tried to tell Max not to shoot you because it could only lead to trouble. And then Max told him you were a government agent. Humph! It was Frank and his yellow spine that caused all this trouble."

A pensive look crossed her face. "Max was only supposed to scare Frank, show him what would happen to him if he didn't calm down. But, as usual, Max was too heavy-handed and got carried away. just like he did when he originally went after you. He didn't even know who you really were until later. He was just afraid your poking around the lighthouse would cause us trouble. I told him to play it cool and we'd keep an eye on you, but Max thought he knew better."

The hard look returned to her features. Her words were emphatic. "Frank was a coward and Max was a fool."

Lauren's premonition had come true again. Another gun. Their lives again being threatened. She glanced at Kyle. He appeared very calm and in control. His face wore that impassive mask that she could not penetrate. She had to remain calm, too. She had to be ready to do whatever he needed. She clutched the collar of his jacket tighter in her trembling hand, demanding that it provide her with some of his strength and courage.

Irene began pacing again and waving the gun around in an agitated manner. The words poured out of her mouth, her distress coloring every utterance. "We gave you Max. He was out of control, making one stupid mistake after another. I served him up for you. That was supposed to put an end to your investigation." She stared pointedly at Kyle. Her words almost had a plaintive quality to them. "You were supposed to stop looking. You were supposed to consider the case closed."

"You're overwrought, Irene." He held out his hand toward her. His voice was soft and soothing, that seductively hypnotic quality that he did so well. "Why don't you give me that gun before someone gets hurt? We can sit down together and talk about this." He started to rise from the couch.

"Don't you move, Kyle Delaney." She angrily spit out the words. Her eyes blazed with hatred. She emphasized the order by leveling her gun at him. "You stay right where you are." Irene kept her distance from the couch as she turned slightly toward Lauren. "Don't you move, either. I've always been very fond of you, but that only goes so far."

Irene stared intently at Kyle. Her voice had turned almost childlike. "Why didn't you just accept it as the end to your investigation and go away?"

"I couldn't do that, Irene, not with the two main culprits still at large. I needed to complete my investigation, which consisted of collecting the evidence necessary to obtain arrest warrants for you and your son."

Lauren's eyes widened in shock. "Her *son?*" She stared

at Kyle in total disbelief. "Irene has a son? Who are you talking about?"

"You're crazy!" Irene screamed at Kyle. She was quickly tipping the scales beyond reason as more and more of her perfect little world fell apart and more of her secrets were revealed. "No one is going to believe that pack of lies. What proof do you have?"

Kyle held out his hand again. "Why don't you give me that gun, Irene? You know there isn't any place you can go."

She took a step backward, blinking several times as if trying to clear her head and get her bearings. "I told you not to move. Now, tell me just what proof you have of these ridiculous charges."

"All right." Kyle's words were deliberately slow and precise. "It all started with the background checks I ran. At first it was a general check on just about everyone I had run into since my arrival. Any irregularities would signal the need for a more thorough check. We couldn't find anything on Mitch O'Connor that went back more then ten years. It was as if he didn't exist prior to the time Max was elected sheriff and he was hired on as one of the deputies."

A noticeable twitch had developed in Irene's left eye. "That...that doesn't prove anything."

"Well, not by itself it doesn't. But I had to ask myself why this man had found it necessary to change his name and alter his identity. It also raised the question of why the sheriff would have hired a deputy who had purposely hidden his background and true identity. That coincided with other bits of information...just small pieces in themselves, but when added together they began to form a pattern."

"Pieces? What kind of pieces? What kind of a pattern?" Irene's nervous tic had gotten worse. Her hands trembled. "You're just making up these terrible things."

"Well, there was the photograph I spotted among all your family pictures. It was you as a young teenager with a boy of the same age and another person, older but with a very distinct family resemblance to the younger boy. I assumed they were probably brothers. Then I saw a photograph in an old copy of the newspaper showing you and the same boy a couple of years later. The caption identified the two people as Irene Peyton and Wilton Brewster, the king and queen of the high school prom. Wilton Brewster was Frank's father, and that made the other young man in the photo at your house Ralph Brewster, Wilton's brother and Frank's uncle."

"So? Why wouldn't I have a photograph of my high school friend? This is a small town. It was even smaller back then. We were all good friends, spent a lot of time together. There's nothing wrong with that."

"You're right, Irene. There's nothing wrong with that. However, it piqued my curiosity. Why would you have the photograph of the three of you framed and sitting in your house, but not keep the photograph of you and Wilton at the prom? Why was the older photograph more important to you than the one depicting an important event? From there, I moved forward and found an item saying you were going away to college. Small town newspapers are really great at listing all the little things that big cities don't care about. But for some reason, the newspaper never made any mention of you graduating from college. That would certainly have been newsworthy back then. Again, I had to ask myself why.

"I checked and found out that you never attended the school listed in the newspaper. So, what were you really doing? A little digging brought to light the hospital record of your having given birth to a son and a birth certificate that listed not your high school friend, but his older brother, Ralph Brewster, as the father of the child. After that it was easy to track that child through school and into the military service, then through several jobs. But the trail came to an abrupt halt ten years ago.''

"No...you're wrong..." Irene seemed on the verge of overload.

"We used your son's military records with his finger-prints and compared them to Mitch O'Connor's finger-prints and we had an absolute match. And, ironically enough, I found that same photograph of you, Wilton Brewster and Ralph Brewster in Mitch's house along with a photograph of you holding your baby son."

Kyle softened his manner. "I imagine it must have been very difficult for you, Irene, especially back then—a young woman from a small town giving birth out of wedlock. Did Ralph Brewster provide the money for his son's up-bringing? Is that what dictated that a small smuggling op-eration running liquor in from Canada during the latter days of Prohibition should seek out new markets and con-tinue to function after Prohibition was repealed?"

Tears formed in Irene's eyes and slowly trickled down her wrinkled cheeks. "I loved my boy. Ralph and I both loved him. Times were difficult, and small-town gossip being what it is, it just never worked out for us to really be a family. My boy was raised by Ralph's relatives back East. I went to see him as often as I could."

The hard edge suddenly returned to her face. It was hate, pure hate, that emanated from her cold eyes as she stared at Kyle. "Why did you shoot my boy? I saw you, Kyle Delaney. I saw you pull the trigger and shoot my boy dead." A sob escaped her throat as she sank into total despair. "Just the way I'm going to do you."

The fear totally consumed Lauren. Kyle had tried to reason with Irene, and it had not worked. Lauren was sure Irene had thrown off the bonds of reality and was no longer rational.

Lauren noted the way Irene managed to stay just out of Kyle's reach. The only way he would be able to take the gun from her would be to rise from the couch. Even Lauren could tell that Irene would be able to pull the trigger before he could reach her. And it looked more and more like that was exactly what she intended to do.

As frightened as she was, she knew it was up to her to make a move. Irene was so focused on Kyle that Lauren felt she would be able to do something as long as she did not make any sudden movements. She knew what she had to do. As much as she hated guns and everything they stood for, she loved Kyle even more.

She took a calming breath and steeled herself for the ordeal ahead. She slowly released her grip on the collar of Kyle's jacket. Her gaze never left Irene as she slipped her hand underneath the jacket sleeve to the holster and pistol that were hidden from sight.

Her fingers touched the cold metal of the gun. She fought her immediate reaction to jerk her hand away from the hated object that only brought death. She paused as she shoved down the queasy feeling churning in her stomach. She forced herself to ease the gun from the holster an inch at a time. Then she brought it out from beneath the jacket.

Chapter Sixteen

Lauren stared in disbelief. It looked like her hand holding the foul weapon, though she could not imagine how it could really be so. The queasy feeling tried to battle its way through her conscious efforts to contain it. She tightened her grip on the handle.

She raised the gun and pointed it at Irene. Her voice betrayed the fear and anxiety she tried so desperately to control. "Please, Irene…hand your gun to Kyle."

Irene's head snapped around in Lauren's direction. Shock immediately spread across the older woman's face, then was replaced by a strange calm. The nervous tic disappeared, and her hand stopped trembling. "You must love him a great deal to sacrifice all those emphatically held beliefs of yours where guns are concerned."

Lauren did not hear Irene's words, she only saw the gun the woman held. "Please, Irene…don't force me to do something I don't want to do. Give Kyle your gun."

Irene had taken her eye off Kyle for only a second, but it was long enough. He lunged forward and grabbed the gun from her hand.

"Thank God." The words came out as no more than a whisper. The pistol slipped from Lauren's hand and fell to the floor. She sank into the couch and closed her eyes as they filled with tears.

Maybe Lauren had not heard Irene's last words, but Kyle heard them loud and clear. They reverberated through his mind, filling him with thoughts of the odious task yet ahead—telling Lauren goodbye.

LAUREN SHIVERED inside Kyle's embrace. She desperately needed the comfort he provided even though it had been three hours since Irene had been taken away. "I think I could actually have shot her." As if to put an exclamation mark to her sentence, a hard spasm shivered through her body. "That realization frightens me more than anything else that has happened. I didn't think I was capable..." She looked up at him. "When I saw that look of pure evil on her face and the hatred directed toward you...well, she was not the person I'd known all these years. She was a stranger, a very dangerous stranger who was saying she was going to kill you."

Kyle smoothed her hair and held her head gently against his shoulder. "It's all over now."

"I don't understand why you allowed her to keep waving that gun around. Why didn't you take it from her right away when you had the chance?"

"I needed to hear it from her. The evidence I had against Irene was skimpy and totally circumstantial. It was an iffy case. We could have nailed her on minor charges, which is what the arrest warrant was for, but I needed to hear her say that she had made the decision to kill Max. That gives us conspiracy to commit murder...well, it gives the state the availability of prosecuting on those charges."

Lauren looked at him. "You mean you didn't have enough on her to make a case?"

"Yes and no. The fingerprints we pulled from the candy wrappers were from Frank's office and Max's house, places she had visited on numerous occasions. No crime there or indication of a crime. Unfortunately, the candy wrappers from the room above the cave were too smudged to get a print match, and the peculiar folding of the cellophane is only circumstantial evidence and not very conclusive. I wanted her confession.''

''All that money she had made from decades of smuggling...what in the world did she do with all of it? She took one month each year to visit a nephew back East somewhere and then threw a lavish costume ball each Halloween. Other than that, she spent all of her time working on the various projects of the historical society. I had always thought of it as an all-consuming passion of hers.''

''The one-month visit to her nephew every year was really a first-class luxury European vacation that cost her a bundle. The money was laundered through a corporation called Triangle Associates. The profits from the smuggling went to the corporation and then the corporation wrote checks to all those involved. We're tracking down Swiss bank accounts right now. Triangle Associates also paid for the cabin cruiser Frank used, made payments to foreign associates for goods smuggled into this country and made large corporate donations to the historical society.

''All of her fund-raising efforts were nonexistent. She was her own corporate benefactor. Those trips to Seattle every couple of weeks to visit her niece and the fund-raising trips were to transport cash. She didn't even have a niece. According to the newspaper article about her high school graduation, she was an only child. No brothers, no sisters, therefore no nieces or nephews. The substantial inheritance she claimed came from her parents was also nonexistent.''

''I feel so bad for poor Milly. Apparently she and Max had been seeing each other for almost a year and nobody knew it. They had even discussed marriage. Max told her he had put away a tidy little nest egg and had inherited a house in Hawaii. I guess it was really all from the smuggling money.''

''It may take a little while, but I think she'll be okay.

Milly strikes me as someone with a lot of strength and courage, the type who can handle tragedy and come out of it without a lot of emotional scars.''

"I hope you're right. I'll do what I can, but right now she says she prefers to be alone to sort things out. It was not only the shock of him being killed, it was learning about all the criminal activity.''

An awkward silence filled the air. Lauren could feel the tension growing in Kyle's body. She knew what was next. Kyle would be moving on. The image of him as she had found him—passed out facedown in the mud with a bullet wound—popped into her mind. She had seen enough death lately to last her two lifetimes. She knew she would not be able to live with the knowledge that every time he left home there was a very real possibility he could be killed. He released her from his embrace. She felt him pulling away from her emotionally as well as physically.

He stood up and stretched. He tried his best to sound casual. "I'd better get busy. I have packing to do and I have reports to file before this case can be wrapped up. The chief has mentioned another assignment that sounds real interesting, and...I need to...''

He cupped her face in his hands. He saw it in her eyes. She knew...they both knew what had to be, but it did not make the words any easier for him. "It's better this way, Lauren. You'll see that I'm right. In the long run—'' He turned away from her without finishing his sentence. The pain in his heart was greater than anything he had ever before experienced. But with time maybe that, too, would heal.

LAUREN SAT in the front parlor next to the fireplace sipping her herbal tea. The early-morning drizzle obscured most of the predawn light. It was the same type of morning as when it had all started. It seemed so long ago now. Kyle Delaney had appeared out of the early-morning mist and turned her life upside down, then he had gone away leaving a hole in her heart that could never be repaired.

The only thing that had kept her from wallowing in her own misery was her need to help Milly get over her pain. Finally Milly had told her it was time for both of them to get on with their respective lives. Lauren had decided she would take a trip. She picked up one of the travel brochures, staring at it without really seeing it. The tears welled in her eyes, then ran down her cheeks. A little sob caught in her throat.

While Lauren sat in front of the fire, Kyle put his plan into action. He crossed the parking lot and stood outside her side door for a minute while he tried to compose the nervous tension that continued to tie his body in knots. He opened the door, then walked silently through the living room and dining room. He came to a halt in the kitchen at the door separating Lauren's living quarters from the business. The look of despair that covered her face tore at his insides. He watched her. The love he felt welled inside him, forcing his fears aside. He stepped through the door.

"I thought I warned you about keeping your doors locked."

Lauren was not sure she had actually heard it or only wanted it so much that she imagined it. She held her breath as she slowly turned. He stood framed in the doorway. She had not heard him come in and was still not sure he was real.

Her voice quavered with uncertainty. "Kyle? Is that really you?"

He quickly crossed the room to her, grabbed her hand and pulled her into his arms. "Oh, Lauren...I've missed you so much." He ran his fingers through her hair, then cradled her head against his shoulder. She felt so good in his arms. It was so right. He held her tightly, relishing the sensation of her body pressed against his.

Several minutes passed in which they both seemed content to merely hold each other without the intrusion of words. It was finally Kyle who broke the silence.

"I tried to put this behind me, but I couldn't. Everywhere I looked I saw only you." He caressed her shoulders. "I'd wake up in the middle of the night and expect to find you next to me." His words were soft, barely above a whisper. "I'd reach for you, only you weren't there." He lowered his head to hers and captured her mouth with a soft kiss. It was a kiss that spoke of caring and warmth—of love.

He pulled back a little, just enough to be able to look into her eyes. "We have to talk, Lauren." He took her hand and led her to her living room. He settled her on the couch, but he continued to stand.

Kyle nervously shifted his weight from one foot to the other. He swallowed his anxiety, then took a calming breath. "I've, uh, I've given this a lot of thought." He ran his fingers through his hair, then stuck his hands in his jacket pockets. His voice became soft. He could not keep his apprehension from showing. "Hell...I haven't thought about anything else for the past week." He hunched his shoulders and stared at the floor for a moment as he tried to organize his words.

Lauren watched him. There was an uncertainty and hesitation about him, the type of thing she had never before associated with Kyle Delaney. He had always had such a strong, decisive manner. Everything about him radiated self-assurance. He exuded confidence and left everyone around him with a sense of security. At that moment she knew the man she loved was about to bare his soul. It was a flash of reality more vivid than any dream or psychic image that had ever come to her. She held out her hand to him. Her insides quivered to the point where she feared she might lose control of her outward calm.

Kyle accepted her hand and seated himself next to her on the couch. He kissed her palm, then held her hand between both of his hands. "Lauren..." He glanced at the floor, then looked up into her eyes as he drew her into his embrace.

Her words were a breathless whisper. "If you don't tell me you love me in the next ten seconds I'll have to do something drastic."

An amused twinkle danced through his eyes. "Oh? Like what? Are you going to cast a magic spell and turn me into a frog?"

"No, I'll let you stay the handsome prince that you are. It'll look much nicer for the wedding pictures."

"Wedding pictures?"

"Well, you were about to ask me to marry you." She had not asked a question, she had made a definitive statement.

"This reading my mind stuff is going to take a little getting used to." His manner turned very serious as he plumbed the depth of her emerald eyes. "I love you, Lauren. I love you very much."

A soft warmth spread through her body, touching every part of her consciousness. "Oh, Kyle...I love you."

"About my job, Lauren, what I do for a living..."

She looked into his eyes. Her words were tentative. "I have a suggestion for a compromise between your world and mine."

The wariness showed in his voice. "A compromise?"

"There's an opening for county sheriff. You're qualified and I think the county supervisors would be thrilled to have you. It's not a desk job, but neither is it the type of adrenaline-rush excitement you're accustomed to." She took a calming breath before continuing. "Do you think you'll be able to conform to a *normal* existence?"

His voice cracked slightly as he spoke. "I can do anything...anything, that is, except live without you."

Harlequin® Historical

If you're a serious fan of historical romance,
then you're in luck!

Harlequin Historicals brings you
stories by bestselling authors, rising new stars
and talented first-timers.

Ruth Langan & Theresa Michaels
Mary McBride & Cheryl St.John
Margaret Moore & Merline Lovelace
Julie Tetel & Nina Beaumont
Susan Amarillas & Ana Seymour
Deborah Simmons & Linda Castle
Cassandra Austin & Emily French
Miranda Jarrett & Suzanne Barclay
DeLoras Scott & Laurie Grant...

You'll never run out of favorites.

Harlequin Historicals...they're too good to miss!

HH-GEN

LOVE *or* MONEY?
Why not Love *and* Money!
After all, millionaires
need love, too!

**Suzanne Forster,
Muriel Jensen
and
Judith Arnold**

bring you three original stories
about finding that one-in-a million man!

Harlequin also brings you
a million-dollar sweepstakes—enter
for your chance to win a fortune!

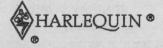 HARLEQUIN ®

Look us up on-line at: http://www.romance.net   HTMM

HARLEQUIN®

I N T R I G U E®

Cheyenne Nights

by Carla Cassidy

As little girls the Connor sisters dreamed of gallant princes on white horses. As women they were swept away by mysterious cowboys on black stallions. But with dusty dungarees and low-hung Stetsons, their cowboys are no less the knights in shining armor.

Join Carla Cassidy for the Connor sisters'
wild West Wyoming tales of intrigue:

SUNSET PROMISES
(March)

MIDNIGHT WISHES
(April)

SUNRISE VOWS
(May)

HARLEQUIN Temptation

and

HARLEQUIN INTRIGUE®

Double Dare ya!

Identical twin authors Patricia Ryan and
Pamela Burford bring you a dynamic duo of
books that just happen to feature identical twins.

Meet Emma, the shy one, and her diva double,
Zara. Be prepared for twice the pleasure and
twice the excitement as they give two
unsuspecting men trouble times two!

In April, the scorching **Harlequin Temptation** novel
#631 **Twice the Spice** by Patricia Ryan

In May, the suspenseful **Harlequin Intrigue** novel
#420 **Twice Burned** by Pamela Burford

Pick up both – if you dare....

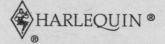

HARLEQUIN®

It's hot...and it's out of control!

Beginning this spring, Temptation turns up the *heat*. Look for these bold, provocative, *ultra*sexy books!

#629 OUTRAGEOUS
by Lori Foster (April 1997)

#639 RESTLESS NIGHTS
by Tiffany White (June 1997)

#649 NIGHT RHYTHMS
by Elda Minger (Sept. 1997)

BLAZE: Red-hot reads—only from

BLAZE

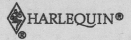 

COMING NEXT MONTH

#417 HOTSHOT P.I. by B.J. Daniels
Lawman
The first time Clancy Jones sleepwalked onto a murder scene, she
was a witness; this time she's the prime suspect. For all those years,
P.I. Jake Hawkins harbored desire for her as well as anger, and now
he doesn't know whether to find her innocent—or guilty.

#418 WED TO A STRANGER? by Jule McBride
Hidden Identity
Fritzi Fitzgerald's search for her missing husband led her to a remote
Alaskan village. Accused of murdering the very man she sought, the
new mother was suddenly rescued by dream man Nathan Lafarge,
who claimed *he* was her husband—and alibi.

#419 SUNRISE VOWS by Carla Cassidy
Cheyenne Nights
Someone knew Derek Walker would protect Belinda Connor—but
who? To draw out the killer, he proposed to save the Connor ranch in
return for Belinda's hand and her signature on child-custody papers.
If the scheme worked, the marriage would end—but could he endure
losing Belinda again?

#420 TWICE BURNED by Pamela Burford
Double Dare
Zara Sutcliffe had always been the tough twin. But one six-foot-four-
inch so-called FBI agent Logan Pierce had her quaking in her high
heels the moment he spirited her away to a safe house. Who posed the
most danger—her stalker or her bodyguard?

AVAILABLE THIS MONTH:

#413 LOVER UNKNOWN
Shawna Delacorte

#414 THE REDEMPTION OF
DEKE SUMMERS
Gayle Wilson

#415 MIDNIGHT WISHES
Carla Cassidy

#416 HIS KIND OF
TROUBLE
Vivian Leiber

Look us up on-line at: http://www.romance.net